THE WATERS OF
FORGETFULNESS

THE WATERS OF FORGETFULNESS

An Augustan-Age Memoir

As Revealed by

Yorick Blumenfeld

QUARTET

First published in 2009 by
Quartet Books Limited
A member of the Namara Group
27 Goodge Street, London W1T 2LD

A catalogue record for this book
is available from the British Library

ISBN   978 0 7043 7172 9

Typeset by Antony Gray
Printed and bound in Great Britain by
T J International Ltd, Padstow, Cornwall

EDITORIAL NOTE

As a result of grave robbers ransacking Etruscan tombs, all kinds of unexpected and exciting discoveries have resulted over the past few centuries, among them the scrolls of this manuscript. The original is in Latin and was found in a carefully hidden amphora which was unearthed about a decade ago in Cumae, just a few miles to the north of what we today know as Naples. Written around 18 BC, it describes events which took place in the preceding decade at about the time Augustus Caesar first became Emperor. The manuscript, although in a surprising state of preservation, required extensive editing. Roman texts of the period were written entirely in capital letters without any form of punctuation!

. . . the Ferryman is the foul and dreadful Charon,
A frightful figure, transporter of the deceased across
the Styx.
His wild beard grows hoar, his staring eyes aflame,
His wretched cloak hangs knotted from his shoulder
As he poles his solitary flimsy coracle
And ferries the souls of the dead in his craft.

VIRGIL , *Aeneid*, Scroll vi, lines 301–7

I

It is said that the waters of forgetfulness are clear, while those of remembrance are murky. The story of our *familia* has, until now, remained the most fabulous untold tale of our Romano-Greek world and the obscured memories of it are fast fading. I, Rufus Longius, the clean-shaven, toga-clad Roman citizen and elder of the Orphic sect above ground, was Charon, a dirty, unkempt, white bearded, sinister and near mythical figure underground. My wife Lydia and daughter Calliope, did not know me as Charon at all. To them Rufus was just a stable husband and loving father. How this may have affected my persona will come out as I write.

Never before have I taken goose-quill and black ink to *pergamena* – those treated and long lasting animal skins from far-away Pergamum. But it seems these days that every general is writing his memoirs, every Roman senator is eager to compose some treatise or other. Poetry, texts and pamphlets are coming out in such numbers as to rival the floods of the Tiber. Anyone can 'publish' a volume by hiring slaves to make scrolled copies which are then sold cheaply in the arcade stalls of Rome, Pompeii and even our own Baiae. Alas, I cannot synthesise oysters and roses like some of our famously talented poets can. And in spinning this story it would seem that I sometimes get caught in intricate webs of my own making.

After more than six hundred summers of Homeric fame, the history of both our Sibylline oracle and our fabled underworld, or Hades, deserves to be recorded for posterity. Where else in this world has anyone ever been able actually to see and question the shades of the dead? Yes, I have been one of a long line of myth-promoters of Graeco-Roman civilisation, a purveyor of the grandest of scams, the most long-running and audacious fraud thus far perpetrated by any culture. And while I am fully aware that the Egyptians believed in the transmigration of souls, such belief was just that. It was not an elaborately staged performance which ran for profit. I, Charon, on the other hand, was born into our *familia* to play my part in deceiving the Roman believers – in other words, almost everybody.

Our *familia*, which ran this 'establishment', consisted of about three dozen members. Of course this did not include the large number of our surrounding suppliers – of oils, wines, sacrificial animals, candles, torches and incense, or provisions like fish, onions or cereals – who knew nothing of our operations. We were proud that our *familia* had been an ongoing concern for more than sixteeen generations! (Although our Greek pre-decessors had been running it for some centuries before that.) Being in the bosom of our *familia* was important to me. It nourished my identity.

Some family! Our Sibyl, Sulpicia Galla, who in her public ecstasies manifested heaving breasts, a foaming mouth and wild, deeply dyed red hair, somehow held our complex group together. Often intoxicated, frequently prophetic, and per-petually demanding, this flamboyant, captivating personality never let go once she held you in her clutches. Her command: 'Have done with it,' always brought one to a prompt halt. Our high priest, Marcus Quintius, is one of those rare souls with a spiritual disposition who also happens to be a deep thinker. Somewhat detached from reality, he would have been far more at ease in the worlds of Epicurus or Pythagoras. He remains my closest friend. Our financial comptroller and 'heavy', Gaius Valerius Maximus, also known as 'Captain Max', should, by his own admission, have been a manager (or *lanista*) of a Roman gladiatorial circus where he would have controlled thousands of unruly combatants. Max thought big and had about half the weight of a pregnant sow. In addition to being married to the slightly ordinary but charming Hebe, Max also had two part-time concubines, Glycera and Myrtale. How he juggled all of these I shall never know. Our trainer and organiser of the underground 'tours', Peleus Atenius Vatinus, would have been entirely at ease in Rome's underworld instead of luring the gullible to descend into our next world. With his tousled, scare-crow hair, Peleus had dreams of a rather lurid kind of theatrical glory: that of being the impresario of bath-house orgies.

And I, Charon, the mythical boatman of antiquity as well as being an Orphic cult elder above ground, was probably something of a categorical misfit in this *familia*. My wife, Lydia, was a counterbalance of normality. She was considered by many as a true disciple of Minerva. Our *familia*, when in council, had high regard for her wisdom. In truth, there were at least two opposing camps in our family, as there are in most extended families. The first wanted to hold on to all the traditional ways, and keep our establishment small and intimate. They were led by our Sibyl. The opposition wanted to open the Oracles up to meet the energy and expansion of the new Augustan Age. They were led by Captain Max. We were painfully aware that the Oracle at Delphi, with all its celebrated glories, had totally eclipsed ours at Cumae in the past – but we were also cognisant that this fame brought about Delphi's very downfall. The limited lifespan of celebrity provided us with a nagging reminder of the fate which threatened all of us. Delphi had been repeatedly looted of its treasures over the past three hundred years and its Oracle is now just about to close its doors . . . perhaps for ever.

We were ready to believe that our prospects could be golden. Our truly resplendent Temples of Apollo and Jupiter at Cumae were thronged with visitors and the Sibyl's oracular pronounce-ments were much in demand. The Oracle of the Dead, close to our neighbouring wealthy resort at Baiae, was definitely on the itinerary of the Roman rich, the celebrated, as well as the needy. The guides in the area told visitors the most incredible tales about our Sibyl and the dramatic and exceptionally dangerous descent into the underworld. Even that outstandingly wealthy patron of creativity Caius Maecenas recently descended into the Infernal Regions and my grandfather once told me that Hannibal (although he sacked the area around Cumae two centuries ago) had felt the urge to perform sacrificial rites to the deities of our underworld! Years before I ever thought of writing this account, it was rumoured that Virgil, the most favoured poet of our new Emperor Augustus, was considering a visit to 'our' kingdom of Hades.

Certain places on this earth are endowed with a special sanctity and are holy. This is certainly true of the Sibyl's fantastic cave at Cumae and the underground complex by Lake Avernus, which was cut into the hard volcanic tuff by our ancestors even before Homer's time. I would not say that the sulphur-laden mists rising from the nearby Phlegraean Fields are unworldly, but they certainly are awesome. I shall avoid mapping the complex mythical regions of this underworld for now, but merely explain that for me it is basically comprised of a long, narrow and steep passage which divides into several corridors down to a slowly flowing stream, which purportedly is the River Styx (the River of Hate). Greek mythology had it that the Styx winds around Hades (the underworld) nine times. At a man-made landing beside this stream, my rather flimsy, skin-covered, basketwork coracle was docked. Homeric tradition has it that among the tributaries of this underground river are: Cocytus (the River of Lamentation), Acheron (the River of Woe), Phlegethon (the River of Fire) and Lethe (the fabled River of Forgetfulness). My own perspective on these dread waters is that if they exist in our imaginations, they possess a reality of their own, and if writers, priests and boatmen can describe even a fraction of this reality, then the popular imagination will fill in the details.

Was I miscast into this doleful role of boatman to the dead, destined to release the shades of many men from toil? Indeed, who was I before I became 'Charon'? Who would/could I have been without the disguise of a long beard and Charon's filthy and torn cloak? After some twenty-five years of assuming a surly demeanour, speaking in curt, clipped phrases as I ferried superstitious, wealthy Romans who wanted to contact the souls of their departed dear ones, I do not think such questions are superfluous. When I was some five hundred hands below the surface, I had to be austere, cold, mechanical – pretending to be half-human. I had to play the role of an aged man. I suppose I now am an old man, although I do not feel that is me. Most of those who came to the underworld did not regard me as being of this world. They saw me as a threatening and somewhat mythical figure hovering somewhere between life and death who held their very lives in his hands as he ferried them across the dreaded Styx. However, most of those passengers in my coracle were too nervous (as well as too afraid) to be curious about me: they had to face the prospect of their own death even as they sought to communicate with those no longer alive. Death was on the prowl in this underworld, hovering around the watery mists of the Styx and the Acheron. It is said that wandering sorrow can take the shape of the shadow of death. I felt very much in control of my destiny as I pushed my flimsy coracle through the sulphurous waters, but my passengers did not. They imagined danger – perhaps death – lurking. The over-whelming number of visitors who did return above ground believed, usually with a huge sigh of relief, that they had travelled to the lowest, darkest depths, to the extreme limits of Hades, and were now proud to be able to look back on death itself.

My almost daily footfalls down the dark, torch-lit passage to Hades still echo in my memory. As a young man it was par-ticularly wrenching to descend into a world of mostly silent and vacuous solitude. It did not take me many years of being focused

11

on death and this ghoulish underground performance truly to appreciate the wonders of breathing fresh air. Heraclitus once pronounced that souls smell in Hades. I would have none of that. There was indeed a strong and dreadful stench in these bowels of the earth. It was the noxious combination of sulphurous gases, human and bat excrement, urine, and smoke from the hundreds of burning candles and torches which lit these caves. Clouds of throat-searing smoke also were intentionally produced by burning straw before the visitors descended in order to create a murky atmosphere. This was crucial not only to permit disguises and masks to be used but also because it limited the reality of perception. This encouraged our select visitors, our explorers of death, in their somewhat intoxicated and hallucinating states, to transform evanescent visions into fondly remembered faces.

All this unreality naturally affected me. I was the captain of my tiny, greased-skin coracle. But was this becoming a vessel of my dreams? If the whole underworld was staged, was my coracle not a theatrical vehicle within it? As an actor in the play of Styx, I could abandon the limitations of being Rufus. Crossing the Styx, I was able to enter a world of my imagination where a completely new order of things was possible; where death was entirely unreal. I know that this dichotomy of above- and below-ground personalities also affected and troubled my father from whom I had inherited the time-worn mantle of 'Charon'.

Until I had my voice change, I never knew what my father did underground. No one ever talked about it and he never mentioned it. Sometimes father told me tales about Hades or magical stories of Osiris, the Egyptian god of the underworld. I listened, enthralled, to his description of how the dead were embalmed and mummified. Their voyage in celestial boats, fitted with bathrooms and lavatories and amply stashed with all kinds of provisions, took them to a distant galactic afterlife. This filled me with youthful wonder. This Egyptian fantasy in some ways seemed more real than our own, and somewhat vague, Graeco-Roman Elysium.

My initiation to the darkened ways of the underground came right after my first visit to the barber's. My voice had changed and my father wanted to hear if I could bark like a vicious dog. I passed his test and for a couple of years apprenticed as half of the great three-headed dog, Cerberus, who guards the gates of Hades. This beast greets all newcomers by wagging his snake-like tails and pricking his ears. But should the visitor want to turn back, then this cloth-and-plaster monster growled in all of his three throats and his fierce barks reverberated and rumbled through the caverns of Hades, thoroughly frightening the impressionable. I must confess to enjoying my canine role and the sight of powerful men in my father's coracle shaking with fear. Improbably, on one occasion an old Roman, obviously well prepared, tried to appease Cerberus by throwing him a bone and calling out: 'Good dog, good Cerberus. You'll like this bone.' I growled back loudly, hardly able to control my laughter. Fortunately the bone did not hit me on the head, and I can never recall the incident without a smile.

Gradually I was given other roles as well. For example, I was instructed on more than one occasion to be a young warrior who had died in battle. I had to put on an appropriate mask and a suitable wig whose projected shadows would resemble the deceased. I then had to learn a range of responses to questions in the nature of which the visitors had been thoroughly coached. Assistants to Archaeon, the father of Peleus, who in turn became our camp trainer and coordinator, would pass me instructions on how to prepare for any given role. One day I would be a slaughtered gladiator, on another a young man killed in a fire, or murdered by robbers, or drowned at sea. I was told how tall each youth was, how he spoke, if he stuttered or stammered or lisped. I would also be given the names of his parents and grandparents, brothers and sisters, friends, lovers, etc., some of whom had to be given specific greetings. In a slightly wavering and shaky voice I would say: 'Remember me to my uncle Julius and to my niece Candia.' Impersonating pale and wondrous phantoms was truly a challenging and entertaining introduction to the theatre of the dead. It proved an excellent training period for my ultimate role as Charon.

Above ground I was able to pay my tribute to Bacchus's sacrament: my goatlike lust. The beaches of Baiae, as our celebrated Roman writer Propertius duly warned, are fatal to chaste girls. Along these shores unbridled licentiousness took place, with heavily rouged *lupa* of uncertain age wiggling their hips, passing flirtatious glances and even embracing passers-by. I only vaguely recall 'Tits' Mammarion, 'Lovie' Erotion and 'Tickles' Uranus, a transvestite. But after some youthful escapades I learned that keeping away from the public roads enabled me to enjoy sweeter tastes. Women who were not at all provocative I found the most arousing. The honey of genuine passion is not only delightful in and of itself but also represents the most profound kind of human pleasure.

I only assumed Charon's mantle when my father suffered a stroke and could no longer paddle the flimsy coracle across the fabled Styx, in reality but a short stretch of underground water. At first this seemed like more play acting to a small and select audience, but time took its toll. Waiting sometimes for hours in the dim light of flickering candles for the visitors to descend the long tunnels, I began to feel confined by my bleak sur-roundings. I came to understand the meaning of the phrase 'perpetual boredom' as used by the Greeks. The eerie reflections of the burning torches in the waters often proved hypnotising. The fumes could be suffocating. Scorpions and huge black spiders crawled on the walls. I wanted to blot out the real hell that was growing in my head. After my father died I remember shouting to the reverberating tunnels: 'Father! Father! Don't leave me here. Don't leave me alone.' And the response was total silence. No response from Echo whatsoever. Even Dis paid no heed. Everything seemed stained with the black stillness of death. Once I even thought I heard my father's familiar voice cry out brusquely to me: 'What! Have you joined us here?'

Perhaps in such moments I was very close to madness. I not only missed my father's voice but also the terraced furrows which were often to be seen on his forehead, clearly expressing his scepticism.

Although I ferried dozens of visitors across the fabled Styx every week, I still knew absolutely nothing of what really happened behind death's veil. The darkness of uncertainty haunted me. Helping others believe they had seen the realm of the dead in no way helped me. The music of false beliefs was still music to some ears, but not to mine. Such base, flutelike tunes were simply off-key! Poets have said that the way to hell is easy, but as the years have passed I would say that in the Infernal Regions of Avernus it was not. It was impossible to accept that the fear of death was simply fear of the unknown. Meditating for hours on end, watching the bubbles of air rising in the waters, I began to accept that life needs death because death stimulates living. Trying to cheat death was sheer folly. Simply assigning fears to the Jovian gods, as most of my passengers in the coracle did, merely chained us to ignorance. Underground, I hoped death would be a long and forgetful sleep . . . a fading of consciousness in the eternal pitch-black. And there was good reason for me to wish this – and not only to preserve my sanity. I saw myself reflected in the water and on occasion it seemed to me that my hands were dripping in black blood.

As Romans, we are accustomed to bloodshed all around us . . . and not only in the pools of sacrificial blood of animals in the temples of Jupiter and Apollo. In the past a small number of the select visitors to Hades who refused to go along with our story, who – even though inebriated with less than celestial wines – rejected the whole mythical experience, were murdered

15

as they disembarked from the coracle and their bodies were thrown into the slowly flowing 'Styx' never to be seen again. They were later reported lost as 'shades' to a vengeful Hades and most unfortunately had been unable to make their return journey. This particular practice more or less stopped in the time of my father. In the past few decades we had to resort to poisoning those few who it was thought could ruin our *familia* and close down our entire operation. The very survival of the descent into Hades, known to all since the days of Homer's *Odyssey*, was at stake. So were our lives. Although I never took a life with my own hands, I was an accomplice both because I sometimes gave the order and on account of my silence. I never reported these sinister activities to the authorities in Baiae. Indeed, this is the very first time this information has ever been written down and no member of our *familia* has ever talked about it to an outsider for fear of being swiftly eliminated.

What are the facts of this matter? Well, I would estimate that on the average we have had to poison about two visitors in every lunar cycle, or close to thirty 'casualties' a year. It may have been slightly more, but we never counted. All such arithmetic would have been suspect in any case. Admittedly the total was not an inconsiderable number. In return for this we helped many thousands to make a treasured contact with the hereafter; to turn the fables of Homer and the mythical underworld into a genuine and unforgettable experience. That is no small achieve-ment and other religions have slaughtered many more to preserve and enhance their particular beliefs in the hereafter. People have always had and always will have a desire to communicate with the deceased. We enabled a few to do so at a relatively low cost. Visitors were able to gain the entrance to the afterworld where they purportedly contacted the dead spirit of a loved one or of some ancestor. They were fully aware of the risks involved in visiting Hades and knew that a few just did not survive their journey. After many generations, some members of our *familia* accepted this furtive practice as a given. They tempered the management of the lurid details so that they would not overwhelm or transform us. The hundred-faced deceptions of our *familia*, as well as the clandestine proceedings of our enterprise, were seldom mentioned. Regular prayers were made at the Temple of Apollo asking for the understanding of the gods. It was said for many years that our former manager, Archaeon, had been struck – but not killed – by a lightning bolt as a show of Apollo's anger. We recognised that slowly dripping poisonings should never be allowed to become banal. The manner in which the truth is hidden is often critical. As one of our more cynical priests, Lysius, whose mouth had a caved-in look resulting from the falling out of his teeth, once suggested as an afterthought: 'Death is merely a side of life that is turned away from us.'

I have also paid a price in my frequently repeated and haunting dreams of the dead – that is, of people I suggested should 'disappear' because they might talk. It is fair to say that some years back I was caught up in a spiral of frightening halluci-nations and circling apocalyptic thoughts. It seemed possible to me that life and death were merely an exchange of masks. I was unable to accept my own death or understand such a fate for others. I tried to evade responsibility with the recourse that the souls of those departed did live on. Timeworn questions arose in my mind, such as: Where exactly in the body do our souls reside? Do they have a separate existence from us? Are they more ancient than our bodies? Is their transmigration possible? Do souls have their own identity, or are they interchangeable, passing from one body to another? Infinitely debatable questions with no possible conclusions. It was a long time before I came to accept that Dis is composed of such obscure profundities as to be practically incomprehensible. I thought in circles and sometimes found myself talking to the excavated walls. On occasion, the flickering light provided by the mirrored torches confused my fragile hold on reality. In the presumably more sane atmosphere

17

above ground our high priest, Marcus Quintius, who had become my mentor in our *familia*, patiently tried to explain that Plato had seen the soul as an intermediate between intelligibles and sensibles. I understood very little of all of this. It was too learned. But then Platonists also had argued that looking into ourselves was not the proper way to proceed in ethical enquiries. Some sick people, for example, might think they were doing well, when in truth they were not. This was particularly true for the mentally disturbed. Quintius cautioned me, saying that Jupiter did not like mortals prying into heavenly secrets; that he might even hurl thundering headaches into fertile brains as punishment. Or, I silently thought to myself, as punishment for murder.

Ghosts or shades had become familiar to me in the theatre of the dead we conducted underground. I was deeply perturbed, however, when in my mid-twenties I one day recognised the face of a 'sceptic' whom I had marked for extinction a month earlier. I was sure it was him even amidst the masked faces that were partially obscured by billows of smoke and the dimness of the flickering torches. Had someone sculpted a mask in his likeness? Was it all in my imagination? Where had he come from? Was it really a 'shade' that had come to haunt us? This figure kept on recurring with regularity and enormously distressed me. I tried to get help from Marcus Quintius, who came down to observe the phenomenon. But whenever Marcus came down the 'sceptic' failed to appear. This led me to believe this particular shade was a phenomenon of my guilty conscience.

Forgetfulness could have been a blessing. The Greek myths held that drinking Lethe's waters brought about a blissful oblivion of the past. According to the ancients, the spring of Lethe, which rose under a white cypress, was the first thing seen in the underworld by the souls, or shades, of the departed. Being very thirsty after the long journey, they would be tempted to drink from it. One drink from the spring would erase all memories of past incarnations and render them no wiser than the rest of humanity – which is always born into this world without remembrance. But these same spirits also drank Lethe's waters in order to forget the sorrows of their former lives before entering the Elysian Fields.

I no longer need to drink from the waters of Lethe – everything is becoming more unknown to me every day. What is memory anyway? Perhaps we should find another name for the distorted way we remember past events that are still somehow alive within us. Do not memories often become a record of what has not been? Are they like dreams which turn more real over time? Marcus Quintius contends that memory is our coherence, our source of feeling; that without memory we are blanks. He preaches that life has no meaning without memory. Remove memory and all of history, time and reality as we have known them, simply vanish. I respond that, as far as I am concerned, there are seasons when I think memory is overrated. He disputed my observation that oblivion was the road of man's destiny. Personally, I felt I could do with a bath in cool oblivion and achieve a degree of the tranquillity I so desired. How good it would be if I could shout at the entrance to the underworld: 'Oh, visitors, beseech no more the hapless shades of the dead!' Of course they would have thought I was simply demented.

I admit that perhaps our *familia* became over-committed to giving our fellow Romans a taste of the next world. Ours was turning into something of a long-running Homeric theatre of the afterlife, providing not only a stimulus to the popular imagination but to our own. I felt there was creativity in interpreting and expanding on what our forefathers had bestowed on us. Perhaps it is inevitable that under such pressures we sometimes experienced a loss of reality. The Sibyl, who with the priests exercised full control over the religious rites of the oracle, certainly was no great help in this respect. Her grasp on reality was often restricted by all the hallucinogenic mushrooms she consumed, not to mention the laurel fumes she inhaled in order to make oracular pronouncements in a state of Apollonian ecstasy.

Although it was the Sibyl who nominally decided who could and who could not enter the nether regions, most of her attention was focused on prophesying: The offerings of visitors who sought resolution to problems facing them was the *familia*'s principal source of income. These 'contributions' to the Temple of Apollo and to the 'Oracle of the Dead' never made us wealthy – but our communal income was kept confidential by both the Sibyl and Quintius. I did not enquire about the exact figures. I was not privy to the secrets of the priests and others around the Temple of Apollo and the Sibyl's Oracle.

When our oracular circle held discussions about tactics and the problems facing us, I was treated with respect not only because of my length of service but also because of my close friendship with Marcus Quintius and my access to our Sibyl, Sulpicia Galla. It is true that on occasion she instructed me on the best approach to take with famous visitors and afterwards would deeply interrogate me about their reactions, questions, fears and so on. However, she almost never took part in any of the discussions, meetings or daily activities of our *familia*. She was above that. She only descended from the clouds on important occasions.

As a family we ate many of our meals together. We often sang together. We observed religious festivals – which frequently would end in drunken revels – together. We bathed communally at our own baths almost every day of the year. Yes, we all knew how we look naked. And we also enjoyed the occasional, almost ritualistic, group orgies. When we were happy as a family, we were united. All this bound us in the most profound ways – to the extent that there were moments when we got on top of one another. And, of course, there were also the arguments which all human activity can arouse. In more than one sense, our lives depended on our most unusual 'business'. And, as this occasionally involved murder, it also demanded our absolute silence.

II

'The Sibyl would like your visit,' was the way I was summoned one bright autumn morning by the charming young Clymene, one of the Sibyl's three devotee-priestesses. This was an invitation not to be refused.

The Sibyl was the spiritual centre of our *familia* in Cumae. It was not only that the Oracle had become a widely renowned institution but, more importantly, that this particular Sibyl was regarded by Romans as just about the sole source of contact with the gods, and in particular with Apollo. Hers was the poetry of cataleptic knowledge. When not drunk, drugged or in a trance, she seemed to know of worldly horrors well before they actually happened. She had a prophetic imagination and also skilfully manipulated all the possible ambiguities of language whenever she really wanted to do so. I admit to envying and admiring her immense powers of concentration.

She did not summon me often and when she did the reason was always political. Highly calculating and supremely manipulative, she knew that with me, who had the reputation of being fiercely independent, and the priests on her side she could outmanoeuvre the others of our tightly knit and self-contained group. Besides being awesomely imperious, she was invariably surprising. Certainly never dull. Highly theatrical when she needed to be, she had visitors never knowing what was coming next. This suited her, but made life difficult for the younger priestesses surrounding her. One moment charming and confiding, the next moment terrorising, the Sibyl kept them all on their toes with her constant demands, needs and threats. She knew there were numbers of young Roman women eager to learn from her and win the much sought-after opportunity to live at the Oracle.

21

This situation was particularly hard on Mentula, who was her chief assistant and 'understudy', if I may put it in theatrical terms. There had been many such favoured 'virgins' over the years. Mentula was in her late thirties and my heart went out to her because she was truly gifted. She somehow read the minds of the members of our *familia* and who can say this is not a true gift of Apollo? Sulpicia herself was selected by the priests after the previous Sibyl died at the self-proclaimed age of ninety-one. She was then already in her early forties. I was frequently asked the age of the Sibyl by strangers – and always replied, 'Miraculously young for her age.' The fact is that Sibyls always seemed to go on and on until only skin and bones remained. Mentula must constantly have been wondering how many years she would have to wait until it was her turn, or until the Sibyl tired of her? Patience itself could be most wearying, especially when catering to the Sibyl's whims.

The Sibyl's sanctuary was a separate world of its own. When I walked into the sanctuary, which is located below the Temple of Jupiter on a small, rocky hill overlooking the Mediterranean, I was struck by the powerful impression its portal made on all visitors. In the entrance hallway of the immensely high-domed cave into which I was ushered by one of the Sibyl's slaves, one's attention is meant to focus on the painfully realistic images painted on large and movable wooden wall-panels. On the first were horrid human shapes, representing grief and resentful care. The next was a vast and ugly scene illustrating pallid diseases, old age, fear, hunger, pain, poverty and finally death. The third was a calmer presentation of that kind of slumber which is closely related to death. This was followed by a picture of Mars, portrayed not as the god of agriculture but as a warrior and thus as a harbinger of death. This panel was also in bright colours but was slightly more blackened than the rest from the soot produced by the oil-soaked torches. Then there was a portrait of Insanity herself: she had a bloodstained ribbon binding her forehead and hair. And finally, concluding the sequence, was a large portrayal of Strife and the Furies – Tisiphone, Megara and Alecto. These female spirits were carrying out the vengeance of the gods upon sinful humans. The images were selected to put those seeking to pose questions to the Sibyl into a fearful state. To me this portrayed assemblage seemed far more frightening than the underworld of Hades in which I worked.

I waited. A couple of slave cleaners came in and scattered sawdust over the floors and then swept away the accumulated dirt. I could imagine the Sibyl inspecting them and commanding: 'Get that dusty spider's web down. Do I see a baby scorpion in the corner over there?' Despite her failing vision, the Sibyl had an excellent eye when it came to detail. More waiting.

The young priestess, Cytheris, came in and lit some incense. In a soft whisper she confided: 'This is one of the Sibyl's favourite scents. She calls it "Dead Syrian"!' Then a slow-moving slave told me that the Sibyl was ready and I was guided through an ancient and eerie tunnel carved into solid rock about two hundred paces long and sloping gently downwards until it reached a depth of some thirty-five paces. Natural light streamed in dramatically from strategically placed holes in the long, sharply pointed ceiling. There were also a few burning torches to illumine the darkest spots.

At the entrance to her chamber was yet another ante-room where all kinds of gifts from past generations were displayed: wonderful Persian caldrons, fancy Egyptian harps, terracotta amphora with oil, ancient bronze tripods, marble statues of Apollo, onyx wine bowls. Objects offered, treasures sacrificed for the privilege of consulting the Sibyl. From these gifts came ghostly voices of the past and also historical meaning. They told of visitors who had come before and left something behind. These sacrifices were a metaphor for a balancing of the accounts of life as well as the finances of the Oracle.

Finally I was ushered in to meet her eminence. She was dressed in a dyed Phocaean purple tunic which was longer than mine and reached her heels. There was a certain nobility to her features, particularly her strong jawbone. Her painted cheeks detracted somewhat from the skilfully applied make-up at the corners of her intense, black eyes. Her (as always) heavily rouged lips and fiercely drawn-back, flaming pomegranate-coloured hair, with its occasional grey streak, dramatically rounded out her face in the most outrageous fashion. The colours revealed her need to assert herself: to declare a forceful and demanding presence. But if she had been walking in the night in Baiae, all would have mistaken her for a prostitute. Possibly even an aged male prostitute.

'You look divine, Sibyl!' I exclaimed as I entered.

She took my hands in her wrinkled and cold fingers, which were like moveable antennae. 'Stop flattering me, Rufus – or relegating me prematurely to your afterlife,' she said in a voice that had once been crystal clear but now had a crackle of the throaty in it.

'Well, you do look positively sibylline!' I said, carefully down-grading my compliment.

'And you, much beloved Rufus and equally excoriated and reviled Charon . . . look . . . pale. I hope it is merely the pallor of the underworld and not because I summoned you here.' Her eyes did not waver from mine as she spoke. They seemed to be piercing through me.

Obviously she was at her sharpest that morning. I used to see her more often, but her age was slowing her down and she was frequently unwell.

'How is your appetite?' I enquired.

'Irreverent,' she snapped. At first I thought she had meant 'irrelevant'. She was not always understandable, but I heard a slight stomach rumble. Then her eyes sort of rolled and her voice changed as if the god within her was speaking. 'Apollo be praised! My fortune is beyond my mouth and my stomach. It is too soon to look into my entrails to see what the Fates have in store for Rome.' As she uttered the tail-end of this sentence, a wry trace of a smile crossed her lips.

Our Sibyl frequently prefaced her comments with references to Apollo's arrows of inspiration. Her pace and poetry changed markedly when she was professionally intoxicated. Then she often babbled non sequiturs and repetitive sounds much like an infant. No one could understand these sounds, much less interpret them, but the priests often pretended.

'I have heard rumours that the Pythia has left for Athens,' she said, apparently rather pleased with such reports. Generally the Sibyl considered herself high above the normal, day-to-day problems of this world. And she placed 'her' Oracle rungs of importance above any visitations to Hades, that is, 'my' underworld.

'So have I,' I replied. 'It is good news, but as we all know Delphi has long been experiencing a decline in supplicants.' The Sibyl was extremely competitive with the Delphic Oracle and was currently pleased that her rival, the Pythia, had nearly given up – in good measure due to the loss of foreign patronage with the defeat of rich Persian, Syrian and other oriental rulers by the Roman armies.

'It is a heaven-sent opportunity for us to move in on her regular customers,' she said. 'On the other hand, it is also a warning. For my part I would rather die than abandon Cumae and slink away to Rome. We must remain strong and dream up ever new ways of increasing our reputation and attracting attention to our Oracles.'

'The tallest flowers often get picked,' I retorted. 'Being noticed also entails risks.'

'We will talk about this later,' she commanded. She was going to set the agenda. 'I have not seen your Calliope of late – but then I don't get around as much as I used to.'

'She is learning to play the flute and is more of a butterfly than ever,' I said of my cherished eleven-year-old daughter.

'I, who am confined to this windswept cavern in order to convey Apollo's messages to this world, find myself out of touch with the young. My inspirations are continually interrupted by the pedestrian.' There was a long pause. Then she resumed along the same line: 'I, who devote myself to Apollo, who am intoxicated by him and for him, must stoop to cope with mortal ambitions – with Max's rubbish!' Now I was beginning to gather the drift of her thoughts. Silent, I waited for her to continue. There was the chirp of a sparrow rustling some leaves that had scattered on the stone floor of the ante-chamber.

'I will not tolerate turning this Oracle into a circus . . . or a brothel,' she fumed. 'There are enough of those in Baiae and Pompeii I am told. There is only one world-famous Oracle now and that is here at Cumae.'

'So where, prophetic one, do you stand on the projects being proposed by our *lanista*?' I asked rather tentatively.

'Apollo is beyond money and material rewards. Because he is not silence or words, only I can comprehend him.' And she drew a deep breath. 'As ever, Max is overly ambitious. He recognises no boundaries. He wants to attract larger crowds in order to make more money. He cannot comprehend that greed in the world of the spirit is a sin.'

'Might it not be true that we may be too narrow in our appeal to the rich?' I ventured tentatively. 'There are many rich. Perhaps bringing more of them in on special gambling boats to Baiae could increase your . . . your meagre revenues?'

'Boats full of naked prostitutes?' And here she pounded her breasts so that the rubies jangled.

'I wouldn't put that past him,' I replied amused.

'I have had it reported to me that Max suffers from a neurotic tic of the prick. Perhaps that is at the root of his problem,' ventured the Sibyl, revealing the naughty side of her psyche. I laughed heartily at her description. She brushed my response aside with a wave of her hand and continued in a more typically Sibylline way: 'Apollo will not stand for this. Radiant Apollo who joins music, time and divination. How could he put up with such a shameless circus?' Then she stopped. I was used to respecting the Sibyl's silences which spoke so loudly in between her measured words, her succinct phrases. After a few moments she continued normally. 'And the other half of your *lanista*'s dreams?'

'That's quite another matter,' I replied, 'but a most political one. A joint celebration of Apollo and the Emperor could bring Augustus here. We couldn't fail there. It would attract the widest notice.'

The Sibyl nodded her head in agreement. 'Yes. There would seem to be a consensus on that one. We shall have to sound out his joint ruler, the sinister Agrippa, before we move ahead.'

'That may prove tricky,' I countered. 'You know Agrippa still resents the Oracle because an ancient prophetess told him when he was a youth that he would always be number two.'

'I have often regretted that,' she said. 'That was a politically motivated misinterpretation by the priests. By Apollo! That was sheer opportunism.' Then she stopped herself and paused. 'Yes. It is true. We also need money but how to find it? I doubt the Senate would give us any. Perhaps we should consult Maecenas. Such a lovely, soft man. Such . . . elegant style. And so much money.'

'You don't find him somewhat . . . dainty?'

'By the breath of Apollo! Pederasty has all kinds of consequences, including odd propensities in manners, dress and even manner of speech. Wild bores, wild poetic bores, as much as they curry favour with the gods, are driven along by their greed for fame.' Here she prodded me, knowingly and with familiarity, in the ribs. 'But the main thing is that he has means and influence with the new emperor. Which brings me to the reason why I invited you to come here this morning. I am most troubled by *your* Orphics and so, it would seem, is Augustus.'

'They are not *mine*,' I said with mock indignation.

'But you are one of them. You are an elder and an Orphic leader in Cumae,' she said with great determination.

'Yes. I am proud to be one of them. I feel very much that while pantheism is a wondrous concoction, it does not truly address my spiritual needs nor that of most people. Romans now have far too many gods. In fact, these have descended on us almost like a plague, from Egypt, Syria, Persia and even beyond. There seems to be a god for everything these days. And these gods don't seem to listen to our inner selves. I believe people are looking for something deeper, which will offer them hope and even redemption in the next world . . . which as you yourself know, Sulpicia, they do not have now. Olympus truly presents chaos while Orphism focuses on one single almighty force which all can believe in – which I believe in.'

'You mean you would reject Jupiter?' she asked half-incredulously.

'He is supposed to control the other gods, but cannot. He is purportedly too busy chasing earthly nubiles. Now you know that this entire Olympian construct is an extended fairy tale, Sulpicia. No more pertinent to Romans than that of the Persian magi or of Horus in Egypt.' She looked directly at me when I used her own name. It reminded her that she was also human.

'I will not get into a discussion on comparative religion, Charon. But if you look with such disdain on our wonderful gods, why must you hold your meetings in *my* temple?

'*Our* temple, Sibyl. The Temple of Apollo, who is your divine transmitter, also belongs to the people of Cumae who built it.'

'I do not need to be told what Apollo does,' she said with disdain. 'You don't seem to realise that given the Emperor's new direction of a return to our Grecian spiritual heritage, to a renewal of our ancient Roman faith and to our old morals, staging mysterious rites in the Temple of Apollo represents rebellion and could lead to this entire Oracle being shut down.'

'But Augustus claims that Apollo is his special – not to say favourite – divinity. He treasures Apollo. How could he close his temple?' I asked. It must be remembered that Octavian regards Apollo as his protector and in his role as Augustus, the first Roman emperor, he must fulfil the auspicious prophecies the ancient Sibyl gave to his purported ancestor, Aeneas.

'By Apollo! By the tune of the insects, I know it is the time of the harvest moon. Charon, you know how the Romans are hankering after Egyptian "knowledge" and Persian "wisdom" in their search for the afterlife. These are like alien invasions. Octavian, I mean the revered Augustus, is our Roman emperor. He is half-god and half-mortal. His birthday is now a holy day and a national holiday. His name has been added to those of the gods in our official hymns.'

'Not bad,' I interrupted, 'when one considers that he is a money-lender's grandson!'

'I want to hear none of that,' retorted the Sibyl. 'Let us make this clear. Augustus is suspicious of all these new cults and he regards the Orphics as one of those potentially subversive of our ancestral Roman gods.'

'So what do you propose, Sibyl? Forbid our meetings?'

She was silent for an instant, then decided: 'Hold the meetings underground.'

'You mean in the caverns by Lake Avernus?' I asked incredulously.

'Not necessarily . . . but you know: on the quiet. Hidden. Behind closed doors. You hold those super-secret mysteries which no one knows about. I have always wondered . . . '

'Come now. We don't pry into your secrets, do we, Sulpicia?'

She took that question quite defensively. 'I am also a priestess, although some would deny it,' she declared. 'Our secrets are jealously protected by the gods.'

29

'Just as ours are sanctioned by our one all-powerful God.'

'I should like you to recall that Sibyl in Greek means god's will,' she countered in proud defiance.

'And Charon was merely the son of Erebus, now remembered as that gloomy space through which the souls pass to Hades,' I said mockingly.

'So? Have you been endowed with the power to know the future?'

'Apollo was not so generous to me,' I responded.

'As Apollo would whisper: "Sings the whole day and the skylark is still not satisfied." . . . Rufus, you are so insistent. You are beginning to sound like one of those Jews who are absolutely unshakeable in their faith. Theirs is also a harsh and vengeful creation. It would seem to me most unusual – not to say unnatural – for such a lonely and solitary divine up in the galactic heavens to be so impatient and . . . and . . . impulsive.'

'I believe our God is compassionate, understanding and for-giving, but I shall not try to convert you or convince you, Sibyl. You in your oracle have direct access to the gods. I, in lowly Hades, possess no such powers of communication. I don't want to belabour the point, but what we are seeing today is a return to ruler worship. Augustus is spending vast fortunes on the upkeep of the holy places in Rome, resplendent with new temples to his radiant 'patron' Apollo, blessed be his name, but as one can tell, not a sesterce is being given to this ancient and holy establishment.'

'Alas! You are right about that, Rufus. On the mountainside there are old trees – with cracks and holes . . . That's me . . . The sanctuary is short of funds. Our expenses are too high. And so far there has been no help from Rome. We have precious few benefactors . . . ' And here she faltered, looking somewhat forlorn.

Of course I was dimly aware of the financial problems facing the Oracle and the Sanctuary of Apollo. As they were sacred and religious institutions, we could not charge entrance fees or the like. All our income came from non-monetary gifts which we had to convert into cash. On receiving visitors, the Sibyl told them right away what was usually expected for such consultations. She would explain that Aeneas himself had to provide seven ewes and seven bullocks to the Sibyl of Homer's times and that expectations had risen in the intervening centuries. These visitors would then have to go to the local merchants working for us who would sell them oxen and other animals at high prices. Only a small portion of this livestock was used for offerings. True, their entrails were used for divination by the priests, but all the meat, fat, hides and wool of the animals killed went into the *familia*'s kitty. The remainder of the cattle, goats and sheep went back to the merchants for resale to the next lot of visitors. Of course the olive oil used for roasting, the candles, torches, flowers and so forth, would also have to be bought from our merchants, as would the expensive bronze tripods, the cakes and the wines which were special offerings to the Sibyl and her priestesses. The general rule was that the more anxious the visitor to the Oracle, the more generous would be his gifts.

'Let us not talk more of finances,' she declared peremptorily. 'I have ordered one of "my little spirits" to get us some of those delicious oysters from Lake Lucrino.' She used a high-pitched and condescending voice when referring to her attendant 'virgins', who were always lurking in the shadows. Then, her face tightening up, she said: 'I have been getting reports on our Lydia's health. The prognosis does not look good. May the Fates be with her.'

I nodded my head in agreement. 'It does not.' My wife, who once had served as a personal attendant to the Sibyl, was suffering from severe intestinal problems and had been unwell for many moons now.

'I have asked Marcus Quintius to lead special prayers for her in the temple. I – I . . . ' She wavered.

'Thank you. She is most appreciative of your concern.' It was, in fact, highly unusual for Sulpicia to express genuine feeling or sympathy for others. Empathy was almost beyond her. But few noticed this. They were far too preoccupied with observing her carefully staged 'image'. One day she had admitted to me in a moment of rare confidence: 'All my life I have been alone. I am no longer able to show many kinds of feeling.' Then she mumbled something to the effect of:

'The naiad of the weeping spring . . .
In these cavernous echoes no ear can stay true . . .
Apollo . . . Little . . . so little . . . we can do –
Next to nothing and merely avoid
Zero . . . cold . . . nothing . . . then the void.'

The Sibyl seemed to be going into one of her light trances. I could never tell whether these were somehow induced or a natural phenomenon. This time she seemed simply to drift away into her own, distant world. I thought about getting up but decided to wait. Indeed, after a short while she suddenly roused herself again.

'Please excuse me. I have had a minor spell. Sometimes I do not know how to stop and keep on babbling when it gets me nowhere. Pitiful. I know when I am on the right path, when I can go no further. Now let me see. Where were we? Yes, I remember. Let us plan our proposal to the *familia* for the Apollonian celebration of our new Emperor Augustus.'

'By all means,' I said, much relieved that she was back on track. 'But let us not make it too festive. No gymnastics. No dancing. Lots of laurel leaves.'

'Absolutely,' she nodded in agreement 'We must emphasise honour and solemnity. I should like to have some poetry read – perhaps by Virgil, although they say he does not read well. However, he would be good at immortalising Octavian's political and social ambitions. Getting Virgil to come would assure the visit of the Emperor.'

'It would,' I nodded in agreement.

'And then,' she continued, 'I should like to be able to come forth with some inspired prophecies in front of a highly select group . . . ranking senators, high priests, magistrates, the Emperor's family – something that has never been done before.'

'Capital! That is truly inspired, Sulpicia!' She had always enjoyed an excellent sense of the dramatic and carefully staged all of her flamboyant seances.

'And, if possible, I should like the *sacrificia* to Apollo to be kept to a minimum. I can't bear looking at them,' she said wincing.

The sacred rendering of a lamb, goat or calf forms an integral part of the ritual offerings to the gods. I knew that burning their entrails was especially distasteful to Sulpicia. Although my parents took me to witness the 'rendering sacred' of little lambs and goats at a very early age, I never liked either their slaughter or the spirit in which this was performed, namely: 'I sacrifice so that you, Jupiter (Apollo, or any of a hundred gods), may give in return.' This contractual aspect at the very basis of Roman religion continues to disturb me. It was not what bothered Sulpicia. She simply didn't like the sight of blood.

'I am entrusted with prophecy, a gift of divinity,' the Sibyl declared. 'I play no part in all those rituals of sacrifice. The "truth" and the path of "purification" are recognised in prophecy.' Then she abruptly asked if I thought we should have any milk-fed serpents crawling about her Persian rugs for 'atmosphere'? She claimed that a display of writhing snakes was an imperative for her Oracle. I replied that I never liked them crawling about my ankles. Although I had to admit their weaving motion was most sensual and suggestive, I didn't even like them swimming around my coracle in the underground river.

'Ah, I see our oysters are coming!' exclaimed the Sibyl, as Tappo, a slave to the high priest, brought them in on a large pewter platter.

This was a most unusual honour. The Sibyl usually treated me quite differently above ground from below. In her own space she was habitually far more distant and aloof. In her quarters, when I flattered her, she put up with me but expressed her disdain for my Orphic convictions. However, on the rare occasions when she descended to Hades, she became almost deferential. I suspected this possibly could be because she feared crossing the Styx might end her life. Afterwards she always told her priestesses that I should bathe more often. Apparently I stank! They then passed this unflattering comment back to me.

Sulpicia launched into the oysters with genuine appetite. She accompanied them with her special drink: boiled red wine which was then cooled and mixed with fuchsia juice. But she did not talk while eating. I had been told this was because she feared choking to death on her food.

At the end of our oysters, she returned from her sofa to sit on a bronze tripod, decorated with lions, which perhaps in former times had served to prepare roast kid. It was inscribed in Latin: Sacred to Apollo. With a certain grandeur she pronounced: 'Our land is brimful of sacred fury. The gods are still angry at our impiety. Oh, Apollo! Give me the strength to do more to appease you.'

'What can any of us do, Sibyl, to assuage their anger?' I asked politely.

'Stop listening to the silly magicians!' she exclaimed with a sweeping gesture of disdain. 'I don't have my curls trimmed under Venus,' she said imperiously. This last reference was to the wandering Chaldean astrologers whose pseudo-science is sweeping our land.

'But we at Cumae have no interest in their nonsense,' I countered – although knowing that was not entirely true.

'I spit at the evil eye,' she volunteered. 'It doesn't even have proper make-up. Oh why, oh why, can't those astrologers leave the gods in peace?' She moaned. An awkward silence followed.

I did not know what to say. Then she continued: 'If you must, and have matters that can't be settled, go to our augurs and let them make their pronouncements.'

'I wouldn't want to take up their precious time,' I protested.

'I am tired of those enquirers who want to know how to invest their money. Should it be property or should it be trade? If property, should it be houses or land? If trade, should it be in Rome or Baiae? It's disgraceful. The Sibyl is no real-estate fortune-teller.'

'Of course not, Sibyl,' I agreed.

'When the Greek gods vanish together with the great Pan, who has ruled our flocks and pastures, the forests and all their spirits, then nature will have lost its divinity. My relationship with our ancient gods is one of respect, mutual exchange and trust. I take my responsibility to transmit their messages most seriously,' insisted the Sibyl.

'Naturally, you do,' I responded in a rather fawning voice.

'Well, if we go ahead, I shall perform to the very best of my ability in front of the Emperor,' she said. 'In the next few days I shall invite your *lanista*, Max, and sound him out. After that we could invite one of the nobility to the Oracle so that he might extend our invitation to his holiness, Augustus.'

'That seems like a sound sequence. Most sensible,' I agreed.

'And you be sensible too, Rufus. Next time you stage one of your mysteries, do it in Baiae in their Temple of Venus. Let us keep your strange oriental rites out of Cumae.'

There was no point in further discussion. I sensed she had brought the meeting to an end. I rose, thanked her for the superb oysters and said my goodbyes, formally kissing the embroidered hem of her perfumed toga. It was real silk – worth its weight in gold. What luxury! In her presence, much as in that of the Emperor's court, ceremony had to be observed. Sulpicia favoured those who played her game.

III

'I can read your mind,' said Max, the general manager of our Oracles, relaxing naked in our *tepidarium*.

'You always can,' I said – half in flattery.

'So what is our holy bitch up to now?'

'Hardly the way to talk about our world-famous seer, the nominal head of our *familia*.' The truth is that Max had married into our family. Early on in his life he had been an officer in Caesar's army in Gaul and was extremely proud of his military record. None of us ever knew what to believe of his stories as he was as much of a compulsive exaggerator as a confirmed self-deluder.

'Come on now. *Familia* be damned,' said Max tightly clenching one of his large fists and pounding it against the marble wall of the baths. 'You and the Sibyl have been plotting to do me in.' As he said this the short hairs on the back of his balding head seemed almost to rise.

'By Jove, you know both of us better than that, Max. I have always been fiercely independent and don't like running conflicts in our *familia*. For her part, our Sibyl is focused on her status and doesn't care a bean about much else.'

'Not quite true. Rare is the family that does not contain one grubby miser in it. Sulpicia is anally concerned about money and is unbelievably tight-fisted. You know she has rooms full of treasures.'

'That's an exaggeration!'

'Perhaps even gold ingots?' Max prodded.

'That's just a rumour and you know it.'

'Wasn't she scheming again? Now be truthful, Rufus.'

'Well, she also wonders what schemes you and Peleus are up to.'

'Nonsense. I do not plot against cataleptic hags.' Here his round face flushed with anger. Max's alternating moods were truly tidal. 'I may not pay her the respect she thinks she deserves, but I am close to being obsequious when acknowledging her public role. She is our Oracle's mouthpiece. Some figure. Ugh! And what a crazed head of red-dyed hair!'

'And in turn she thinks of you, Max, as a power-hungry, money-crazed *lanista*. More suited to a Roman gladiatorial circus than to an oracle. All of this is not exactly conducive to harmony in our *familia*'s concern.'

'I hate being called an impresario of the gladiatorial circus. Julius Caesar praised me for the way I led our legion's attacks against the Gauls. I made it high up the military ranks. I earned my commission by blood. By Jove! I've earned respect as well. Let us face the facts, Rufus, but not in a two-faced way like Janus. This whole operation in Cumae has been stagnant for far too long. Half-asleep for more than three hundred years. We need to change. To move ahead dramatically with the new Augustan Age.'

'I'm not sure change for its own sake is a good idea and I certainly don't enjoy open-ended family drama.'

'I know, I know,' said Max bursting with impatience. 'You, Rufus, make a great Charon. But could you handle two hundred visitors in your coracle a day? No.'

'I would never need to. It's Peleus's job to separate the welcome kernels from the popular chaff. Few visitors are ready for or likely to profit from an actual encounter with the dead.'

'That's from your underground perspective. I know that there are countless thousands of the rich – scattered all over the vast Roman empire – who are waiting to be convinced. Who have the money but are fearful.'

'And with good reason. They hear of those visitors who never come back. They may even have seen some who return home with 'Cumae fever' and never recover. Most are incoherent and die within a few weeks. We must try to change this, but how? If those who go down and do not believe what they have seen were permitted to return home and tell the world, our ancient descent into hell would be swiftly shut down.'

'It's in reading those fucking entrails that the trouble lies. I have said it all along,' cursed Max, once again pounding his fist against the marble sides of the bath. 'Those *haruspices* examining the sacrificial lamb or chicken livers, or whatever, are total frauds anyway. We must make certain that they become more demanding. It would be easy for them to deny positive readings to any but the most exceptional. And negative readings warning them against any descent into hell could only be changed by massive donations of gold, olive oil or livestock.'

'Expensive consultations with the gods are all well and good, but Lysius and Balbus are independent priests with their own agenda,' I protested.

'And corrupt to the core. With a slightly larger cut of the take, they will instantly agree to anything.' Max always felt he could manipulate and intimidate all those around him.

'What if we brought them only sick animals with defective or even rotting entrails?' I countered.

Max burst out laughing, his large naked belly shaking. 'The underworld may be affecting the grumpy Charon, but it has certainly not touched his resourcefulness or imagination, Rufus.'

'Call mine the charm of Hades, Max.' At this point in our morning discussion in the Cumae baths, the bearded Peleus and his assistant Alfernus joined us. All of us were addicted to the slow, enjoyable routine of our bathing establishment. It was the best way for us to relax and at the same time to talk frankly to each other.

'Good-morning, you disciples of Bacchus,' Max greeted his closest friends in the family.

'And a fine autumn morning it is,' retorted Alfernus.

'You should be joining us a bit more in our rites,' said Peleus, patting his flat and lean stomach.

'I don't know why!' responded Max as he patted his protruding belly. 'I fuck every day, but I don't lose any weight.'

'It's not the regularity, Max, it's the force with which you do it,' said Peleus and all four of us laughed heartily.

'Expansion! Expansion!' said Max, again patting his belly. 'I've been talking forcefully to Rufus, here, about the Oracle's need to expand. For years I have been dreaming of bringing Romans down here on carpeted ships which would offer wine, women, song and gambling and bring profits rolling in,' he asserted proudly.

'Not a bad idea,' said the balding Alfernus, trying to be supportive.

'Not a bad idea? Bloodless Hades! It's an incredibly good one. I feel myself on the point of making history . . . heading towards immortality.'

'Towards immorality?' chuckled Peleus. 'Then count me in.' We all laughed again. Even Max.

'I'm going to make the vision of sex, money and risk that Romans only dream about a reality in which they will be able to take part.'

'But won't the priesthood in Rome want to know whether this is the kind of thing the Oracle should be involved in?' I asked, not wanting openly to ally myself with the opposition.

'I say, let the ship of Fortune steer men's lives,' responded Peleus.

'The arseholes of these priests show greater refinement than their mouths, for they have no teeth,' almost shouted Max, paraphrasing Catullus.

'You sound more like the Charon of Aristophanes, loudly hawking his services: "Any more for Lethe, Blazes, Perdition or the Dogs? Come along now, any more for a nice trip to Eternity?

No more worries, no more cares, makes a lovely break," ' I retorted, trying to lower Max's visibly rising temperature.

'Well, my project has the best of prospects: travel in carpeted luxury before getting access to the next world,' countered Max.

'You are babbling like a bleating sheep,' I pronounced with a broad smile.

'And I find you are bubbling like a *blatero*,' retorted Alfernus.

'It sounds positively and decadently Egyptian,' remarked Peleus.

'All my life I have been searching out opportunities,' continued Max, on a roll. 'I love to put one over on those pretentious Roman rich. I love to sniff out suckers and then milk them of their gold and silver. A bit of creative bullying helps raise the initial cash. When it starts coming, others with their silver will join in for the kill. That's how it always is and always has been.'

'Impossible' was obviously not a word in Max's lexicon, I thought to myself.

'Your charm will get them to succumb even though they know they are being taken for a donkey-ride,' said Peleus.

'What I want to know is: Are those in the Temple of Apollo so pure they can censure me?' challenged Max.

'Our *familia*, as you know, Max, governs by consensus. It will take all of your powers of manipulation to convince them and the upper echelon of priests,' I replied.

'I'm with Max,' said Peleus. 'But what about you, Rufus?' His face approached close to mine. Often we like to look very closely and directly into each other's eyes.

'It will take time to convince me,' I said evasively. 'Meanwhile may my genius protect me from Max's dreams.' (In our world each individual has a divine double, or 'genius', to whom he may appeal.) At moments like these I felt our *familia* had too many dynamic characters in it for its own good, even for its survival.

'Is it not the destiny of the obscure to be looked down upon and the privilege of the dynamic to be hated?' asked Max rhetorically. 'I comfort myself by saying that whoever hates me proves and feels himself to be a lesser person than I am.'

'Well put, Max,' applauded Alfernus, 'but I suspect this splendid project of yours may have to be put on hold. Last night in Baiae I met up with Anicius, who is the slave to Virgil, and he told me that, having been commissioned by Augustus to glorify the new empire, the poet would like to come and visit both the Sibyl's Oracle and the Descent to the Underworld.'

'Whew!' blew out Max in huge astonishment. 'By Jupiter! That will present major challenges!'

'And demand preparations,' added Peleus, suddenly looking rather glum.

My brain was racing as to what a visit to my underground by such a renowned poet would mean . . . I got stuck somewhere between my longing for immortality and my desire for profitable exposure.

'Ours is a great story, I tell you . . . among the greatest ever,' opined Max.

'You are going to have to go back to Baiae and contact Anicius to get more details,' Peleus told Alfernus. 'We can't have anything unexpected happen. No impromptu visits. We must be fully prepared.'

'Could you imagine the panic if Virgil suddenly came un-announced!' I agreed, shaking my head at the prospect.

'Max, I also heard that an assistant to Atreus, who in turn is close to the "near-immortal" Agrippa, has been talking to your slave Vectius,' said Alfernus, who obviously had been snooping around on his visit to Baiae.

'Yes. Vectius told me he had been to Baiae. It's been bothering me like a mass of fleas in my bed. How could my own Vectius, who has been mine all his life, whom I have looked after and upon whose informal education I expended so many hours – no, so many years, and such energy – would want to abandon me?' asked Max, adopting an injured expression.

'Indeed. Indeed. How could he do that?' asked Peleus with a broad smile.

'The ingrate says I have promised to set aside much of his pay for the day when he can ultimately buy his freedom,' replied a seemingly perturbed Max.

'Have you done so?' demanded Peleus with an incredulous look on his face.

At this point Max became slightly evasive. 'Well, hmm, no . . . not exactly. But it will be me the boy pays, which comes to the same thing.'

'That sounds fair enough,' I said, knowing how demanding and tight-fisted Max was. 'He's served you loyally all his life.'

'I always thought I was good to him. Maybe a bit hot tempered or impatient once in a while. But I only hit him when he deserved it. It couldn't be that I've been too demanding, could it?' he asked with mock innocence.

'Come on, Max. You know you don't exactly have a good reputation in that respect. Berating slaves never increased one's status,' said Peleus. 'But never mind. Personally I have never liked our trusted slaves leaving the *familia*.'

'Exactly,' said Max, seeing a new possibility for delaying the departure of Vectius. 'And how should I cope without him? He's run my accounts for years, kept my records. Fortunately Augustus has now made it more difficult for a slave to be freed. Property rights have been placed firmly above any slave rights. For the boy to gain his freedom is now going to take far more time and papyrus work,' said Max a bit more cheerful at the prospect of indefinite delays.

'Alfernus, what else did that official tell Vectius?' enquired Peleus.

'He said that he would try to find him a place on their staff looking after the accounts.'

'Which means Vectius would have to get a recommendation from you, Max,' said Peleus.

'I know, I know,' said Max again rather doleful.

'Could this give our *familia* an ear into the Imperial network?' asked Alfernus. Obviously he hoped to have yet another informant with the administrators in Baiae.

'Perhaps. But I don't like it,' said Peleus. 'Far more worrying – it also could give Agrippa information about us.'

'Then, indeed, it might be better to try delaying this for as long as possible,' I reflected.

I observed Max raising his eyebrows as he managed a light smile. He was rather pleased at my reaction.

'Maybe the gods have not abandoned me,' said Max. 'I was counting on the Sibyl to back me in my project because she would smell the perfume of money, but now our first priority obviously has to be Virgil's visit.'

'Yes. We need to hold a *consilium* of our *familia* on how to deal with this,' I added, sensing that this visit could bring us all together at a time when there was a danger of a division into two self-interested factions. A tug of war between the egos of Max and the Sibyl simply was not in our communal interest. After these many generations, tradition is important. Neither Sulpicia nor Max had been born into the Oracle, like Peleus, myself and most of the others.

In our *familia* each of us has developed his or her own role and, in the context of the communal mythology, we are all expected to play our part. Whenever one thinks one can escape from it, and play another role, there are eager members, such as Lysius and Mentula, who are ready to point out that one is straying. Of course once one is expected to manifest certain familiar characteristics, one is encouraged to grow into that role. If you are seen as a clown, you find yourself playing that role for all it is worth; and if you are seen as a miser – like the Sibyl – you will be expected to manifest those attributes. Sexually, as well, if you are a known seducer, like Peleus, certain women are likely to pursue you.

43

I must repeat that when we have been happy as a family, contented with our achievements, we were united; when we have been unhappy, we were each discontented in our own way and tended to be disruptive. Being in the bosom of our *familia* was important to me. I wanted to do everything I could to protect it and strengthen its reputation. Sometimes I wished our *familia* could revert to the ancient but infrequently observed practice of silence.

One could say that we are as cohesive as any troupe of actors or seminary of priests. We are not in the same league, of course, as our Roman nobility, but we too are quite separate from the ordinary, from the masses. Sometimes we even speak our own dialect. Our speech is laced with a few words of Etruscan origin, understandable only to us. I have heard it argued that the language of the *familia* is rooted in our ancient connections with both Hades and the Sibyllic tradition. Frankly, I doubt this. But it is true that occasionally our Campagnian atonality is a source of amusement to Roman visitors.

I got up out of the hot bath and went to take a quick cold plunge. The others stayed behind. Hebe, Max's rather portly wife, and Larissa, his eldest and most shapely daughter, were just entering the *natatio* where they swam every day. Although mixed *thermae* had been prohibited at various times in our long history, we never felt obliged to conform. There was something wonderful in our being able to mix without any feelings of embarrassment. In our naked state, we had our bodies accepted as much as our faces or our hands. Lust might be stimulated on both sides but apart from specially designated occasions, like the rare orgy, our baths were chaste. All of us need the space to be able to converse, relax, and enjoy the waters. I talked to Hebe for a few moments about my dog, Corso, who had been pestering her bitch, which was in season. I knew Hebe did not want any more puppies right now. It was a harmless and neighbourly conversation which ended when I returned to the heated waters.

Max was now holding forth to his small audience, which had been added to by our *lector*, Lysius. Romans have a somewhat, to me, humourless fascination with violence, sex, self-sacrifice and historical context. It always 'gets me' that rape is unfailingly good for a laugh with Max and Lysius. Admittedly, Max is a skilled storyteller who, as such, assumes his listeners are not particularly interested in the truth. 'The best lies are those that help me to sleep at night,' he was fond of repeating.

'If we take the broad historic perspective on the main challenges facing us Romans, I believe that the range of negative assumptions being made about our future is unnecessarily impressive,' the ever-optimistic and often pompous Max was saying.

'The positives may be few in number but I find them more appealing,' agreed his friend Peleus.

'In Rome I have often heard it said that our downfall will be our greed for money and power; that the rest of the Empire will rise up against us,' continued Max.

'If the miserably starving, the wretched poor and the exhausted slaves do not first burst out of the underbelly of the Trojan horse we have brought into our capital,' retorted the sharp-tongued Lysius.

'Certainly the ongoing importation of slaves from all over the Empire does pose a threat to our stability,' admitted Max.

'But they all have a chance for self-improvement and ultimately for freedom if they work for it,' rejoined Peleus.

'Well spoken,' said Max. 'And are these threats really more dangerous than those posed by odd believers in the Egyptian gods, barbaric practices, miracles and secret rites which are undermining our morals and the core of our ancient beliefs?'

'Cicero told us to beware of the invasion of barbarians from the north,' said Lysius.

'But haven't we always been successful in repelling all barbarians?' asked Max rhetorically. 'I was there when we finally crushed the serious threat of Vercingetorix,' he said proudly. 'And despite initial defeats, we ultimately resisted Hannibal's invasion. I know that whatever happens, Romans will always be ready to defend their heartland.'

'The Emperor deplores our falling birth-rate and escalating divorce-rate,' I said, entering the discussion from another perspective.

'And his co-adjutor, Agrippa, claims that piracy is now so rampant it threatens our very survival,' said Alfernus.

'Yes. Yes. Yes,' said Max, putting on a mock-weary face. 'But I say that if we managed to survive all the slaughter and dreadful bloodshed of our civil wars, none of these challenges are going to do us in. I see the positives more clearly. Our imperial trade has never been more impressive. One can see an endless queue of tightly packed freighters waiting in Ostia to be unloaded. This trade and our solid way of doing business are civilising our entire Mediterranean world.'

'Our army, too, has proved itself the best and will continue to defeat all others until we have a truly Roman world,' said Peleus.

'Quite right,' said our self-proclaimed hero, Max.

'But without enemies might life not become rather boring?' asked Alfernus.

'Remember that the gods have brought us not only bread, order and security, but circuses as well. With a steady diet of such gladiatorial spectacles, no one ever need be bored,' said Lysius.

'We cannot try to match what a Jupiter or an Apollo have tried, because we are not divine,' I said, 'but even they have not been able to achieve harmony on Olympus. I maintain that Rome is in a state of spiritual crisis and that this whole concept of multiple gods is doomed. That is why I believe Orphism, the vision of the unity of the One, will ultimately win out. Until then the masses throughout much of the Empire will regard Octavian, now become Augustus, as something of a divinity.'

All this was quite daring to say and I never would have spoken so openly outside of our *familia*. I totally trusted that my sacrilegious words were safe here.

Max countered skilfully, 'We Romans and our Greek ancestors have never thought the differences between men and gods were unbridgeable. After all, even Jupiter often assumed human form so he could fuck whoever he thought desirable.'

'Yes. And we all know that if he chased your Larissa, you'd try to string him up by the balls!' said Peleus.

Here everyone burst out laughing – even Max. His shaved head turned cherry pink, revealing his genuine embarrassment.

'If toads or bulls were able to speak about the gods, they would of course tell us that their gods were in the shape of toads or bulls,' I said.

'And that they would croak before making love!' said Peleus. Here everyone laughed again.

Our morning bath then came to an end and so did our fraternal exchanges. We were all agreed that our immediate priority was to prepare ourselves for the impending visit of the great Virgil. As we once more put on our tunics in the dressing room, I smiled at the mural of representations of coupling. These had originally been painted to ward off the 'evil eye'. They made newcomers laugh and supposedly prevented them from looking at the 'equipment' of others who were undressing on their first visit. Far better, I thought, than the suggestive scrawls in chalk and ink which pollute so many of our walls, offering assignations or pricing sexual practices. Personally I preferred erotic dreams which featured the god Pan, that sexually voracious satyr, who played his pipes in many of the sacred groves of the imagination.

IV

The shadows of the dead cannot shake a blade of grass or even utter the lightest of whispers. That was the core of the problem facing us. Our entire *familia* had gathered in the large atrium of our high priest, Marcus Quintius. It had been decided beforehand that no slaves would be permitted to attend the highly sensitive strategy meeting dealing with Virgil's visit to the Oracle. In my view his trip presented a hydra's head of problems. Whichever way I looked at it, ever more wiggly snakes seemed to be threatening our future.

The lanky Quintius, who was seated on one of the four long benches placed in a square, formally opened the meeting by praying: 'O patron Apollo, to whom we are so devoted, help us to resolve our dilemmas. We are here to examine exactly where we stand on the forthcoming visit of Publius Vergilius Maro, during which the poet intends to celebrate the achievements of his great patron, Augustus, and to discourse on the supremacy of Rome.' At this he opened his right hand and gently motioned it towards the seated Sibyl.

Our Sibyl, heavily rouged as always and dressed in one of her full-length purple-silk *stolae*, replied in unusually straightforward terms: 'O beloved Apollo, generous patron of our Oracle, to whom we sacrifice so much and so often! O inspirer of music and poetry, help us in this, as you have helped me in the past, to draw down the moon.' Then she stopped and took in a prolonged deep breath. 'This Oracle of Oracles is fully prepared to greet our honoured visitor and to lead him through all the ceremonies preceding my own prophesy. As I foresee it, our problems do not arise above ground, but below. The underworld is a realm of fears, cold sweats and nightmares. That is why I am counting on you, our most skilled Lysius, to prepare a potion which will intoxicate Virgil in such a way as to allow him to create fantastic and poetic visions which he then will be able to recall and pass on to all Romans. Enough said.' Upon which the Sibyl closed her eyes and folded her hands.

Lysius, on whom an enormous responsibility now seemed to repose, stood up to reply. I thought he was trying to cloak his usual arrogance with a rather detached voice: 'From the reports which I have been able to gather, Virgil is in a rather frail state and generally abstains from drinking wine. He will sip it, symbolically, at ceremonies. This will not permit me to serve my usual, delicately balanced concoctions. I am considering offering him a powerful pomegranate juice doctored with a low dose of poppy extract and blended with minuscule portions of essence of hemp and extracts of non-identifiable hallucinogenic mushrooms. I believe this will produce the effect that the Sibyl has requested. Of course we shall first test this out on several of our slaves.'

As Lysius sat down, Max shifted his drooping tunic and rose to speak: 'I thank you for stating solutions to our problems so clearly and directly. I agree completely that we should drug, not poison, such a distinguished guest. His death would not only be a tragedy for the Roman language, but it would also cause a scandal and lead to an investigation in which many of us might be tortured in order to extort information. We must therefore be extremely careful with regard to the dosages, and I commend Lysius for the precautions he is taking.' Here Max took a deep breath, even more profound than the one our Sibyl had taken. 'I have been considering two propositions. The first: Is Virgil corruptible? The second: How much can we let on? For example, should we allow him to see Cerberus or our performing shades?' Here he pushed the fingers of both hands up through the thin hair above his ears and took a significant pause. 'As to the first, Virgil is for sale. That much was clear when he accepted the

49

large commission from Augustus to glorify him. However, I do not think that we could offer a sufficiently large sum for him to embellish a projection of our own imagined afterlife. I don't think money really interests him sufficiently. He is too focused on his poetry. Another form of corruption might be sexual. I sent my "boy" Vectius to spy on Virgil over the past two weeks and he reported back to me that Virgil appears to prefer young men to nubile girls, but has a low and diminishing sex drive. So there is little we can do there, alas. More important, Vectius also found out that Virgil had sent one of his slaves to Cumae to find out as much as he could about us. And this is crucial for us. This slave of Virgil reported back that the trip to the underworld was a truly nerve-racking experience from which some never returned and others came back crazed. The slave told Virgil that after crossing the Styx in a coracle it might be possible to talk to the dead. This slave reported to Virgil that there were literally thousands of "shades" flitting about, disconsolately waiting for decades to be ferried. The tale he told was apparently received with profound interest by the poet. So, I am happy to say, the story – our story – is already in Virgil's head ready to be transposed into poetry.' Having delivered his speech, Max sat down rather heavily, thereby shaking the others seated on the bench.

'This new information is most encouraging,' said Peleus, who was in charge of training for the descent into Pluto's realm. Spreading his bronzed and muscular arms through his tunic, he went on: 'This does open up all kinds of possibilities. Looking back on our experience in selecting visitors to the underworld, I would suggest that our Sibyl convince Virgil that he is too fragile to take the entire trip; that the risks simply would be too great; that Virgil should take, at the very most, only a small part of it. This could include being ferried by Charon. We could induce one of Virgil's assistants to give him reports from the underworld confirming the rumours he has already learned from his spy. However, I do think it essential that Virgil be put through much of the elaborate pre-descent training in order to prepare him for the possible ordeals ahead. The training camp will stir his imagination. It will then be easier for the Sibyl to guide him down to the water and in his somewhat hallucinating state fill him with details which he can later use in his epic.' Peleus seemed relieved when he in turn sat down.

'I heartily endorse the proposals Peleus has just made,' said Quintius, rising slowly from his bench. 'I had been hoping that Homer's *Odyssey* might provide us with some ideas on the visit to the underworld, but Homer had little to offer in this instance. Although Aeneas had countless meetings with dead heroes, he gave no accurate descriptions of Hades. Apparently drinking the blood of slaughtered sheep temporarily brought the "shades" back to a state of suspended animation, but this certainly put no flesh or bones on them.' I chuckled at this thought. Quintius went on: 'Thank Jove we don't have to go through that charade! I feel that at this stage we can already sense the direction we should be going. I believe that any attempt to corrupt Virgil must be ruled out. It could explode in our faces and at best would arouse his suspicions. Drugging Virgil may be essential but poisoning is not to be considered. As Virgil already knows so much of our "tourist" descent into hell, I would encourage all of us to focus on making these rumours seem as real as possible. For this reason, I think we should conduct a step-by-step rehearsal of all the stages from Virgil's arrival to his departure.'

All seemed to nod their heads and I volunteered: 'I think we truly have a consensus on this and I would like to have Max express our special thanks to Vectius for having made this possible.'

'I have already promised his manumission and he shall, alas, be leaving me a freed man within the month,' replied Max. 'But there are still other matters to be considered. I should like to ask what level of "gifts" we should suggest to Virgil for his consultation with our Sibyl? I would propose a somewhat modest fee, as the poet is well-to-do but not rich, of seven bullocks and seven unspotted ewes.'

'And for his descent into the underworld?' I asked.

'Would one lamb, a ram, a calf, a pair of strong bull oxen and four bullocks, as well as six amphora of olive oil, be about right?' asked Peleus.

'I suppose that depends on the current market rate for the oxen and the bullocks,' I said, knowing that most likely only the ewes would be sacrificed.

'I believe Virgil understands that when it comes to the divine Apollo there is no receiving without first giving,' said the Sibyl. 'After being greeted by Quintius and saying his prayers, Virgil will be guided first into the temple and then to my cave for a consultation during which I shall have him take the sacred oath which will put his life "on deposit" with the gods of the underworld. Later, when the animals have been sacrificed and roasted, he shall be escorted at night into our painted cave, with its various scenes depicting disease, old age and death, and left there to meditate with only some water lightly "flavoured" with the extract of mind-altering mushrooms. I am certain that the portrayals of earthly sins and evils not only will disturb him but also will be properly noted for inclusion in his narrative,' she declared pointedly.

I thought to myself how ugly and terrifying these images were. There was nothing soothing or beautiful about them. I knew that in this confined environment many visitors experienced a deep sense of unreality. After three days of being isolated and in total quiet some went into mildly hallucinatory states abetted, no doubt, by the drugs and morbid images. Most often their thinking became temporarily befuddled.

Fully in command of the process to be followed, the Sibyl then continued in her most forceful manner: 'Balbus will then conduct his usual reading of the entrails. He should express strong foreboding here. Virgil will doubtless impart his desire to please the gods and do as directed. Balbus will inform Virgil that it would not be wise for him to explore the underworld after crossing the Styx but that he should return above ground promptly.' There she stopped. No one uttered a word. Then, closing her eyes, she continued: 'Let Deiphobe help him find the golden bough we shall insert into the tree by the lake and then I shall be his guide, helped by Quintius, through the grotto by Lake Avernus and into the underworld.' I recognised that this would be most unusual for the Sibyl, because she intensely disliked underground visitations. 'Yes. And there should be the usual impersonations of the shades,' she declared. 'And Cerberus should bark ferociously and I shall cast him a pretend potion which he shall devour. This will cause that fierce animal to fall asleep. I prefer sleeping dogs. I so hope Virgil does as well.'

'What do you think, Sibyl? Should I converse with him or remain silent?' I asked.

'Better let Quintius do most of the talking,' she declared. This hurt my feelings. I should have liked to have some exchanges with the poet. But I felt it inappropriate to say so.

'And what about the shades? Will he ask them questions?' Peleus wanted to know.

'Of course. You must coach them as ever. On this one occasion, Peleus, you yourself should put on a mask and perhaps respond to a few of Virgil's specific questions.' The Sibyl left no doubt as to who was in command of the programme.

I knew from my long tenure as Charon that the visitor's first experience of the underworld's profound darkness and deep stillness often had a pronounced effect. After a time some saw stars trembling and shooting up from the depths. They imagined these were produced by daemons. The rolling clouds of black smoke which were carried upwards by the draught in the tunnels and which came from the many torches burning olive oil convinced the visitors that they were indeed on the narrow path to hell. The applicant would also hear the bleating of a terrified lamb or goat that had been dragged below for the sacrifice which was to follow.

As the visitors were drawing near the Styx, it was usual for half a dozen of our members to cry out in agonised moans and drawn-out wails. The visitors thus were led to believe that the souls of the deceased were troubled by memories of their sins and crimes. They were supposedly expressing anguish at the realisation that they would soon have to appear before Pluto and other gods who would punish them. The visitors were also informed that those who had not been properly buried could not cross the Styx, but would have to wait on the bank for a hundred years before Charon would ferry them. Some visitors found such potentially long queues by the River Styx unacceptable. Making souls wait for decades on end for a judgement to be passed seemed grossly unjust. But souls ferried by me supposedly had paid a copper *obolos* which they had somehow transported under their tongues after death.

Our artificial shades were created by means of thin, faceless papyrus cut-outs glued on to sticks. A lamp held below them projected a shadow on to white sheets draped on wooden stands in the front of the 'river' bank. Billows of smoke were generated by special powders dropped on the burning torches, thus partly obscuring the vision of our visitors. These make-believe shades were thus able to flit about, wafting through the air, flouting the draughts and mocking the lights. Sometimes the actors would produce rustling cries, not much louder than the squeaking of bats, which would heighten the overall chilling effect of a nightmare.

Now came the point, the Sibyl said, at which I would take her, Quintius and Virgil in my little coracle to the other side of the Styx. I again asked her if I could converse with Virgil, if he posed any questions, or if I should remain absolutely silent? 'Restrict yourself to grunts of disaffection as you paddle, Rufus. These are far more expressive than words,' the Sibyl replied in a matter-of-fact way. 'Once we have disembarked on the other side, a bit downstream, I believe would be the moment when we should let Virgil ask his questions of specific "shades" such as his own deceased father.'

Peleus then asked the Sibyl what would happen if Virgil asked them hard questions, not like the ones usually asked by visitors, such as: 'Is it difficult to move without wings or a physical body?'

'Tell him that souls are not fluttering about in the dark with bat wings. Virgil is a poet. He has imagination. It is up to him to come up with the answers,' she declared.

'But what should I tell him if he should want to know from a shade whether good and evil exist down there?' Peleus asked, stroking his trim beard.

'You know all the answers by now, Peleus. Tell him that those sinners who have been cruel to their relatives, traitors, perjurers, adulterers and even misers receive their just retribution from Pluto. No point in answering the question directly. Let Virgil think the shades are a bit hard of hearing,' said the Sibyl with a look of delight at her masterful exposition.

'But what if he should ask a truly ticklish question, Sibyl, such as: 'If the soul comes to us at birth and leaves us at death – is it part of us or a separate entity?'

Here Quintius chose to reply for her: 'Peleus, this will not be an occasion for Virgil to discuss theology with a shade. The soul is an abstraction and has no locality, such as the heart, the liver or the brain.'

'But if the soul is incorporeal, are our souls then on loan to humanity?' I asked with a teasing smile on my face.

Quintius took this in his stride. 'Virgil will not want to engage his readers in this kind of speculation, Rufus. He will want to charm them with his verses or frighten them with his descriptions, but he is not a philosopher and in the past has seldom alluded to quandaries for which there are no absolute answers.'

'Must he examine all the heroes whom Aeneas met in Homer's *Odyssey*?' asked Peleus. 'Usually we coach our actors on what roles they are to play, depending on whether the visitor to the underworld wants to meet his mother, father, uncle, former partner, fellow soldier or someone else of that sort. We have never had to face up to a situation where we might be asked to play dozens of dramatic roles.'

'It is a good question, Peleus. It makes us realise that we must limit and filter the number of possible "shades" Virgil can meet,' said Max.

I suggested that when Virgil was being readied for his descent we could ask, just as we always did, whose shades he would like to talk to. We would also suggest that because of his health he could only have a limited time underground and could thus have a request list of no more than half a dozen names. Most agreed on such a formulation, but Lysius expressed doubts about the overall strategy.

'Do you really think Virgil, who claims he next wants to take up Stoic philosophy, is so gullible as to fall for our impersonations?' Lysius asked. 'And what about . . . '

Here Quintius, who knew more about the Greek philosophers than the rest of us put together, interrupted him. 'Virgil may on occasion have quoted the Stoics, but his outlook has always been Epicurean. Virgil read and admired the poetry of Lucretius at an early age and Lucretius was an acknowledged and devoted Epicurean. There can be no doubt that Lucretius brought Virgil to a new understanding. Lucretius, it will be recalled, proposed two theories as to the fate of the soul after death: the first that it perishes with the body; the second that it visits the underworld of Tartarus.'

Peleus, probably sensing that this was going to develop into a protracted lecture on Virgil's philosophical outlook, about which the rest of us were not knowledgeable, joined in by asking: 'There may be strains of both Stoicism and Epicureanism in

Virgil's writings but does this matter, since writing wonderful verses is his aim not the propounding of a particular philosophy?'

'Absolutely not,' said Max in his most commanding voice. 'His philosophical outlook is of no importance to us. The issue Lysius raised is vital. As something of a non-believer in the pantheon, who will see Homer's version of the descent into hell as pure fantasy, Virgil could spot us as frauds who are treating him to cheap theatre.'

'He may arrive that way, even after all he has heard, but once we have plied him with our specially spiked liqueurs all doubts will disappear,' declared our Sibyl. We all acknowledged both her experience and her expertise in this matter.

Upon returning from underground, most applicants were in quite a dazed condition, awestruck but convinced of the reality of what they had encountered. Each one would be escorted to the Room of Memory, seated on a chair and interrogated by Lysius and Atreus. They would ask him to tell all that he had seen or heard. If at this stage there were the slightest suspicion that the visitor had not accepted his underworld experience as genuine, the priests would have him drink some of the specially prepared 'waters'. Their immediate effect was one of profound disorientation. This would soon be followed by nausea. The victim would then be entrusted to his waiting friends and relatives who, delighted to have him back alive, would take him home where he would die a couple of weeks later.

As such an ending was not possible with Virgil, we had to make certain he was at least partially convinced – or at least convinced enough to write beautiful verse relating to what he had seen. That became our plan, now reinforced by our shared, but undeclared, hope for literary immortality.

V

We started making preparations almost immediately, once Virgil's visit became a possibility. All of us were most excited by the plans. We felt truly challenged by both the threats and the possibilities offered to us as a *familia*.

Amidst all the unusual turmoil surrounding the impending visit of the Maiden (for this was Virgil's nickname among his neighbours in Puteoli), we were diverted by the annual festivities of the Lupercalia in which we had to join the inhabitants of Cumae. My Calliope, like most of the young people – no, like most of the people of Cumae – loved the annual festivals. These are celebratory occasions which feature pantomime, acrobatics, conjuring, poetry reading, hymn singing, young ones riding donkeys and sometimes even one of our priestesses driving a chariot drawn by a tame brown bear. Female diviners work the grounds, along with heavily rouged prostitutes. The air is always redolent with the smoky scents of roasting lamb, goat, pig and duck. Every other year I would be involved in the acting or the staging of one of the Greek myths or raucous, zany parodies. I enjoyed putting on a mask, getting into a costume and applying make-up which made me look strange or different – unlike my truly tiresome disguise as the much-feared Charon.

This year I was deputed to stage and narrate a traditional favourite, *Echo and Narcissus*, next to our fountain of Diana and its pool. Narcissus was being played by Antonius, the son of Peleus, and Echo by the charming young concubine of Max, Glycera. I liked working with both of them. On the opening afternoon, a small crowd had assembled in anticipation of the performance. It was a tradition that heckling and a range of catcalls were an integral part of the festival fun. And I knew, when I saw Max with his young daughter Phoebe by his side, that there would be lively repartee.

I started off by describing Echo, the beautiful nymph, who happened to be in the woods which Juno was scouring for her oft-straying husband Jupiter, whom she suspected of amusing himself with some of Echo's fellow nymphs.

'You mean nymphomaniacs!' shouted Max. There were loud giggles but I chose not to reply and continued.

'Echo, who realised this, kept on chatting to Juno, trying to distract her with small talk about the weather and the latest silk underwear from distant Lydia' ('Who will give me some?' shouted one of the prostitutes in the audience) 'until she felt that all the nymphs had had time to vanish. When Juno later discovered this she became so enraged she passed sentence on poor little Echo saying: "You shall forfeit the use of your tongue – " '

'What about for kissing and licking?' loudly interrupted Max.

'That was excluded from the contract,' I replied, tongue-in-cheek, and continued: ' "Yes, that tongue with which you cheated me shall retain only the right to reply, of which you were so overly fond. Forevermore you shall have the last word, but never again will you have the power to speak first." '

'Thus incapacitated, a while later, Echo saw Narcissus, an incredibly beautiful young man, chasing a deer on the mountainside. Utterly smitten by him, she followed his footsteps, hoping he would talk to her. But he seemed to have no interest in speaking to her at all . . . '

'Was he sick?' again interrupted Max patting his rotund belly. 'I mean with a naked nymph following him like that he must have preferred the company of boys.'

'He was Greek, after all,' I replied. 'But let me go on . . .

'Days passed with Echo always patiently following him through the deep woods. Then one morning the young Narcisssus, hunting with his friends, got separated from them. So he shouted out loudly – '

'Anyone here?' yelled Antonius, playing the part of Narcissus.

'Here!' came the playback – delivered by Glycera aka Echo from behind a column.

So Antonius shouted more loudly – 'Out you come!'

'Come!' answered Echo.

At which my dog, Corso, started jumping wildly up and down and then began to wail loudly. I spoke to him sharply: 'Stop! Stop butting in on the act, Corso!' Everyone laughed and Corso wagged his tail, as if on cue.

'Narcissus could not see anyone,' I resumed, 'so he shouted – '

'I can't see you!' called out Antonius.

And Echo parroted back. 'I can't see you.'

'Let's join up!' shouted Narcissus aka Antonius in reply.

'That's more like it!' heckled Max.

'That's enough, you warped penis of a mind!' Peleus retorted.

Loud laughter from an appreciative audience followed.

'Let's join up,' Glycera answered with all her love and ran to throw her arms around Antonius's neck.

He started back exclaiming rudely: 'Get away, I would rather rot than you should have me!'

'Have me!' Glycera repeated in despair.

But Antonius ran away as fast as his legs would carry him.

I returned to my narration. 'So Narcissus left our lovely nymph to grieve in the mountain recesses. She was disconsolate. Slowly her form faded until her flesh began to disintegrate and her bones changed into rocks. Only her voice was left, ready to reply to anyone who called her.'

'What a waste!' exclaimed Max.

'But she is still with us wherever we walk in the mountains,' I replied.

'Then what happened to Narcissus?' asked Calliope, eager to know when Antonius would return.

'The gorgeous youth continued to avoid any nymph he might encounter in the woods. But one day one of Echo's companions, despairing of attracting his attention, uttered a prayer that he might some day also feel what it was like not to have affection returned by someone to whom he was attracted. Diana heard her prayer and granted her wish.

'Soon thereafter Narcissus, hot, thirsty and tired of hunting, came upon a clear mountain pool sheltered by surrounding trees. He stooped down to drink and saw what he thought was a beautiful water-spirit staring back at him. He continued, bent over, to admire the bright eyes and beautiful golden locks that resembled Apollo's – '

'Never have I seen anyone so wonderful' declared Antonius, looking at himself in the pool. 'His eyes are so radiant! The gold of his locks so incredible! He is so full of health and vitality! Oh how I love that face!' Whereupon he brought his lips closer to the water of the fountain as if to kiss it and plunged his arms into the water to embrace it. But there was no body there to grasp.

'Go on, drink the water! Get drunk on your reflection!' shouted Max.

Others in the gathered audience joined in the refrain: 'Drink the water! Kiss the water!'

Antonius, blushing, actually bent down and kissed the surface with his lips. The audience promptly applauded.

I went on: 'We all know how the story ended. Narcissus was so consumed by love for his own image that he could not tear himself away. Bit by bit he lost his colour, his strength and his beauty. Pining for love, he would cry out – '

'Alas! Alack!' (Antonius, saying this, was out of sight by this time.)

'Alas! Alack!' replied Glycera.

'Eventually Narcissus died. The wood nymphs prepared a funeral pyre and would have burnt the body but he was nowhere to be found. The gods, however, wanted a memorial to him where he had collapsed. So a flower sprouted which today bears his name.' And here the whole audience shouted in unison:

'Narcissus! Narcissus!' And loud applause followed for Antonius, Glycera and myself. Obviously all had enormously enjoyed the retelling of the ancient tale.

Quintius and Max both walked over to laugh with us. Quintius, as was manifest from the first words of wisdom he uttered, was in another world – his own. 'As ever, Rufus, this great myth shows us that encounters with the gods are but the visions and voices of our own minds.'

'I have often mistaken beautiful women for goddesses,' said Max, bringing us back to reality.

'Which man has not?' laughed Quintius.

'Love is seen by many of us as a condition caused by Juno or Eros or some other divinity because it is godlike in its power, linking love and the beloved one, who is regarded as having some divine characteristics,' I said.

'I have the suspicion,' said Quintius, picking up my mood, 'that erotic love manifests the desire of many for transcendence, for a perfection that is close to divine.'

'Fine words for a high priest,' said Max. 'But to paraphrase the last words of Socrates: "I owe cock to no one!" '

Here we all laughed.

'Obviously continence and self-control are not words in your vocabulary, Max. Many women aim to be seen and regarded as goddesses – '

'And don't I know it!' exclaimed Max giving a lascivious glance towards Glycera.

' – while males pride themselves on their animal function,' continued Quintius.

Max immediately picked up on this more earthly level: 'Love and sex are the best known cure for melancholia – even though the loss of sperm is a loss of "vital spirits",' he said with a smile.

Quintius chose to ignore this remark. 'Lucretius tried to convince us that with the removal of illusion, all the wonders, mystery and excitements of Eros vanish,' he said.

'It is extraordinary how often love is a matter of perceptual error,' I added soberly. 'Lovers would appear to be mostly blinded by desire.'

'Yes,' said Quintius approvingly. 'Both Catullus and Lucretius have satirised the inflated male perceptions of the women they love: A dwarf becomes "one of the graces", a thin, wiry female is turned into "a gazelle", a tall giant of a woman is "a wonder", and a dark Persian becomes "honey-skinned".'

'You've sold me. I'll take the lot of them!' laughed the irrepressible Max. 'Me, I am lucky. I often have gods visiting me in my dreams. Particularly Aphrodite.'

'The Sibyl has said that those men who have dreams of Aphrodite do not need to worry about getting to heaven – they are already there!' said the priestess Mentula, who had quietly joined our little group.

'Sometimes in our dreams we recognise divinity but not the identity of the particular god,' I volunteered.

'Even I can experience joy, awe and exaltation on waking up after having met a god in my sleep,' admitted Quintius.

'It does seem strange that Romans show no shyness about having nightly contact with a particular god or goddess,' puzzled a mocking Mentula.

'It's easy,' confessed Max. 'In my dreams I say to Aphrodite, "You are the one and only." '

'Don't you say that to every woman, Max?' Mentula suggested laughingly.

'Don't give my secrets away, Mentula. But Aphrodite may merely reply with a word or a phrase like "You!" or "Only you!" '

'And that is enough to give you a wet-dream!' Mentula exclaimed amidst the general merriment.

'Almost. Aphrodite is so divine, omniscient, so gloriously confident. She radiates such incredible emotional warmth,' continued a nearly ecstatic Max.

'Divine presence was described in Greek as *epiphaneia*,' said

Quintius. 'The wonderful thing is that in dreams the gods can suit their appearance to the needs or capacity of the dreamer.'

'As one who speaks from experience,' said Priestess Mentula, 'gods may be somewhat hard to cope with.'

That promptly shut us up. How to reply without being blasphemous or irreligious? Quintius, taking an historical approach, finally broke the silence: 'Some Homeric gods were spies who, in disguise, would enter the world of men – usually to take sides.'

'The best thing about them was that they could disappear in a flash!' said Max. 'Wouldn't want that sort to spy on me!'

'Nor would I like them to come and spy in our underworld,' I said, blushing.

Everyone else seemed to show similar embarrassment at such a prospect.

'For all that we know, one of the gods might come in the guise of Virgil,' said Max.

'Yes. Except for a statue of him, none of us has ever seen him,' I added.

'See how easy it is for our real world to turn into a fable!' rightly concluded Quintius. 'After all, none of the gods has any need to spy on us. If we believe they can read our minds, as Diana could read the mental prayer of her nymph, well then they certainly don't have to come down and spy on us – ever.'

The real Virgil, I suspect, may be almost as clever as most of the Roman gods, excepting Apollo and Minerva. That thought further unnerved me in view of the increasing likelihood of a visit by the poet. Was Virgil the kind of man who could be fooled by flickering shadows on underground walls or impersonations of the voices of deceased members of his family? There was the potential for so many slip-ups. One of our actors might bungle his lines. An immediate cover-up would then be imperative. Could we carry this off? The risks involved were staggering and the thought of them troubled me during my sleepless nights.

VI

All my nagging worries about Virgil's visit were shelved when Lydia, my wife, my love, died of cancer after a lengthy and painful battle. She was only in her mid-thirties. I had wanted to deny her malady. Despite our recourse to the disciplines of Aesculapius, her appetite dwindled and she steadily lost weight. Quintius, Lydia and I had prayed together for recovery, but it was not to be.

Our tender daughter, Calliope, then aged eleven, was disconsolate. She cried and cried, unable to understand how her beloved mother could have left her. What was I to tell her? That we are hostages to Fortune is an explanation only brought in by most of us to cover up our ignorance. One small consolation for me was that as Orphics we all believe death is followed by the transmigration of the soul. This did not impress grieving Calliope at all. Lydia and I had named our daughter Calliope after the legendary mother of Orpheus. Her son came to be worshipped as a god because of his songs, his poetry and his intimate understanding of our human trajectory. Now my only real contact with Lydia would rest in Calliope, who in most ways was more like her mother than her father. I told Calliope a fable that Lydia had been carried away by Aurora, her cloud chariots drawn by white horses taking her through the very gates of heaven. Calliope looked at me with her wide-open blue eyes, which were rose-red from crying. I too missed Lydia terribly. My Lydia had believed that Necessity was above the moon while Chance was below it. Her luck had simply run out.

The entire *familia* gathered for the funeral in the small Cumae cemetery the day after she died. Immediately upon decease we believe the corpse is sacred because it has no proper status in either this world or the next. That is but one reason we must pay our respects. Sulpicia, for whom Lydia had worked for many years as an attendant, looked genuinely mournful. Calliope held on to me throughout the rituals. Unlike the adults, most of whom pretended to good cheer, Calliope was in tears. I felt strangely detached – as if I were floating through the service. I kept on hearing sounds in my head that resembled Lydia's deep, warm voice. Was she trying to communicate with me?

There was a small spread of cakes, bread and cheese and lots of red wine from Campania for all of us. There was also a similar small offering of food and drink set aside for Lydia. Max walked around with pitchers of wine and kept on filling people's cups. He himself got quite drunk. So did Peleus, Balbus and Vectius. The funeral oration itself was nobly delivered by our high priest, Quintius, who had been a close confidant of Lydia's.

'What is the nature of the soul?' Quintius began his sermon in a clear and strong voice. 'The truth is that we do not know. Was Lydia's soul born Minerva-like by, of and for itself? Did it find its way into her body when she was being born, to die with her yesterday? Or did it flit away into the ether, the Milky Way or Elysium? As an Orphic she believed that the soul comes into us from space as we breathe, borne by the winds, and departs in a similar way. Lydia was partly of earth and partly of heaven. Her heavenly part was increased through her pure life on earth where I believe she steadily became more ethereal.'

'Pythagoras, following the beliefs of Orpheus, taught us much about the transmigration of souls and said that the soul, or the incorporeal part of us, once formed part of the soul of the universe itself and is now diffused throughout nature. For Pythagoras the soul is a temporary prisoner of the body. The life of the world to come is our ultimate goal. Yes, many Orphics believe that life on earth is, for the soul, a punishment for previous sin. Being fettered to a body is its sentence. Such entombment is to be regarded as part of its trial through which it may eventually be purified.' Quintius took in a deep breath and looked around at all of us in a significant pause. 'Where may our Lydia's soul be now? One great thinker said that in his previous incarnations he had already been a maid, a bush, a bird and a dumb fish of the sea. The truth is we do not know.'

'Plato, in his *Timaeus*, explained that when the creator first fashioned souls, "he made them equal in number to the stars and assigned each one to a star". The creator also taught them about the nature of the universe and that their fate was to be implanted in bodies. When the soul lived one good life, it went to the Islands of the Blessed – a marvellous place but one where bliss was only temporary. This is where we hope Lydia will go. Ultimately, after multiple reincarnations, her soul will travel back to its original star, to what Plato said was "a place no poet has ever sung nor shall ever sing worthily". We all hope and shall now pray that eventually Lydia's soul will escape the wheel of incarnation and continue a blessed existence for all eternity.'

With these words Quintius closed his eyes, folded his hands together and our *familia* observed a prolonged silence. I hugged Calliope and then went up to thank and embrace Quintius. There were tears in his eyes and in mine. Lydia's body was then buried in a simple wooden coffin and each threw a handful of earth over it. I knew that her pure soul was already elsewhere on its journeys.

Afterwards my dear Calliope was full of questions for me, the sort only a young person can ask and to which, as a loving parent, I could provide few intelligent replies:

'Father, is there light where mother is, or is it all dark?

'Can she . . . could she see me?

'Will you and I rejoin her when we die?

'If it is always dark, is there still time in the afterworld?

'Is Lydia deadlocked in time?

'Is death the result of a loss of heat?

'I didn't understand everything Quintius said, but is mother's soul fluttering around like a bat? Can she, I mean her soul, feel any joy or pain?'

The truth was, Calliope didn't want my guesswork replies to the flow of her questions, she wanted my reassurance and comfort . . . and, above all, to be sure that I, too, was not about to leave her for the next world.

The full mourning of Lydia lasted nine days, at the end of which we all gathered once again in the cemetery for the unveiling of the simply engraved marble headstone:

DIS MANIBUS
LYDIA
HSE
Ø

To the Spirits of the Dead
Lydia
She Lies Buried Here
[Hic Sita Est]
Ø

The last was the sign of the Orphics. Quintius kept strictly to all the usual formalities. I felt, however, that in spirit we were becoming less tied to these ancient rituals. Such ceremonies still commanded our services but no longer the hearts and beliefs of people like the members of our *familia*. I had talked to Quintius about whether he agreed with me that prayers now were being formulated in the style of legal contracts and asked him how he felt about this? He replied that Romans were generally showing increasing indifference to moral values. Despite the efforts of rulers like Augustus and poets like Virgil, the ancient religion was losing its power over the hearts of men. Quintius felt that after the long civil wars, Romans were becoming more materialistic and showing a marked lack of metaphysical curiosity. I suppose that was one of the reasons he had become more involved with Orphism after he had been appointed at the time of Julius Caesar to become the high priest at the Oracle in Cumae and the Temple of Apollo in Baiae.

Marcus Quintius was my closest friend in our *familia*, just as Peleus was Max's best friend. All of us had intimate friendships except for our Sibyl, who was too close to Apollo in her own mind to have room for true earthly friendships. I adored spending hours with Quintius – listening to his discourses on religion, philosophy, the afterlife and many other subjects as we walked through the woods or along the sandy beaches stretching past Cumae. Most often we talked about Orphism, which had been officially banned by the Senate many times, but which continued to be practised in semi-secret everywhere. Sometimes at night when one could see all the constellations, he would tell me: 'Your star shines brightly in the firmament, you *Bacchoi*!' (This was the term we all used for the initiated Orphics.)

Quintius's tall, lanky frame was most un-Roman. His deeply recessed eyes were always searching, roaming like his mind. Yes, he was intense: 'Only a burning faith could make life meaningful,' he often said. Frequently he waved his thin, sensuously veined index finger to emphasise some point or other that he was making. For a high priest of noble origins, he was also extraordinarily irreverent. 'Jupiter never had time for philosophy: he was too busy chasing nubile women,' he would say with a naughty smile.

For Quintius, spirituality implied a breaking away from the given material world. It was the breath of life itself. The animating force within all living things. He opined that the best in man, his spirit, could have no form. It could not be imprisoned. Orphism is based on the belief that life is to be lived for the joys it gives on this earth. Beyond the world of the captivating senses, we Orphics believe it is possible to regain the sphere of the cosmic divine. For Orphics, hope is important, so is the realisation of inner calm resulting from a deep faith.

My belief in belief itself, which I often discussed with Quintius, strengthened my faith as an Orphic. It remains the basis of my expectation that Orphism will one day triumph universally.

The dark tunnels of grief I descended in this time were labyrinthine . . . I struggled with my sorrow as if it were a fever I had to bring down. I missed Lydia's deep warm voice so keenly. I resented the silence of the wall of death: it was invisible and yet unpenetrable.

At the end of the mourning period, confirmation of Virgil's visit came through. The intense preparations which now began included full dress rehearsals at the Sibyl's cave, the Oracle of the Dead and the Temple of Apollo. I assumed the role of Virgil for several of the run-throughs above ground.

In 'Hades' I was Charon, as always, but we faced continuous problems in preparing for the variety of questions Virgil might pose to such shadows as that of his own father, his deceased brother, and even Dido. Minor slip-ups continued. What to do if a 'shadow' suddenly stumbled in his or her reply? This was usually no problem with ordinary visitors, but with a writer eager to describe his descent it could be crucial. We tried to devise techniques to provide swift diversions, like the torches blowing out or smoke filling the passageways, should the occasion warrant. Of course we were also relying on the usual wine and drugs to lower the alertness of our prestigious visitor. Lysius had painstakingly and successfully tested various potions on the unfortunate slaves. Much would depend on what kind of information we could insert afterwards in our 'interrogation' of Virgil. Admittedly our nerves became as frayed as those of warriors about to engage in battle. I found my own rising level of anxiety made it even harder for me to sleep and the consequence of this was debilitating. However, the pressure did prevent my dwelling morbidly on Lydia's passing.

VII

During the final countdown to Virgil's visit, I wondered, as many of us did, whether we could really 'pull the wool' over the eyes of someone of Virgil's intelligence? Personally, I thought this would depend on how much the poet truly wanted, or needed, to believe in our Oracle of the Dead. Virgil arrived at the foot of Cumae's glistening marble acropolis on the afternoon of a budding spring day. The omens were all positive. I believe there are few such blessed places on this earth as Cumae, with its Oracle of the Sibyl, its temples to Apollo and to Jupiter and its proximity to Avernus, with its ancient Oracle of the Dead.

These Oracles were a centre of pilgrimage even before the myths of Homer. Odysseus presumably visited the underworld of Hades at the time that Cumae became the first of the Greek colonies in Italy. Already in those days it was the custom for augurs to be consulted before any major voyage, military campaign or other operation was undertaken. This meant such supporting services as provided food, oil and sacrificial animals were all well established in Cumae and neighbouring Baiae. In those days many diviners and priests became rich. This was well before my own era, when there are long queues at the stalls in Baiae of women seeking to have their dreams interpreted or to acquire love potions to arouse the flagging passions of their husbands. In our Augustan Age selling magic spells and counter-spells to the fashionable Roman women who frequent the opulent baths in the area has also become most profitable.

None of our casual visitors recognised Virgil as he approached the cavernous abode of the Sibyl. I was close by as the poet, dressed in a sparkling white toga, was formally greeted by our priestess Mentula who, as the principal interpreter and assistant to the Sibyl, one day might inherit the mantle of Deiphobe from Apollo. By way of a reply, Virgil solemnly declared in a soft but somewhat tremulous voice: 'I am making an offering to the temple of seven young bulls from an ungelded herd and seven well-chosen ewes, as I was instructed to do by my slave, Anicius.' This price had been negotiated weeks beforehand. As I observed him over the next few days, the great poet seemed somewhat listless and pale. Although he was in his mid-forties, he seemed older – perhaps because he was slightly stooped. The masculine side of his persona was weak. His feminine side, especially the delicacy of his hands and the fragility of his fingers, was most evident. Much of the time Virgil wore a somewhat bemused expression, as if he couldn't quite believe he was actually consulting an oracle.

Before meeting the Sibyl herself, who had been preparing for this visit for many days – just like the rest of the *familia* – Mentula led Virgil to the Temple of Apollo. There the priestess helped to assist in the formal sacrificial rites which were led by our high priest Quintius and seconded by Lysius. Balbus had rehearsed the reading of the entrails of the sacrificial lamb to make certain that the omens for Virgil's visit would be favourable.

Quintius delivered a short discourse, in his most reverential voice, in which he expanded on a theme borrowed from Cicero to the effect that 'all men are brothers' and that 'the whole world is to be considered as a common city of gods and men'. Quintius concluded by recalling, for Virgil's benefit, that Cicero had written at length about life beyond the grave in which the high-ranking enjoyed the eternal bliss of Elysium while those who had committed grievous sins were to languish in a deep underworld hell, known by all as Tartarus. Balbus then carefully interpreted the slight irregularities in the triangular shape of the liver of the freshly slaughtered lamb and declared the omens were favourable for Virgil's consultation with the Sibyl.

Virgil was promptly accompanied by a small procession, in which I was included, from the temple to the gaping sandstone mouth of the oracular cave. There the Sibyl, dressed in a blazing purple *stola*, had been waiting, progressively working herself into an extreme state of agitation.

'Now is the time to ask your questions!' she cried out excitedly to Virgil. 'The god! Look there! The god!' she screamed, pointing with her hand to the Temple of Apollo, where I assumed she beheld a vision. Her voice resembled no mortal sound. Let it be understood that the Sibyl doubled as the mouthpiece of Apollo and the priestess of Hecate. The sacred frenzy made her the organ of divine utterance. Like one transported, she seemed almost out of control: her dyed hair was flying above her head in the wind; her ample breasts were heaving. Again she shouted, this time to a decidedly startled Virgil: 'Are you always so slow in your vows and prayers? The gods will never open up until you show your obedience!'

I could not make out what the stumbling Virgil replied. Obviously it was not the type of greeting he had expected. The Sibyl then turned her back on him and, dramatically grabbing a lit torch, led the procession down the long corridor towards her quarters. This tunnel, which legend has it was dug by the Cimmerians, was also lit by candles but some natural light was coming in from window-like slits on both sides.

As she neared the end of the tunnel and was about to open the first door to her heavily draped underground lair, she turned around and loudly proclaimed: 'Not if I had a hundred tongues, a hundred mouths and a voice of iron could I describe all the forms of crime, all the tales of torments.' Upon which she opened the door and, inviting Virgil in, pointed to the leaves and scraps of papyrus arranged on the floor of the ante-room and commanded him to 'commit no verses to the leaves . . . or they may be confused, shuffled and whirled by playing winds. Chant them aloud and remember.' So that Virgil coud have a few moments to stare at the leaves on the floor, she made a point of waiting before opening the next door. When she did so it immediately produced a draft which scattered the leaves about so that the message on the leaves which had been carefully arranged in order – possibly an acrostic one – was lost for ever. Quintius, who was there, later told me that the effect on Virgil was unsettling. Perhaps it reminded him of what could happen should his own verses on parchment be blown about by the wind. Virgil looked at the strewn disorder on the floor and picked a leaf up at random. It read: ' . . . the barber's plaster of spider-webs soaked in oil and vinegar rarely stops the bleeding . . . ' He promptly let it drop and decided to follow the Sibyl into her private quarters, the floors of which were covered in highly colourful oriental rugs.

The Sibyl was calming herself and was no longer verging on the hysterical. Instead, she was divagating – perhaps from the potions she had taken. Virgil found it difficult to decipher the sentences which she sang out in garbled Apollonian riddles: 'Never shrink from blows,' she declared. 'Backwards is dangerous. Boldly – more boldly where luck permits. Go forward, face them. A way to safety will open where you reckon on it least. Most fortunate is the cave bat.'

This made no sense to Virgil, or to Mentula, Quintius or myself, all of whom were on hand to help decipher or interpret possible hidden meanings in her messages.

Virgil replied in a slow, calm voice, 'No novel kinds of hardship, no surprises loom ahead for me, O Sibyl. With your and Apollo's help I hope to have foreseen them all. Carefully I have gone over the challenges Aeneas faced in the *Odyssey* and feel myself prepared.'

The Sibyl stared straight ahead and seemed oblivious of what he was saying. I was not sure whether she had indeed gone into a trance or whether she was acting. Mentula then asked us to grant the Sibyl some time for solitary meditation. There was no option for Virgil but to go back and await the Sibyl's pleasure.

He got into a discussion with Quintius about Fate. From Virgil's perspective, deities of Destiny could be guiding not only our daily lives but our entire world. The ancient Greek Moirai – those daughters of Night: Clotho, Lachesis and Atropos – were ever to be feared. Virgil did not make it clear to Quintius whether Jupiter's will was subordinate to that of Fate or indistinguishable from it. Both agreed that the Parcae, as we Romans call them, are divinities of violent death. Virgil wondered whether there was a possible escape from the final sentence of Atropos. Quintius could sense that the descent into Hades was worrying Virgil.

Nevertheless, when summoned again by the Sibyl, Virgil asked to go to the underworld: 'Teach me the paths, show me the entrance way so that I may once again, after these many years, see my father,' he pleaded with genuine sentimental longing.

The Sibyl, who now sat majestically erect on her bronze tripod, answered directly and without hesitation: 'The way down is easy from Avernus. Black Dis's door stands open night and day. But to retrace your steps to heaven's air, there's the challenge. If you really want to go down to Hades, you must first find the golden bough which is sacred to Juno and tear it off. You must take this with you on your descent.' There she paused. When she once again had collected her thoughts, she told Virgil to 'sacrifice black oxen for the unburied body of a deceased friend', but then fell silent and closed her eyes, once again leaving the poet looking puzzled.

Two of the Sibyl's priestess assistants, Clymene and Cytheris, escorted Virgil out of the cave. Although dressed in their finest white tunics, they led him through the thick underbrush of a nearby forest. I followed them, along with Balbus, until they arrived near a white cypress. There they showed the poet where to find a 'golden' bough of mistletoe growing from a white poplar. He was helped in cutting this off and, armed with this purportedly magical branch, returned several hours later to seek out the Sibyl.

This time the Sibyl was surprisingly lucid. That was one comforting aspect of Sulpicia: she was predictably unpredictable. Graciously she invited Virgil to take the long walk with her down to Lake Avernus where lay the principal entrance to the underworld. 'As man originally came from Mother Earth so to Mother Earth he must return when he dies,' she told him in a studiedly casual manner.

'Is my life in danger?' the now increasingly nervous poet enquired of her.

'You will need all your courage,' she replied evasively. 'You will have to show your stout heart.'

'Do you think Homer made this particular descent?' he asked, perhaps hoping the historic precedent might comfort him.

'I am certain Apollo must have vouched for his safe return,' she replied evasively.

'And mine?' asked Virgil haltingly.

'There shall, of course, be another reading of the entrails, and if there is any sign of danger, I shall forbid your descent,' she told him, dismissing the matter.

I descended with the small procession as Virgil and the Sibyl took the long winding walk along a well-worn path through the thick woods and rocky crags to Baiae. This journey lasted several hours as neither of them was accustomed to such a long hike. Virgil was not in good shape and was frequently so out of breath that he asked for a brief halt. One of his slaves brought him a triangular stave on which he could rest and compose himself. In addition, our Sibyl's ankles seemed to swell from the weight of a body not used to exercise. At the end, as we entered Baiae, both Virgil and the Sibyl seemed equally exhausted.

Baiae had become the most fashionable watering-hole for wealthy Romans and a place where sufferers from diseases took their cures in the abundant sulphurous hot springs. Once in Baiae, the little party entered the sacred area of the Temple of Apollo where Quintius somewhat perfunctorily offered the appropriate prayers. From there, the Sibyl conducted them across the forecourt of the religious complex and into a dark and sombre room, with barely visible images on the walls, where Virgil nervously asked if he was indeed approaching 'the first jaws of hell'.

'Aeneas would have drawn his sword at these images,' replied the Sibyl, pointing her finger at the painted horror nearest to her. Then she told him: 'This is where you will spend the night,' and peremptorily left the great poet alone in the chamber. Lysius entered after a short interval and told Virgil that he should undress and take a cold bath, to refresh himself after his walk and to prepare himself for what would be a minimal supper.

The poet asked him a number of questions about the regimen he was about to follow and how this might differ from that usually accorded to those seeking to descend into Hades. Lysius said it was only exceptional because he would not spend the usual three nights in isolation looking at the suggestive portrayals of disease, old age, fear, war, poverty, hunger, strife, insanity and evil. What Lysius, who was in charge of preparing all the potions, did not tell him was that his overnight stay would be just long enough for him to take the various drafts formulated to render him more susceptible to the unreal conditions of his descent into 'hell'. Lysius had been testing numerous compound solutions of belladonna, datura and henbane, certain opiates and a variety of hallucinogenic mushrooms on three of his slave assistants for a couple of weeks to be certain of arriving at the desired dosage. His experimental approach had been methodical. He carefully noted the dosages and their cumulative effects on his unfortunate victims – one of whom actually died as a result. Lysius's terse comment to us was: 'Accidents will happen.'

Early the next morning two young men escorted Virgil to the forecourt where a black ewe was being sacrificed. Here Lysius and Balbus inspected the entrails and pronounced that the prospects for his consultation looked only mildly favourable.

This verdict had been decided upon because Virgil was not the usual credulous and unsuspecting visitor but something of a sceptic who would have to be convinced.

Virgil was then taken to bathe in a room which contained 'the waters of forgetfulness', which were lightly drugged with hemp extract. After further fasting, prayer and meditation – which lasted until noon – he took another bath, this time in the 'Waters of Remembrance', which were spiced with hallucinogens. Virgil came out of this latter bath feeling rather dizzy and found it difficult to walk. Lysius dismissed this as the usual state of awe in one facing a descent into Hades. Virgil, although increasingly uneasy, remained eager to visit the fabled underworld and to make contact with some of the shades reputedly dwelling there. 'Sunt geminae Somni portae' (There are twin gates of Sleep), he was overheard saying by Lysius. Apparently he even mumbled something to the effect that he had been dreaming of how he could improve upon Homer's famous account.

At sunset, Virgil was told to offer yet another sacrifice of a black lamb to the mother of the Fates, dread Night, and her sister, the goddess Earth. He was then dressed in a short white linen tunic which was held at the waist by a belt into which his slave, Anicius, had carefully inserted a decorated bronze sword. Virgil's longer strands of grey hair were bound at the back of his head with white ribbons. Once he was ready, his branch of 'golden' mistletoe was brought back for him to carry.

At the entrance of the Oracle of the Dead, which is not far from the Temple of Venus, Virgil was joined by the scarlet-robed Sibyl who told him all the omens had been sufficiently favourable for him to make the descent.

'Are you certain?' asked the wavering poet.

'Now is not the time to ask your destiny,' she replied firmly. The Sibyl was exuding confidence and determination, but this did nothing to improve Virgil's state of mind. I think I was almost as nervous as he was. So much of our future seemed to depend on the outcome of this descent. This was the moment we had been preparing for during the past weeks. I was fearful something entirely unexpected would happen to catch us out.

Walking to the opening of the tunnel, they were joined by Quintius and Lysius who were dressed in rough black cloaks with pointed hoods which were only punctured by narrow slits for their eyes and incisions for their mouths. These 'holy men' led the sombre procession, holding branches from a black cypress and slowly chanting eerie dirges as they began the downward march along a corridor about two hundred paces in length but only some four hands wide and nine hands high. The gradual descent was lit every five or six paces with oil lamps placed in the ancient, carved-out recesses. About halfway down, the sheep that was to be offered to Hades joined them to bring up the rear of this mournful group. The sheep began bleating in the worst sort of way, being pinched to do so by Tappo, a slave of the high priest. At the same time, clouds of black smoke started to billow up the tunnel and this truly did made it seem like a descent into hell. Towards the end of the corridor the Sibyl stopped to tell Virgil: 'It is here that the road splits in two. On the right it goes to Hades, where can be found the house of Persephone and the path to Elysium. To the left it leads downwards to godless Tartarus, where evil men are condemned to suffer endless torments.'

They made a turn to the right down a stairway where the tunnel widens and ends in a series of steps which form a landing stage beside the mythical River Styx, a small underground stream fed by two springs. This was the place I called my 'second home'. Here was docked my coracle, ready to take the four of us across the fabled river.

Tradition, fed by rumour, had it that Charon ferried the shades across on a one-way journey. They were warned that they would never be brought back. We had collectively decided to omit this warning to Virgil.

In a highly strung state, I asked in a raspy, heavy voice: 'Who are you with armour, visiting our rivers? Speak from where you come. This is the region of the shades and sleep. It breaks the eternal laws for this Stygian craft to carry living bodies.'

'Don't fret, Charon,' replied the Sibyl softly. 'These weapons don't threaten anyone. Our celebrated visitor has the approval of Apollo himself, who has spoken through me. Even the Fates have expressed no opposition. So let Cerberus howl on, terrifying the bloodless shades.' Having thus spoken she took out a golden bough which she had concealed under her cloak and waved it imperiously before her.

I did not reply but simply motioned them towards my coracle. I was wearing my filthy, unkempt wig, which once had been white but now was a dirty grey. My formerly white tunic was full of holes, stained and torn in many places. Some brownish patches covered old holes. I stood straight, holding the coracle pole against the river's stone bottom as Quintius helped the Sibyl into the fragile vessel before stepping carefully into it himself.

My little coracle groaned at the weight and took in some water.

I kept silent and then started to paddle very slowly to the opposite side. The reverberations of the loud barking of what sounded like several dogs continued. Soon we passed the landing where the plaster dummy of the three-headed Cerberus – operated by two crouching slaves – was partially obscured by the heavy smoke-screen. First this 'beast' growled menacingly. I could see Virgil was visibly alarmed. Then, as the Sibyl threw the cake we had prepared, Cerberus stopped growling and one could observe the slow wagging of his snakelike tail. The Sibyl explained to Virgil that legend had it that this beast allowed the shades to enter but never to leave. Cerberus would soon be asleep because she had drugged the cake. I could see he looked much relieved as I rowed on.

When all three of my passengers had descended from the coracle at the landing on the other side of the Styx, the Sibyl led them up a long steep stairway into yet another corridor. Virgil was still holding on to the mistletoe he was going to offer to Persephone, the goddess who had married Hades, the dread lord of the underworld. When they arrived in front of the door of the inner sanctum, Virgil sprinkled holy water on himself as he was instructed to do by the Sibyl. Then, prompted by Quintius, Virgil stuck the mistletoe into a small, gilded niche carved into the rock wall.

Of course I do not know what Virgil might have felt as he entered the house of the Queen of the Dead – a most frightful place. Knowing Homer by heart he must have been aware that Persephone could call forth the lethal Gorgon, with snakes for hair, who turned to stone all those whose eyes met hers.

But instead of finding Persephone, Virgil seemed surprised to discover a bound sheep on the sanctuary altar. He must have wondered how the sheep got there. Quintius told Virgil to advance. Then the Sibyl said, 'Draw your sword and be ready to prevent any shade from approaching.' At this point Tappo cut the throat of the sheep on the altar. Its blood immediately started to flow into a small trench below. At the same time, from behind a screen in the room, shadowy faces were projected by mirrors reflecting the light of the flickering torches on to the vaulted ceiling and the walls. Wailing and stifled screams came from all directions – created by Clymene, myself and the other actors who were crouched behind the narrowly open doors of the sanctuary.

'Be prepared, Virgil, the next shade to appear may be that of your father,' warned the Sibyl. 'Do not try to clasp his hand or embrace him, for he is but a shade.' Before a stammering Virgil could think what to say, the shade briefly projected on the wall had already started to grow more faint and his form wavered unevenly. Peleus, assuming Virgil's father's voice, started to pontificate from behind the screen. I had helped him compose alternative scripts and rehearse them many times.

'My son, at long last you have come. But what is it? You look like a lost one,' said Peleus in a deep and scratchy voice.

'Father! Are you wel . . . ill?' asked a Virgil almost at a loss for words.

'Being ill is a concept from your world, my son. The body is the cause of fear and desire, of sorrow and of joy . . . souls must accept punishment for their ancient offences.'

'Does your shade wish to re-enter bodily life, father?'

'Some souls are destined to live in the body a second time,' replied the shadow of his father dolefully. Peleus was reciting his lines most artfully.

'Oh, father, am I then to believe that some of these souls go soaring up to the world beneath our sky and return once more into ordinary matter?' enquired Virgil.

'I'll tell you, so as not to leave you mystified. We suffer each our own lot. Each soul finds the world of death most fitted to himself,' replied Peleus. 'Eventually, after some have turned time's wheels for untold years, they may again see the heavens and wish re-entry into new bodies.' There he paused. 'My dear son, you shall grow famous as a poet and shall be remembered . . . as . . . long . . . as we . . . an . . . ' And his voice trailed off.

I could see that Virgil's dimly-lit face registered both slight bewilderment and frustration as the voice of his dead father faded. He had, alas, a limited range of personal expressions. His eyes failed to reflect much of a shift when moving from calm to fright. But suddenly Virgil tried to reach out to his father's shadow. The attempt was in vain, of course. Other shadows began to flit around the ceiling, crowding out the rapidly disappearing shadow of his father. At the same time different whispering voices began to be heard from three directions. These voices, which included my own, grew louder in intensity.

'I would like to . . . could I speak to my dear mother, Magia Polla?' the poet asked beseechingly.

We had prepared for Virgil to ask for Dido – but knew next

to nothing about his mother. This was totally unexpected. Could Clymene's projected shadow of Dido fill the role? I whispered to her and tried to move her in front of the mirror. She was wearing the headdress we had arranged for her possible role as Dido but Peleus promptly pointed out her shadow as that of Virgil's mother on the cavern's chalky walls.

'Virgil, is that not Magia Polla there?' he asked.

'Doesn't . . . I . . . how? I want to hear her voice again,' replied a bewildered Virgil.

Alas, at that moment the elaborate wig Clymene was wearing toppled off and in a panic I swiftly pushed her away from the reflecting mirrors.

Peleus, sensing disaster, blocked Virgil's view. The great poet seemed quite distracted, obviously not understanding either the commotion or what he was only partially seeing. Quintius, Lysius and Balbus swiftly crowded around Virgil and the Sibyl said it was time to return before they were overwhelmed by the shades, who wanted to drink of the sheep's blood. So, led by the priests, who opened the sanctuary's ivory door, and followed by the Sibyl, the small procession started up the long corridor which led them directly to the world above. Virgil was soon out of breath and coughing from all the smoke. He looked both confused and distraught.

Once above ground, Quintius guided him to the Room of Memory, where supplicants are usually interrogated about their underground experience to make certain they believed and understood all that they had heard and seen.

As the poet sat down he said somewhat plaintively: 'I think I need some time to recover from this journey. I feel weary and both throat and head are suffering.'

'I hope this abbreviated tour has not overly taxed you,' commiserated an anxious and solicitous Sibyl.

'My age is showing. O Jupiter, if you would but restore me the years that are fled!' slowly pleaded the tired poet. 'How truly I wish to thank you, Sibyl, for this incredible – if somewhat frustrating – journey. Almost nothing in my life has been as evocative. Indeed, I . . . I hope to use it to advantage in my epic.'

The Sibyl, much relieved by his favourable reaction in spite of the uneven conclusion of his trip to the Oracle of the Dead, told Virgil that after such an exhausting and emotional experience he first should have a drink of water. Then he should rest for a few hours, after which the priests would help him go over the entire experience. Embracing Virgil warmly – a most unusual gesture for her – she bid her farewells. Virgil, still quite unsure on his feet, was escorted to a large bed which had been prepared for him. He almost immediately fell into a deep sleep. His water had been carefully, but minimally, drugged yet again.

After the group had left the sanctuary underground, I discarded my entire outfit and pulled off my long paste-on beard. After a quick dip in the Styx, whose waters were actually pure and quite warm, I felt like Rufus once again. This time I put on an almost pristine toga and rushed up to rejoin everyone gathered around the sleeping Virgil.

We were all glad the descent was behind us. But foremost in our thoughts was: What will the poet remember? Our entire scenario now depended on the sketch we might be able to implant into Virgil's head when he woke up. Virgil slept for most of the night but still complained of drowsiness when we brought him some restorative fresh milk. Quintius decreed he should remain quiet for a day and decided to sit on a stool near Virgil's bed. He introduced Lysius and myself as fellow priests who would look after him. Virgil seemed to have a dry throat. 'Could you bring me some cold water flowing forth from the Fountain of Memory?' he asked somewhat plaintively.

'So you too are familiar with the Orphics?' replied Quintius as Lysius went out to fetch the water.

'I am not yet entirely certain whether I am dead or alive,' replied Virgil. 'I know that the dead are always thirsty and in need of water from the lake of Mnemosyne, from which only those souls whose purity is vouched for can drink.'

Obviously Virgil was still rather befuddled. Quintius responded by saying, 'Plato in his *Republic* wrote that some tended to drink too much of the waters of forgetfulness. It was best to drink as little of it as possible and that the wisest course for souls on the threshold of full divinity was not to drink from Lethe at all.'

I felt we were all tottering on the edge. Nervously, I tried to bring a note of levity into this exchange. I volunteered, 'Perhaps I would rather lose my memory than my teeth. The first has its own remedy. We know not, or know only in a somewhat hare-brained way, that it is gone. But with teeth we are reminded of our loss at every meal and curse all the hard bits in the food.' As soon as I had uttered these words I felt I had struck a false note.

Virgil managed to produce a wan smile, however. Rather drowsily he owned up to having been disturbed by a long-drawn-out Homeric dream. 'Part of it had to do with Anchises leading Aeneas and pointing out to him who were to be their descendants. Among these were my own father, my brothers, Cebes and Alexander, and myself. We were all being led to Clotho who ratified each of our destinies within the revolution of the spindle she was turning with her withered hand. It was all somewhat confused,' admitted Virgil. 'In my dream there was a thunderstorm with lightning and then suddenly the whole group of us were hurtled liked shooting stars into the present, where the Sibyl was guiding us up the forked road out of Hades towards the light.'

'That was a most promising and important vision,' opined Quintius. 'It shows that you have found a connection between the heroes of our past now confined to the subterranean abode of the dead and a most glorious dawn for Rome itself.' As we spoke, slight earth tremors could be felt. I thought this was a sign from Hades but had no way of interpreting its import.

'Homer generally accepted the notion that death is the negation of everything that makes life worth living. His helpless dead were witless shadows uttering thin, batlike shrieks as they darted aimlessly about Hades,' said Virgil. 'But travelling in the underworld I have seen for myself that the "practice for death" could be invaluable.'

'We must see it as but a stage our souls go through in the long transmigration process,' rejoined Quintius.

'Personally, I have no love of death. I sense that "Hades", or "Acheron" in the popular imagination, is rapidly developing into a locus of seemingly endless suffering and misery for those who have died . . . almost irrespective of how they lived in their previous lives,' I cautiously ventured.

'*Amor mortis* is also an expression of the longing for the ultimate and the limit of all desires,' interjected Lysius who had been following the thread of the conversation most intently. I think all of us wanted to be in conversation with Virgil, somehow to connect with greatness. Virgil, on the other hand, seemed anxious to overcome his drowsiness, to prove to us, but mostly perhaps to himself, that his mind was as sharp as ever.

'Once caught within the vortex of desire, what most Romans would appear to fear most is the death of desire – the end of wanting itself,' declared the increasingly conscious Virgil.

'It is easy to descend into a lust for death if you are overcome with the boredom of endless repetition,' proffered Quintius.

'All this shows that the Roman fascination with the afterlife is much more profound than simple curiosity,' observed Virgil. 'But seldom is there any contemplation of the plain horror of almost eternal silence. There is no waking of the dead.'

Here we all suddenly and self-consciously fell silent. There were more rumbling tremors from the volcanic underground. Which of the gods was sending us a warning, I wondered to myself . . . and why? Would Virgil bring up the incident with the shadow of his mother? None of us would. That much was certain.

'It is fortunate that I can weave these mythical settings into my poetry.' Virgil's words broke the silence.

'Your poetry depends on the divine every bit as much as our Sibyl's often mysterious pronouncements,' said Quintius.

Taking in a deep breath, and not knowing quite where this would lead to, I exclaimed: 'Poetry! Inspiration! Music! Orpheus himself turned to song and music in order to show the power of myth and allegory.' Having pronounced this so dramatically I felt awkward – embarrassed at having somewhat overplayed my role. Could this have been my "shadow-self" talking?

'The Homeric myths were symbolic expressions of inner truths, not literal accounts of creation,' noted Quintius. 'The Orphics propose that every action in this world will be accounted for in the next.'

'Even Plato thought the Orphic myth was a complementary expression of profound truths,' I hastily nodded in agreement.

'Plato accepted the Orphic separation of the lower world of the senses from the heavenly world of ideas,' added Virgil, now speaking more slowly and deliberately. 'I admire those Orphic poems that are suffused with a sense of the mystery and paradox of life. How shall all be One, yet each individual?'

I could sense torpor was beginning to set in as he switched his role from that of the poet to that of the philosopher.

'Orphism's positive side is that it is a religion with a belief in immortality and in posthumous rewards and punishments. But in reincarnation it does hold out the possibility for the soul ultimately to escape and advance towards a state of perfected divinity.' Then he paused while all of us waited respectfully. 'I think Plato, the man, was torn: on the one hand he wished to climb out of the cave into the sunlight, on the other he felt a need to return below and help his fellow prisoners still fettered in the dark.'

'He should have turned more to the Orphic, because it provided the medicine, that is the help, that their souls needed,' I put in.

'Yes. Men's souls need poetry. They need sculpture . . . They need beauty,' agreed a tired Virgil. 'But for now, please excuse me, for I think I need a bit more rest.' And with this he sank back on the bed and we all quietly and respectfully left the room.

I had not expected Virgil to respond so positively to the Orphic ideals. This was a welcome surprise. Welcome because I firmly believe that Orphism represents a balance between exuberance and the measured conduct of our lives. It achieves a calming of the explosive Dionysian energy through the sanity of Apollonian verse. Lysius, who is something of a cynic, had questioned me about this in the past. How, he asked, is one to interpret the dramatic clashes between the gods? Were Apollo and Dionysus false friends or pretend enemies? It was hard for me to clarify the many doubts of Lysius who had ridiculed the ultimate dream of Oneness. I accepted the fundamental Orphic proposition that everything originated out of One and thus will ultimately revert into One. For my part, as an Orphic, I could see a grave danger in formal religions, like that of the Jews. The Orphic offer the myths of Apollo and Bacchus; the Jews offer a vengeful god, a chosen people, and a history of their suffering. Such an excluding religion could lead to fanaticism and intolerance. This did not occur in the worship of our Greek and Roman gods, or in Epicurianism, or indeed with Orphism, where we believe that all the phenomena of the universe are connected in one giant design or pattern. Does the heritage of the great Orpheus not contain the seeds of what all men and women need to believe, I contended with myself?

Lysius, once we were out of Virgil's hearing, asked me quite pointedly: 'So. Rufus, aside from all this philosophico-sophistry, do you believe you'll eventually wind up in Hades?'

'Don't try to wind me up, Lysius! I don't know what shape my soul might assume after my bodily death, but, sure as Hades, I know that if there is one, that's where you will go!' I said this with uncalled-for hostility.

'And you are quite confident that you won't wind up there after all the murders to which you have been party?' he countered. Obviously his malevolent mind had hidden teeth.

'As to that, I shall let Apollo or some other deity be my judge. My own conscience is clear on that point. I have done my utmost to further popular belief in the afterlife.'

'Here I think Rufus is right, Lysius. None of us is capable of passing an after-death judgement on our souls,' said Quintius, seconding my views.

'Holier-than-thou as ever,' said Lysius with contempt. 'I sometimes wonder if the two of you should not consider the religion of the Jews. I spoke to some rather convincing ones on my recent trip to Pompeii who told me that there were those among them who believed that a few "deserving souls" could attain immortality in the afterlife.'

'You too shall turn to "righteousness as the stars for ever and ever",' responded Quintius who was familiar with the scroll of Daniel. 'I think it is fair to say that the Jews simply do not have the same relationship with the dead as the rest of us do. Unlike us, they have no contact with the deceased and no belief in any reunion with dead souls.'

'Could have put us right out of business,' quipped Alfernus, who had joined us. This provoked loud laughter.

'The eternal hope of the Jews is for the coming of their "Messiah". Perhaps we could have made a business out of that,' chuckled Quintius.

'Personally, while I much admire their Commandments, I find their Almighty both vengeful and forbidding, their sexual strictures inhibiting and their dismissal of other religions, such as ours, quite unacceptable,' I said, looking straight at Lysius.

'The Jews are as reluctant to honour our Roman gods as they are to pay taxes,' retorted Lysius. 'They have the conceit to believe they are the chosen people of the one and only deity. Why should they be so favoured? Our knowledge of history tells us that monotheism – a word coined by the Greeks – is nonsense. And if they truly have been "chosen", how come they have not even been able to create a viable state . . . much less an empire.'

'Lysius is right,' chimed in Alfernus. 'The Jews present themselves as a race with a God superior to the rest. Would it not be correct to say that their reluctance to accept any truth outside their sacred scrolls forms a kind of protective coating which some would call arrogance?'

'No mourners at Julius Caesar's funeral were more assiduous than the Jews,' observed Quintius, who, in trying to soften the harshness of our criticism, was demonstrating his usual accommodating nature.

'They wept so publicly because they had lost their great protector,' rejoined Lysius, who was no admirer of Caesar's populism. 'On my recent visit to Pompeii I heard a Jew say that homosexuality is a deadly sin which provokes the wrath of his God and leads to earthquakes and volcanic eruptions.'

'Well, they do see Pompeii as a kind of Sodom and Gomorrah straight out of their Testament. I would suggest that in this they are not far wrong,' countered Quintius. 'Some Jews would appear to be addicted to virtue, but Jewish virtue and Roman virtue work at different levels.'

'I am astounded how Felix Youdaikou, a prosperous Jewish wine merchant in Pompeii, can stuff such unbelievable amounts of guilt into a single sentence,' exclaimed Tappo, to everyone's amusement.

I could see that this discussion was not going to go anywhere and, to no one's surprise, said I was going to relieve myself. At which Quintius decided he would join me and so did Lysius. So the three of us walked over to the polished marble comfort of the *foricae*, with its open, communal seating, and there continued our rambling conversation. I have often thought it interesting that we Romans find it easier to talk and relax while seated and relieving ourselves in public than do other peoples, such as the northerners, who demonstrate a hard-to-explain desire for privacy.

We gossiped for a while about Virgil. Quintius and I were impressed by his familiarity with Orphism. Lysius disliked what he described as Virgil's flattering and fawning ways. It was evident to him that, although somewhat reserved, Virgil had a deserved reputation as something of a poetic arse-licker, insinuating his way into favour with those who could advance or enrich him. I did not agree with the cynical Lysius. Some of those who manifest such unpleasant tendencies did so with a sweet-sour smile. Virgil did not smile falsely. Admittedly, he was not someone one could immediately warm to – unless, perhaps, you were as rich as his patron, Maecenas. Nor was Virgil what one could call a 'crowd-pleaser'. Rather he came over as an adept court flatterer. So much for the personality of the most celebrated poet of our age. I knew we were being hard in judging him. What was indisputable was his most exceptional ear for the harmonies of our Latin language.

One of Virgil's slaves, Anicius, came to notify us that 'the Master' was awake. When we rejoined him, he said he was feeling much better. Obviously the potions were wearing off. Lysius took the lead in questioning him: 'Tell us, Virgil, in whatever way most suits you, exactly whom you met underground? We want to help you to refresh your memory.'

'I thought the special waters might do that,' Virgil replied in a rather sarcastic tone.

'Do you remember meeting Aeneas?' asked Quintius, deliberately trying to avoid responding to his remark.

91

It took Virgil a few moments to answer. 'I must admit to being somewhat confused. I often dream at night that I am Aeneas and that Anchises is my own father. I'm mixing up my writing with reality. But for a poet that is not serious: the line between them is naturally blurred. I think I did meet Anchises amidst a host of shades. I can picture him now, but I can't be certain that we talked.'

'You did, you really did,' said Quintius. 'I overheard your conversation.'

'How remarkable!' exclaimed a truly surprised Virgil. 'Can you remember anything he said?'

'Not specifically. I do recall him explaining how weary he was,' replied Quintius. 'But he did go on at great length about turning time's wheel a thousand years and looking both at Rome's heroic past and her glorious future.'

'That is most remarkable and I know it must be true for I have been writing about it,' said Virgil: 'Illustrious Rome will bind her power with earth, her spirit with Olympus.' Then Virgil paused briefly. 'Tell me, Quintius, did I meet up with Queen Dido?' All of us blushed at this – wondering if his mother would be brought up next.

'Honestly, Virgil, I cannot be sure,' admitted Quintius. 'There were so many shades clamouring about, trying to contact you. There was one woman of stature whose face was about as expressive as stone, but whose form seemed somewhat dis-ordered.'

'Yes! Yes!' Virgil exclaimed with agitation. 'That must have been her.'

I could see from the expression on his face that Quintius was pleased his stratagem was succeeding. Virgil could not differentiate between what happened in the underworld and what was contained in his head. There was no need to continue this particular line of questioning. Quintius digressed by saying, 'I feel confident that Nurturing Venus recognised in Dido the talent to strike love into the breasts of others. Dido's is truly a shade to haunt us all.'

'Alas, Aeneas's great love was but a dim shade underground, much like a moon seen rising through the clouds,' I added softly.

'Well spoken,' said an obviously pleased Virgil. 'As Lucretius expressed it so lucidly, although he didn't say it about Dido, she was "a woman radiating love from her whole body" – and I assume men naturally were drawn towards such a burning source of passion as Dido and longed to unite with her. Alas, such passionate erotic love is a kind of madness that robs the mind of both clarity and reason.'

'There appeared to be such torment in Dido's grief,' said Quintius ingenuously.

'And I had not dreamt her disturbed state might continue in the underworld,' said Virgil.

'Was it not through the malign influence of Juno that Dido's love was kindled to a flame?' asked Quintius.

'Absolutely,' rejoined Virgil. 'Both sorcery and divine intervention led to her madness.'

'It was evident from the way her head bobbed up and down that Dido's madness accompanied her to the underworld,' said Quintius.

'Dido! Oh, Dido! What an infernal descent she has experienced! I must . . . I must try to speak to her!' exclaimed Virgil.

This naturally alarmed all of us, but Quintius cleverly decided not to respond but to return to the theme of the conversation: 'Are the passions not more powerful and immortal than the gods themselves?' he asked somewhat provocatively.

To our relief, and my surprise, Virgil readily accepted the challenge. 'Lucretius certainly thought so. He didn't fall for the kind of hypocrisy, the ritualism and the rampant superstitions which sweep through religions today. The gods of Lucretius were without passions or desires. They did not love or hate and were probably unaware of the existence of men. They dwelled in cosmic isolation far removed from the daily sufferings of our species. Far "beyond the flaming ramparts of the world", these divine creations lived in contemplation of the truths and beauty of their universe.'

'I know you will agree that there are two kinds of religious belief,' said Quintius. 'One for philosophers and thinkers and the other for the masses.'

'Quite so,' said Virgil. 'Lucretius held that the soul is neither immortal nor spiritual. At death its atoms are dispersed in the earth. The philosopher held there is no hereafter. Heaven is here right now in the serene contemplation of the wonders all about us. That is not a perspective suitable for the populace.'

'Serene contemplation is for the very few,' I agreed. 'I hold a disdain for the basis upon which the mass of Romans worship – the contractual principle of "something for something". If I make a sacrifice I want you, Jove, to do me a favour in return. If I do wrong I shall be punished; if I do right, I expect to be rewarded. This goes against the whole spirit of contemplating the world dispassionately.'

'Lucretius is the greatest of our philosophical poets,' declared Virgil, 'but don't expect the Romans to appreciate that. It is likely that his thoughts will be more congenial to future generations than they are to our contemporaries.'

Virgil then discoursed for a while on our aspirations to immortality: 'Lucretius held that the quantity of matter, energy and motion in the universe never changes; that destruction is only a change in form. He maintained that matter cannot arise out of nothing . . . '

'Like our Sibyl does, miraculously,' Lysius interrupted.

Virgil shrugged this off and continued: 'There is an elemental spontaneity that can be observed all around us and ultimately in our own indeterminacy or "free will". My own poetry, in its struggle to cast off the surges of prejudice which infect us, reflects my efforts to compensate for the imperfections of life.'

'It is good to hear you speak so fluently after all that you experienced yesterday in the underworld, Publius Vergilius Maro,' said Quintius, addressing the great poet by his full name.

Such praise seemed to urge Virgil on: 'Lucretius held that all things that grow also must decay: bodies, families, races, planets, stars – only the atoms do not die. Creation and destruction are reverse sides of the same coin of existence. Given the mortality of the universe, one day the walls of the sky will collapse in a gigantic fire-storm. But that will not be the end. New systems will form, new suns will be born. Evolution will march on.'

'Your exposition on Lucretius is most convincing,' I said. 'It will cause me to re-examine my Orphic beliefs and my faith in Apollo.'

Virgil responded by quoting Plato from memory. ' "We must ever maintain a real belief in the ancient and sacred stories, those which proclaim that our soul is immortal, and has judges, and pays full requital for its deeds, as soon as a man has left his body behind." '

All three of us nodded our heads in agreement.

'I suppose Lucretius has been my great model,' said Virgil. 'Virtue does not reside in the fear of Jupiter nor in the denials of pleasure, but in the harmony to be found by having our senses working together with reason. Lucretius pointed out that some men wear themselves out for the sake of fame and larger-than-life bronze statues in their image when "the true wealth of man is to live simply with a mind at rest". That is also my view.'

I could sense we were going to have a prolonged discourse about Virgil's favourite poet. It is true that Lucretius made me understand the structure of our world in an amazingly comprehensive way – one which I, as an Orphist, could broadly appreciate. But Virgil suddenly surprised all of us by asking out of the blue: 'Do you, do any of you, think Homer descended to this underworld, much as I did yesterday?'

Looking around in some bewilderment, Lysius and I decided to defer to Quintius. Our high priest replied with firmness: 'If Homer did visit Cumae, it was more than twenty-five generations ago and we have no record of it. True, Acheron in Thesprotia was fed by the River Cocytus, but they do not claim Homer descended there. Our Sibyl, who is such a natural interpreter of the messages of the gods and feels herself to be the spokesperson for Apollo, does indeed believe that Odysseus visited here and we all tend to agree with her on this.'

'Yes,' Virgil graciously agreed, 'Homer never was able to enjoy the services of such a superb guide and I am most grateful for her supernatural wisdom. I will be direct with you and confess to having been quite nervous about the descent. All too many visitors to the Oracle have never made it back to the surface. On the other hand, I did not feel myself in any danger during the descent and now wonder what could have caused numbers of the other visitors to perish?'

I felt a slight blush rise to my cheeks and glanced towards Lysius, who is such a practised liar. Looking first towards Quintius and me, and then staring straight at Virgil, he said: 'For safety's sake you were taken on a much abbreviated descent into the underworld. Others, although given proper warning, are taken through the Fields of Mourning and then take the fork in the tunnel which leads them down into fiery Tartarus from whose rigours we cannot guarantee the safe return of any visitor.'

Virgil looked quite relieved and seemed convinced. 'For the sake of my poetry, I should have liked to take that path. For the sake of my health and my life, I am pleased I didn't. Thank you. I shall have to use Homer as my model and let inspiration guide me through the rest.'

'I am certain that, inspired by the Sibyl, you shall have no problems in developing those sectors of the underworld from which we protected you,' said Quintius. 'But I should much like to continue our discussion on Lucretius whom you regard so highly.'

I breathed a secret sigh of relief that, seemingly, we had passed this difficult test. Taking Virgil into the underworld at times had seemed as uncertain as taking a rather drunk man through a dark wood: one had no idea what he would remember the next day. Virgil also seemed pleased to go back to the familiar furrows ploughed by Lucretius.

'Lucretius held that the soul grows and ages with the body. His position was that it is not immortal. It cannot move from one body to the next, as some of you who may be Orphics believe. He posited most persuasively that we could not expect there to be a soul detached from the organs of the five senses. Lucretius contended that the soul is affected by wine, sunshine, disease and time itself. It is not immortal like the spirits of the Roman gods.'

'Alas, such a rational system of belief does not suit our Roman flock. The people want mystery and magic. They need doses of the mystic. They take to the emotional and florid Asiatic modes while our martial leaders desire empire and sensual indulgence,' said Lysius, who now seemed pleased at being able to contribute to this serious discussion with Rome's most celebrated poet.

Quintius continued where Lysius had left off: 'There would appear to be a split in Rome between feeling and calculation. Romans show exceptional adulation for the great gladiator, the celebrated poet and the famous actor. But the posturing and posing which has become so characteristic of the city dwellers is entirely alien to us here in provincial Cumae. Natural feelings tend to prevail here.'

Lysius could not resist elaborating on this theme: 'Is not Rome full of idle, scheming and devious people with a scant sense of morals? From what I have observed, the few pursue their quite unbridled craving for pleasure while most struggle desperately merely to survive.'

Virgil did not care to respond to this. 'Romans must do more to recognise the virtues of Venus, like Lucretius did, not only as the goddess of love but also as the ruler of all things natural. Venus strikes love into the breasts of all creatures and assures that they will propagate their generations after their own kind,' was his rejoinder. 'What a splendid portrayal of a rational universe! How bravely Lucretius interpreted nature as being a rule of law.'

As he was finishing, the Sibyl, attended by Mentula and Clymene, entered the room. 'How noble it is to find you holding forth on Lucretius!' she exclaimed. 'It has always seemed obvious to me that we are ruled by immutable heavenly powers.' It was instantly evident that once again she had changed *persona*.

'Virgil, we have come to invite you to join us for supper. We so hope it will be a memorable feast to celebrate your safe return from Hades.'

'Whether you are in truth a goddess, or a prophet most pleasing to Apollo, to me . . . you will always seem . . . divine. Through your intercession I have traversed the realms of death and have returned to earth in safety. Tonight at this dinner we shall burn incense in your honour,' said Virgil obviously not quite knowing how to thank her for her services.

'Perhaps, should you, perchance, receive a fortune from the Emperor or from Maecenas, you could erect a temple in my honour?' she suggested flashing him her most seductive smile. 'Failing that, we shall be content if we are immortalised in your epic.' All of us noticed that she was more concerned with recognition of her own fame than with that of the Oracles. We also noted that the rapidly tiring poet chose not to respond to her boldly provocative proposals.

The candlelit dinner that night, in the large rectangular *cella* of the Temple of Apollo, was one of the most sumptuous we ever provided. The Sybil, surprisingly, wore a white 'synthesis', a lightweight *stola*. She had personally selected the menu: the roast saddle of bear was more succulent than any I had ever tasted; the baked oysters were close to Olympian. Virgil, however, who reputedly was suffering from stomach problems, ate less than a mouse might have. He took no more than a taste of each of the dozen or so dishes. There were also numerous excellent Roman and Ibernian wines, but Virgil hardly took a sip of any during the many toasts proposed to him and to the Sibyl.

The two of them did manage one social breakthrough at the dinner – he called her by her given name, Sulpicia, and in return she called him Publius. Again he repeated how eternally indebted he would be to her.

But far more important than these social niceties was his warning to all of us to keep our profile low: 'Agrippa doesn't like oracles and he considers Orphism as the offshoot of an Egyptian sect. In the past he has been most repressive of what he calls "alien" mystics. I urge caution by all of you now that Agrippa has finished his grand palace in Baiae. This means he will be visiting here more often and listening to the malicious gossip of the Roman social set now swarming in the region.' It was a warning given in good faith but to which we, secretly celebrating the success of our grand deception, did not pay serious heed. Virgil, after all, was seen by us as a poet and not a prophet.

VIII

I tried to distract myself after Virgil's visit. On the one hand we were elated that it was over, on the other hand we were nervous about what might happen once Virgil tried to put his underground experiences on *pergamena*. I wondered whether Virgil's suspicions might be stimulated when he recapitulated the whole visit. True, Virgil never mentioned the incident afterwards, but towards the end of his time in Cumae he seemed somewhat circumspect and increasingly irritable. The farcical matter of his 'mother's' slipping wig haunted my dreams.

Two days after Virgil had departed, Max, Peleus, Alfernus, and I were all relaxing in the baths. After the mounting tensions of the past few weeks in preparation for the visit, we were all in recovery. Max was returning to his normal self. He proposed that as we had all passed this major hurdle we could now start to focus on his pet project: a transport vessel for those wealthy visitors from Rome who wanted to travel in luxury to the oracles at Cumae and Baiae.

'There is no earthly reason to force everyone to go either by foot or by cargo ship!' he exclaimed with his usual flair and conviction, ignoring the fact that most of the rich came in their own vessels or in sumptuous carriages.

'Max,' interceded Peleus, 'before you give us another of your totally convincing lectures on the merits of your dreams, worthy and ultimately profitable as they might be, let's relax. We all need a bit of breathing space. We have not had an orgy since the winter solstice. I need some purification through ritual copulation!' he said with a broad smile.

'Yes. We all need some prolonged bliss,' said Alfernus with

enthusiasm as he extended his body in the rectangular pool of the hot bath along which we were all seated.

'Unlike a cat-house, unfortunately we are not licensed to offer proper screwing!' Max told them with a laugh.

'Even under our new Emperor, proper screwing does not need a licence. Only improper screwing,' said Alfernus. This set off general laughter.

'I have not had intercourse since Lydia's death,' I confessed.

'Really?' asked Max with mock incredulity. Like Cupid he was irresponsible by nature.

'But you must be ready to explode, you poor fellow!' said Alfernus.

'As the *familia* trainer, I would say this is dangerous for your health,' volunteered Peleus. Then, out of nowhere, admitted: 'I would love to plunge into Clymene.'

'Does your wife Thea know of this secret longing of yours, Peleus?' asked Max.

'What she doesn't know won't hurt her,' replied Peleus.

'But she'll see you leaping towards Clymene like a randy goat!' said Max.

'But she won't know the desire in my mind,' retorted Peleus.

'She won't be looking there. Your throbbing priapus will give you away!' said Max chuckling.

'Look who's talking,' said Peleus laughing.

'It sounds as if we'll have to give notice to our women to remove all their body hair in the next couple of days,' said Alfernus.

'Some of us will have to shave as well,' I said, feeling my somewhat straggly beard. It had always struck me that no female statue in Baiae or Rome had pubic hair or even hair under her arms. The Greeks had always been able to see beauty in the naked body. Although I am exceptional, I guess, it seems impossible for a Roman to see a naked body as anything but a sexual stimulus. Small wonder that, for most of us, *nudus* means not only naked but also rough, rude and uncouth.

'They'll all be going to Baiae to get new oils and perfumes for these celebrations,' said Max.

'Well, you'd better join them,' said Peleus. 'Your he-goat smell may put off some women.'

'What do you mean?' asked a somewhat embarrassed Max.

'Eros reserves his favours for men who enhance their sensuality, Max. Do all of us a favour: use orange, cinnabar, mint, any of the scents that you feel most suit you,' responded Peleus.

'Are you telling me I stink?'

'When you get aroused you give off a particular scent, Max. It's specific,' replied Peleus evasively.

'I like women to use combinations of opiates, sandalwood and myrrh,' said Alfernus.

'Are we going to have special touches this time for our Bacchanalia?' I asked eagerly.

'I had thought maybe we could have two all-inclusive encounters,' replied Peleus.

'You obviously have been thinking about this for some time,' teased Alfernus.

'Indeed. I try to plan our rare orgies with care,' proudly claimed Peleus. 'I feel that when we enter the warm room to hang up our clothes, each of us should be presented with something both Juno and Eros would appreciate, like a garland of violets, mimosa, dandelion or daisies. All the garlands would be matched in pairs: some would have dandelion and violets, others mimosa and daisies, some garlands would have only one flower and some might have three. Each person would then match up with his or her flower partner and bang!'

'I like the flowery touch,' I said. 'The women will take to it as well.'

'In the middle of our all-night celebrations,' continued Peleus, 'the men would all gather at one end of the atrium and the women at the other. Then each would be blindfolded and slowly advance towards the other side, meeting in the middle and copulating without ever taking off their blindfolds.'

'Thank the goddess that afterwards I would be able to join up with someone I really fancy,' I said with considerable sarcasm.

'That's a sensible ploy, Peleus,' said Alfernus. 'It will enable all the slaves to feel on an equal footing from the first. I've noticed they've been increasingly shy.'

'We have always followed the same practices in our familial Bacchanalia as those which regulate gladiatorial combat. As you will remember, the first rule is "Any body with any body". Each of us should be free to pursue our own sexual fantasies,' declared Peleus, in an unusually pedagogic tone.

Admittedly our orgies were among the few settings in which no one differentiated between slave and master, between rich and poor, between men and women. All of us were simply naked, erotically fixated beings.

'My father told me – and I know he believed it – that getting what you want leads inevitably to transgressions or simply to the inability to recognise limits,' I said.

Everyone in the waters fell silent, considering how this might apply to them, when Thea, Hebe and Clodia all entered the baths. Although they were not exactly the Three Graces, they did combine sensuality with decidedly seductive elegance.

'Welcome, you angels!' said Max with genuine delight.

'You men looked so serious when we came in, I thought you were plotting the restoration of the republic!' exclaimed his wife Hebe, cautiously dipping her foot into the water.

'Not quite, dears. We have a surprise for you. We are planning a night-time sacrament which will purify your souls and enable all of us to escape briefly from the daily round!' said Peleus with decided relish.

'An orgy!' enthusiastically exclaimed Clodia, a youthful and highly attractive slave of the Sibyl's.

'Well, well,' said Thea with light-hearted insouciance. 'Are you aspiring he-goats planning to go ahead without women?'

'Hades, no!' I responded vigorously.

'Too bad,' continued Thea. 'I was going to recommend that the three of you use lots of oil and polish your arse-holes until they gleam with all the radiance of silver.'

'What's that supposed to mean?' enquired Alfernous, somewhat scandalised.

'Thia's telling you in her own literary way – heavily borrowed from Catullus, I might add – that all of the women in our *familia* are cycling red tomorrow,' said Hebe.

All four of us males groaned.

'Bloody Juno!' exclaimed Max. 'Is this one of Eros's usual tricks to upstage all of us?'

'You would have known at what stage of our *menses* we were at if you had paid more attention to us instead of being totally absorbed in that asexual arse-kisser, Virgil. Every day it has been Virgil this and Virgil that . . . almost as if we didn't exist,' chided Hebe.

'One day you are all ooing and aahing about Jove's amatory exploits – how he carried off Europa as a raging bull, entered Leda as a soft-downed swan and exploded into Danae as a shower of gold – and wishing we 'feeble' men were more like him, but when we offer to stage an orgy, you drip blood all over our plans!' said an obviously frustrated Alfernus.

'Poor, poor Alfernus! Afraid of a drop of a woman's blood are you?' said Thea. 'You know very well that the lunar cycle regulates our bodies and our health.'

'You win. You win!' said Peleus impatiently. 'We'll hold off for three more days.'

'Don't be upset, sweet shrinking phallus,' said Hebe playfully. 'You'll be all the more eager for us at the celebrations.'

'You bet,' teased Max jovially. 'I'll puss you – all – later.' With that the banter continued entertainingly for a while until it was time for all of us to take a plunge in the cold waters.

It occurred to me later that day, while talking to Quintius

about the plans for the orgy (which he said he would not attend), that sex, which obeys no laws and respects no barriers, can at any moment lead to chaos. Youth, I had to admit, disdains orderly procedure and embraces the risks of the unknown.

Quintius concurred. 'An abandonment to passion is also a form of resistance to tyranny of all sorts. Because of their total liberation from social limits, orgies provide a release for those who just want to lose control and give in to unrestrained sexual frenzy.'

'Of course it is the proverbial "forbidden fruit" which attracts men and women to exercise extremes of what is usually regarded as "unacceptable" behaviour,' I observed. 'The orgy is about the expectation of over-indulgence – which is one of our acknowledged Roman weaknesses. As a nation we have never been renowned for either our moderation or our inhibitions.'

'How marvellously free are our ancient beliefs,' exulted Quintius. 'Unlike the Jews, we have no commandments because the gods on Olympus themselves committed every kind of crime from murder to rape. Indeed, how could men be blamed for imitating the rapes of Jupiter or the drunken bouts of Dionysus?'

'We cannot,' I agreed. 'I have always tried to show a respect for women, however, but few men I know share my restraint. I cannot understand why my countrymen think rape is so uproariously funny. Little makes them laugh as much.'

'I often ask myself what our gods Apollo and Bacchus really want from us?' Quintius asked rhetorically, avoiding my digression. 'The answer, it would seem to me, is "awareness of both the spirit and the world of the flesh". Plato contended that Eros is the most ubiquitous of all deities because otherwise he never would be able to enter so many places and fly so readily in and out of men's souls.'

I confessed to Quintius that during a saturnalia in the villa of Varro last year, I wandered about stark naked, singing, clapping and jumping up and down. Yes, I even enjoyed so-called forbidden sexual couplings with members of both sexes. At festivals like these, as well as Bacchanalia and our occasional orgies, we do more or less what we want and there is no fear of divine retribution. To consider nothing wrong is a basic tenet. Our outstanding contemporary poet Catullus, speaking scurrilously of our proclivity to the bisexual, described his two rakes as 'oral Aurelius and anal Furius'. It is true that for us Romans sex with a same-sex partner just to obtain pleasure is fine and does not imply a preference for gender. No one will reproach us for it.

'Sex is holy because it allows us momentarily to halt Chronos's wheel of time,' sighed Quintius. 'Alas, we Romans have always displayed a greater ability to pull our gods down to our level than to raise ourselves ever so minutely to that of the gods.' I noted that my priestly best friend pronounced these words with obvious regret.

Because our households include slaves who live together with us (I only have Porcius, an old family retainer, in my own modest house), this contributes to the far greater sexual access enjoyed by both men and women. The position assumed by a Roman when performing the sexual act is sometimes more a question of social status than gender. Thus the dominator is always someone of higher status and the submissive partner someone of lower status, whether it be a man, a woman or a slave. As popular parlance has it: in any sexual union you are either the inseminator or the inseminated. Our outlook was rather well represented by Marcus Antonius when he reputedly wrote to Augustus: 'Does it really matter so much where or with whom you perform the sexual act?' Indeed, Augustus as a young man reportedly sacrificed his anal virtue to one Aulus Hirtius, then the governor-general of Iberia, for three thousand gold pieces. That said, however, it is considered infamous for a man to give oral pleasure to a woman. Such an act is regarded as servile and weak and is left for slaves to perform. Also for a master to be buggered by his slave shows a lack of self-respect and displays unworthy passivity. It is true that hardly anyone in Rome these days thinks less of a man for loving boys, but then he won't be praised for it either.

Quintius pointed out to me that our Roman sexual mores differed considerably from those of our Greek predecessors. For young boys, homosexual rather than heterosexual relations were considered the ideal, but a Greek adult having a relationship with a young boy had to provide spiritual, intellectual and pedagogical guidance for that youth. I had never known that only boys from the ages of twelve to seventeen were allowed to be loved by Athenian or Spartan men. Getting involved with younger boys was unacceptable behaviour because they were too young to exercise choice. Also, for a youth to continue to have an affair with an older man after the age of seventeen was frowned upon in Athens. I was even more surprised when Quintius told me that for any Greek of the 'golden age', true love of a woman by a man was considered a sign of mental illness. This was because women were regarded as second-class citizens and thus unworthy objects of a man's emotional and physical affections.

'Well, that's not all that different from Rome today,' I countered wryly.

'I believe that among the upper classes this perspective has changed,' Quintius averred. 'We have women doctors and women gladiators. You know several women writers and priestesses. Women in Rome today have infinitely more freedom to manage their business and financial affairs than they ever did in Greece.'

'Well, at least we would appear to be much more advanced in our sexual mores than the ancient Egyptians,' I said.

'That very much depends on what you mean by advanced,' replied Quintius. 'In Karnak prostitution was an organised part of religion. Prostitution was practised and controlled by priests in some of the temples and also in "pleasure houses". Since prostitution was something to be proud of, the women who practised it wore specific clothes, painted their lips red and tattooed their thighs and breasts.'

'The way you describe all of this it would seem you envied those Egyptian priests, Quintius?'

'Their frankness and comfort with sexuality was appealing. As a Roman priest I am much more restricted. If it ever got out that I, as a high priest, attended an orgy, I would be disgraced.'

'I heard that in Egypt sex was quite as important as reincarnation itself.'

'They certainly believed in sex in the afterlife,' Quintius nodded. 'Fertility dolls, clay nipples and phalluses often were attached to mummies before burial so that they could be used in the next life. And as to the gods, well they practised incest, homosexuality and necrophilia. The first human beings to arrive on earth, according to Egyptian mythology, were the twin sons of Atum-Ra, whom he masturbated into existence.'

'I had the wrong impression,' I admitted. 'You make the Egyptians sound possibly even more obsessed with the erotic than we Romans.'

'Perhaps they were. But they were also somewhat bizarre. I read in a papyrus scroll in the library of Atticus that to be sworn in as pharaoh, a prince had to marry his sister or half-sister of the royal lineage. Romans would never tolerate the state imposition of incestuous marriage.'

'Who knows where we are headed? Our future generations may come to admire deified prostitutes, hallowed penises and sanctified orgies,' I smiled.

'I'm pleased I won't be around,' replied Quintius. 'I'm even relieved I will not ascend into the afterlife of the Egyptians. But I have to tell you, in confidence, that I regret not being able to attend your orgy.'

'You should be grateful, since our excesses are not only sexual,' I said, trying to comfort him.

'Overeating has always been an overrated Roman vice,'

admitted Quintius. 'Throwing up in order to eat more has never appealed to me. Some Romans fast not to expiate their excesses but in order to be more affected by the wine they drink. No, I prefer the more modest culinary habits of the plain folk of our past, who were satisfied with barley bread, grilled fish, fresh garlic and ordinary wines. Since Baiae has opened up to trade, we eat dates from Egypt, ortolans from Syria, oysters from the Adriatic, almonds from Mallorca and spices from just about everywhere. I suspect that some of the latter cover up rotting food or are poisonous in themselves.'

'You shouldn't be so suspicious or deny yourself these new delights, Quintius. After all, priests are every bit as human as the rest of us.' He nodded his head in silent agreement. Soon thereafter I heartily embraced him goodbye.

On the day of the orgy I went to the tonsor to have him shave my beard and rearrange my hair. The tonsor's shop was surrounded with benches on which the waiting clients from Cumae always gossiped. Dull mirrors hung on the walls so that the customers could give themselves critical appraisals as they talked. One obese man recounted how he had thought a womanly touch would improve him. He had allowed a middle-aged woman to pull out all the black hairs on top of his head, while his youthful mistress plucked out all the grey ones. Now, he admitted, his bald dome, with dressed hair all around, made him prone to ridicule. We all laughed.

On the evening of the orgy I oiled and perfumed myself thoroughly. My twelve-year-old Calliope wondered why I was taking such care. When I placed a small bread phallus around my neck, she exclaimed: 'Father, you are going to the orgy, aren't you? I hope you have a wonderful time and do everything you like.' What an unusual thing for my young daughter to wish me, I reflected. So even Calliope knew all about our plans but had not let on. Of course she understood that those who were not yet adults were not invited. I could tell she was a bit envious and irritated when I told her to get to bed early. Nevertheless, she threw her arms around me and, giggling, gave me one of her great big hugs.

It was a splendid, warm moonlit night, but the large atrium-like entrance to the marble baths was lit with burning torches. Their flames seemed symbolic of my own eagerness. Already some garlanded members of the *familia* were wandering about the colonnades seeking out their matching partners. Immediately after taking off my tunic, Thea placed a simple garland of dandelions around my neck. So, taking a small phallic drinking vessel filled with wine, I began to look around for my "dandelion partner". All the familiar female faces were flushed with expectation, laughter and excitement. The men were more serious in their various states of bravado. A few were already fully erect in anticipation. Then there was a loud gong and Clymene, wearing a phallus around her neck as well as a garland of violets, stood on a small podium. She paused before launching into a hymn to Dionysus to introduce the evening's proceedings. Had Clymene been a cat, I know she would have been the scratching kind. Her claws of intelligence were always ready:

> Dionysus, we call out to you, inspiring god of wine;
> With your various names, a twofold shape is thine.
> O first-born and thrice-begotten Baccheios!
> Two-formed and two-horned, ivy-crowned with pure Euios!
> Bull-faced yet obscure, bearer of the holy vine,
> Imbued with passion both fiery and divine,
> All-blessed power from Zeus you possess,
> Immortal daimon, hear the voice of a suppliant hostess:
> Hail to you, Bacchus, god of the senses!
> Spread the inebriating elixir of love!
> Let the brain swim in wine!
> Let the senses swirl around!
> Let us leap about and bound!

Let penises throb and breasts heave!
And tenderly let your eyes, your mind, your body go!
Bacchus, you are divine, you are wine, and I am thine!
Thine! Thine!

And opening her arms wide on these last words, she embraced a bronze statue of Eros facing her in the atrium, and placed a loving *basium* on his eternally sealed lips.

At this a couple of slaves started to play a tune on their flutes and another softly launched into a drumbeat. This was the signal for all the men to join in a snake-like column and dance as lasciviously as they could, with suggestive movements of their hands, hips and eyes, as they wound their way around the surrounding colonnades. As I pranced in the winding snake, I looked eagerly for the other dandelion garland. Finally, I spotted Clodia wearing it and smiled broadly at her as she returned my inviting glance. Although she was a slave, I had always liked her saucy spirits. I broke from the snake and walked directly over to give her a friendly *osculum*, then follow up first with a loving *basium* and finally, as our bodies and our breasts met, an erotic *suavium*.* Lifting her in my arms as we were kissing, I rolled her on to one of the many rugs which had been placed in the colonnades. There I took her by storm and I could sense by the way Clodia reciprocated that she absolutely adored it. They say that women's lust is fiercer than ours and more frenzied. In this case I think we were evenly matched. Her fingers dug into my back with passion. We both were rushing quite wildly to a climax, which came with Jovian force for each of us. Exhausted, Clodia looked gratefully into my eyes.

---

* Of the three kinds of Roman kisses, the first (*osculum*) was restricted to friendly lip-to-lip contact, the second (*basium*) featured the flicking entry of the tongue, and the third (*suavium*) was a fully eroticised meeting of two mouths.

I responded with a long and loving *basium*. We then talked lip to lip, our amorous bodies clinging to each other. Around us we could hear all kinds of heavy breathing and moans of delight. When we did eventually look around, we saw multiple limbs moving with animal fervour. The unrestrained sexuality and lack of pretence were comforting. I told Clodia this was the first time I had enjoyed sex since Lydia. 'I could sense that,' she said with lowered eyes, 'but I adored it.' I knew she did. If she were not a slave to the Sibyl, I suspect I would have suggested a longer term relationship right then and there. But we both knew this was an impossibility. Eventually we did rise to drink some much desired and quite delicious red wine of Campania.

I was too drained to take part in the threesomes I saw grouping on the rugs in the colonnades. Some comprised two women with one man and others two men and one woman. To me it seemed that the females wanted to accommodate several men as much as the males wanted to enjoy several women. Then there were also men doing men and women orally pleasuring each other. I did not see any males orally pleasuring females because our social customs as Romans forbade this. As I have already explained, the only exceptions to this were the slaves, whose lower social standing exempted them from all state-imposed inhibitions.

A few hours later, Clymene went back to the podium and the drummers returned to action as well.

'Rise again, Pan, rise!' she shouted. Then, 'Rise again, Max, rise!' accompanied by the laughter of many.

Poor, overweight Max, was totally exhausted by his efforts.

'Rise again, Peleus, rise!' she commanded.

'For you, any time!' he shouted back.

'For Bacchus, for Juno, for Eros, and for all of us!' she responded before continuing with the refrain: 'Rise again, Rufus, rise!'

'I'm doing my best, as always, to awaken a shade!' At which everyone burst out laughing.

There is a certain innocence in desire, I felt, but there was genuine grandeur in sexual dissipation as we were celebrating it. Sex allowed us to honour the cosmic process of creation itself. The gods, they say, know that every kind of sexual excess is divine!

Peleus then got up and explained that all the men, 'irrespective of the state of their phalluses' (and here all the women and some of the men giggled), were to go to the far end of the atrium, and all the women, 'with lips of sorcery as obscene as ever' (and here there were feminine shouts of 'shame'), were to go to the other end. Everyone must then be blindfolded. 'When the flutes start playing, everyone must advance and meet in the middle where rugs have been laid out. The first person you touch will be the one you should take on the nearest rug,' Peleus commanded laughingly.

As the flutes started playing, I began to advance slowly and uncertainly. I suppose I had had too much wine to go on a straight course. I strayed. The first arm I touched was that of a man. I immediately could tell by the hair on his arms. In an orgy anything goes and I soon felt my penis being sucked. Slightly raising my blindfold for an instant, I saw it was Tappo, slave to Quintius. I gave myself up to the experience and soon found myself responding. As we Romans like to say: juicy fruit comes in many flavours.

I can recall the Sibyl saying: 'When Bacchus is sated, then blood and fire and dust shall all blend together.' Indeed I am convinced that the sweet taste of a delightful experience is a legitimate pleasure. Venus, the personification of the voluptuous pleasure of both men and gods, makes her power felt wherever there is life. All those who are under the sway of her sexual spell are truly driven by the ultimate vital energy.

Everyone to their own Elysium. Often I have imagined the

presence of Juno when making love. Usually, in my Elysium, love whispers in the flowering bushes everywhere and I enter the isles of fragrance. The music of the lute is like that of humming birds and that of the drums like resounding waves. I strain to catch sight again of those I have loved. I see my long lost Lydia and she is like a rare bird of passage, her body once again visible through the thin veils of her silken *stola*. Oh, for some more water of remembrance!

IX

My emotional state was admittedly fragile after all the weeks of anxiety and excitement. These pressures caused an imbalance in a couple of my humours (or basic bodily fluids.) Too much earth, associated with my black bile, caused a certain melancholia. I was well aware that Hippocrates had characterised prolonged fears and anxieties as being symptomatic of such despondencies. I know there are non-Romans, such as the Gaellic peoples, who view our belief in humours as just the prattle of toads. I believe otherwise. These fluids are instrumental in regulating my moods. Perhaps that is one of the reasons my attention wandered to Calliope, who was doing her utmost to distract me from my bouts of gloom. After my Lydia's death, I instinctively turned to our daughter for consolation. It is hard being alone after years of marriage. I didn't like the solitude which I experienced underground. I believed Juno sent us Calliope to comfort me. Lydia, as she lay dying, told Calliope: 'Look after your father. He will need you.'

Calliope, she of the wondrous voice, was the eldest and most distinguished of the nine muses. In our Graeco-Roman mythology she is the muse of eloquence and epic poetry, whose harp rings with lofty strains. Beloved of Apollo, Calliope bore him our own, much-heralded Orpheus. Like all the muses, she stimulated our heritage but had contempt for such mere details as style, form and technique, which were to be left to those mortals they chose to inspire. Lydia and I were proud to select this wonderful name for our daughter and it so suited her.

I think it appropriate here to describe our modest home and tell you something about the Roman rituals surrounding sleep. Our simple and ancient *domus*, which I inherited from my family, consists of a square block of some twenty steps by twenty steps constructed of timber, mud-brick and stones. It has just two rooms and an attic. The large front room has an ample *torus*, or bed, a wood chest for our clothes, four chairs and a rickety three-legged table (on which I try to write when not able to use the more ample one in the Temple of Apollo). Our whitewashed walls remain bare. The smaller room has a fireplace for cooking, a corner which serves as a storage space and another corner in which to wash. For light, both rooms have thick opaque-glass windows and there is a wooden door at the back which is open much of the year, but we rely on candles and oil lamps most evenings. Porcius, who is my freed-slave, lives simply in the attic. He is now in his sixties and wishes to stay with us till the end. He looks after the fire and starts off each day by blowing on a small glowing ember until it leaps back into life. Among his many duties, Porcius empties the chamber pots each morning into the compost heap nearby. As our 'cook', he prepares a cup of fresh milk and a slice of bread and cheese for each of us every morning. He also sweeps the cement floors, shops for food and faithfully waters our tiny herb garden. We pride ourselves on our rue, parsley, coriander, fennel and, the most aromatic, *basilicum*. Porcius is the last remaining tie with my father's larger household and is finding it harder and harder to dig up the earth. He has been faithful to me his entire life and has always refrained from gossiping about me to others.

Our family bed, which has a supple wool bolster, is covered by two spreads, one a flaxen blanket on which we sleep, the other an ample damask quilt which is pulled over us. We treasure two opulent swansdown pillows. They are among our few luxuries. Sometimes this bed also serves as a reclining couch for our evening meals. Like most Romans, I do not undress completely when going to bed. I merely lay aside my cloak, if it is cold enough for me to be wearing one, and throw it over a chair. I wear a loincloth made of linen knotted around my waist both day and night. Calliope, like me, wears a loincloth, with over it her short, plain linen tunic in the summer, a woollen one in the winter. It only reaches down to her knees at the front and is lower at the back.

When Lydia was alive, we always slept three in a bed. Once a week or so, when Calliope was fast asleep, we would make love. From an early age Calliope had observed how her mother and father enjoyed sex. For us, it was both passionate and sacred; animal-like and godlike. After Lydia died, Calliope would lie calmly alongside me. We were both shy about touching each other. Sometimes in her sleep Calliope would snuggle her head on my shoulders. We slept with our clothes on as always and shared the pure love between parent and child. Although she was almost a woman, she would climb all over me without self-consciousness as we settled for the night. Her impish good cheer would charm me completely. For her the moon was a source of endless enchantment.

'Oh,' she said one evening as we were sitting on the bench in front of the house, 'I would like to pluck down the moon with my hands and give it to you. If you got tired of holding it, we could play with it and toss it back and forth like a ball.' She would use all kinds of trickery to 'draw down the moon'. Another night, as the moon was hovering in the lingering twilight, she said: 'Can you see, the moon is embarrassed? It is turning pinkish and is blushing.' I could see what she meant as the rose colours of the sunset were altering the moon's hue. Sometimes, when in a contemplative mood, she would ask me: 'Rufus, is the moon afraid of falling?' When I hastened to reassure her, she would put her head on one side and ask me, 'Is the moon happy at the thought of rising?'

I would reply: 'Of course it is, my little moonbeam!'

One night, soon after Lydia's death, she asked me 'What will we do if the moon suddenly gets old and dies?' Drawing on my Lucretius, I told her that everything we know has its own lifespan – but as that possibility is a very long way off, we don't have to worry about it, particularly as we can't do anything about it. Some time thereafter she asked me: 'Is death life's answer to the question why?' I then had to expound to her at some length my views on the transmigration of souls.

At lighter moments she adored teasing me: 'Where were you born, Rufus?'

'In this very house.'

'You were not!'

'Yes, I was.'

'No, you weren't. You were born in the baths. Grandma told me.' And her dark eyes would light up as she giggled with delight. It was not important to her that I was grey and old, and certainly her presence made me feel a lot younger. Calliope had a favourite cat and it brought her live mice to play with. In my daughter's hands, I felt about as helpless as one of those mice.

One morning she asked me why Cicero was thus named. I suspected a trap of some kind and replied that it was because his forebears had raised crops of chick-peas. 'No, silly. It was because of a wart in the shape of a *cicer* on his grandfather's nose.' And she laughed and laughed with pleasure at the telling. She could also be quite serious and ask difficult questions about the nature of the world. 'Does light die?' she asked in earnest. 'Does light have a spirit or a body?' Or, 'What happens to light when it enters a dark room? Where does it go?' Much as I tried, it was very hard to come up with answers to satisfy her inquisitive young mind.

Calliope had been extremely interested in scents from the time she was four or five. This led Lydia and me to wonder if she might wish to become a perfumer one day. We even planted scented flowers and certain species of mints and rosemary and lavender, especially for her, outside the house. Calliope would pinch sprigs between her little fingers and then bring their perfume to my nose for identification and appreciation. I would make a show of how much I liked the smell by taking in exaggerated deep breaths.

At night, after Lydia died, I always kissed Calliope tenderly on her forehead when we went to sleep. Often she would move her curly head on to my shoulder. It all felt wonderfully right. I inhaled Calliope's youthful scent and it was sweet. But as a year passed, our relationship began to change, just as her breasts began to bud. It was she who made the first instinctive moves. It is curious how the most superficial of contacts, barely a touch on the arm, can suddenly shock us and turn us hesitant. One night, when her hand suddenly came to cup my cheek, I became aware that my heart was pounding.

It was Calliope whose lips reached towards mine in the dark. I did not respond. I could sense that she was afraid of her desire yet eager to fulfil it. Then softly, ever so hesitantly, she pulled up my tunic and her hand slowly stroked the skin from my thigh to my hip. I could feel my pulse accelerating. I told her that sex between father and daughter was cursed and recited at some length the tragic tale from Ovid's *Metamorphosis* of how a young girl, Myrrah, was overcome by incestuous desire for her father. The love between daughter and father was both forbidden and eternally damned. Calliope replied that she had heard such myths but was not afraid of the Furies, with their snake-like black tresses. 'I have my own opinion on this,' she said, with all the self-assurance of her twelve years.

I told Calliope that the Furies had much power and that she should not dismiss them so readily, particularly when she was about to go to sleep.

She grumbled a bit in protest, but soon I could feel her breathing slowing and her body relaxing. My stories and her fatigue had won the struggles over the rising feminine passions of her young being.

The next day Clymene, one of the Sibyl's attendants and sometime underground actress, whom I encountered near the

Temple of Apollo cautioned me about the challenges to a father raising a daughter like Calliope all by himself. I did not pay serious attention to this because I knew Clymene had an agenda of her own. I knew that she liked me and would like somehow to enter into my house and bed. I replied that Calliope missed Lydia, of course, but that she had many friends, studied diligently and would most likely be engaged to a member of our *familia* before long.

As we were discussing this, an excited Mentula approached and asked us if we had heard about an outbreak of *pestis* in Ostia, Rome's main port.

As yet we had not, but rumours like this had a tendency to spread like locusts in our community. She told us that a sailor, his ragged clothes soaked with sweat, had been weaving his way unsteadily from his ship and passers-by naturally thought he was drunk. Then the sailor started to vomit yellow and black bile. Finally, after swaying against a pillar near the dock, he collapsed. A whisper of, *'Pestis,'* began to circulate and the streets were soon deserted. Later that day three more dying sailors were dumped from their ship into the harbour and some dead rats were found floating not far away. Spread of a horrible plague seemed by now inescapable.

I had been haunted by nightmares of the *pestis* ever since my father took me to see a powerful staging of *Oedipus the King* in Baiae shortly after I had my first shave. I was bewildered at the time as to why the Athenians believed that the gods on Olympus had sent the plague in revenge for the crimes that Oedipus had unwittingly committed. The progress of the plague was inexorable. Its malign devastation swooped down upon a totally unsuspecting and unprepared Athens, killing thousands of citizens at random: the richest and the poorest, the youngest and oldest, slaves, women, livestock and even cats. For years afterwards in my dreams I was troubled by visions of the rotting, fly-ridden corpses of the Athenian dead, their unburied faces disfigured by maggots. Now, some decades later, I decided I wanted to find out more about this frightening phenomenon which periodically seemed to emerge from the unknown.

As we did not expect any visitors to the Oracle of the Dead in the next few days and I had heard there were to be several performances of *The Frogs* in Baiae's principal amphitheatre, I decided a brief trip would be a good way to cool Calliope's mounting lust. I told her I was going to see the comedy by Aristophanes.

She replied: 'Oh, frogs can always bring on the rain by croaking for it!' Most typical of my daughter's whimsical imagination. I explained to her that this visit would also give me the opportunity to visit the new library of Atticus, to which Quintius had given me an introduction. There I might be able to learn more about the plague and perhaps find how we could protect ourselves against it.

That afternoon, as I trod the lengthy and well-travelled path through the woods to Baiae, I asked myself what were the real reasons I wanted to do this? Little in my daily underground routine frightened me any more. This was a way to re-examine the dread of plagues that had once haunted me. Of course, the trip would also give me a chance to rethink my relationship with Calliope. I needed the distraction. Curiosity was certainly a spur. Were there any other possible explanations for periodic outbreaks besides the anger of the capricious gods? If there were not, why were little young ones among the many victims? Was this *pestis* passed on just like our ordinary colds? I naturally feared that this scourge might take away my Calliope. Indeed, I wondered why we were at the mercy of so many fatal diseases. Was there an over-abundance of life on this earth? Were wars and old age insufficient to keep the human population under control? And then again, how did the gods spread these dread contagions? Through the waters? The air? Our food? Could insects or even moulds be involved? I concluded that the mysterious aura of dark evils surrounding the sweats and fevers of this terror compelled me to go and visit the new and already fabled marble library of Atticus.

In the calm of this splendid new institution, I spent three days scanning the dusty, copied scrolls of the greatest of our ancient historians, Thucydides. Initially I felt ill at ease in this storehouse of papyrus and *pergamena*. My mind had been attuned from my earliest years to the spoken word. Were these records not corrupting our mental processes? Did such libraries not restrict the freedom of our imaginations? Librarians were assembling a wealth of detail and remembrances, but it seemed to me that ultimately they would produce mediocrity. Homer, although Greek, remains our minstrel-in-chief and his narrative is permanently stored somewhere in my head. That seemed like the best and most sacred storehouse. Still, this library was a welcome escape from my dreary routine of daily descents into the pretend realm of Hades. The actual research proved a depressing experience. I learned next to nothing. The exception was Thucydides, who wrote such an extraordinarily detailed description of the horrors inflicted upon Athens four hundred years ago. But he was an historian and did not examine any possible causes or cures. Sophocles had attributed the plague to the gods; Thucydides said it had travelled from the Sudan and then by ship to Athens. This did not enlighten me at all. Life seemed fraught with nagging uncertainties: erupting volcanoes, earthquakes, civil wars, highway murders and robberies, pirate attacks, poisoned foods and now suddenly the plague. We Graeco-Romans are hardy by nature, but the varied assaults on our bodies and our lives seemed unrelenting. Would it always be thus for our species? I speculated that life out in Atlantis might be safer and immune from all such troubles.

I hoped that my visit to the amphitheatre that night would be diverting. I had never seen a comedy by Aristophanes performed there.

I did not know what to expect and I felt a shiver down my spine as I watched Dionysus and Zanthias being ferried across an imaginary Acheron by an ageing and filthy Charon. I could hardly believe that I was being thus satirically portrayed on stage. With some pride I felt I was a much more convincing actor than this Roman performer. But I had to admit to myself that he was funnier. His impudent manner, curious Etruscan accent and his exaggerated gestures were truly comic. I knew his impersonation would stay with me for ever. So would the cleverness and imagination of Aristophanes.

Calliope threw her arms around me when I returned home the next day. Her face beamed with the pleasure of seeing me again. She wanted me to recount all of my experiences in great detail. She laughed uncontrollably when I played the part of Charon in *The Frogs*. She found my strange foreign accent and ludicrous gesturing irresistible. Of course she did not know I was Charon when underground. In turn she told me excitedly that she been talking to one of our priests about some of the minor deities – Murcia, the deity of sloth; Laverna, the goddess of impostors and frauds; and Limentius, the god of thresholds and doorways. All harmless enough distraction for a nearly thirteen-year-old.

That night, as she got into bed, she asked most earnestly: 'Rufus, why should our closeness be my misfortune instead of my happiness?'

I thought it was a question formulated by one much older than my daughter. Then she confessed, with considerable stumbling and embarrassment, that she and two of her friends had secretly watched us all from a small window at the back of the baths on the night of the orgy.

'Why were you happy to have sex with women you barely cared for, father, but are now refusing to have sex with me, whom you love?' She asked this in a pointed yet pleasing manner.

I replied that sex was a form of initiation and that I did not feel I was the right person to initiate her. It should be someone from her own generation. 'Sex is also the meeting place of the sacred and the secret. Making love takes us into another sphere, where sometimes the forbidden attracts us even more,' I said, a bit didactically.

'Is it not true that at the beginning Eros, the fairest of the immortal gods, soothed the limbs and overwhelmed the minds of gods and men?' Calliope asked rhetorically. 'Oh, my darling father, enough of your sophistry and your learning. I want you. Feel the beating of my heart. Feel my breasts, they are burning.' And she firmly took my hand and placed it on her tender, but still small, protruding breast. It was quite hot. 'A year ago, if you had refused me anything, I would have said something silly, like: "May you live to a miserable old age, toothless, one-legged and alone." Now that I am almost a woman, I say, "Take me as Jupiter might and initiate me into the world of the gods." '

And with this she kissed me passionately with her full lips pressed against mine. It was her winning move. Her words had shown me that she was indeed no longer a young one. The sensuality of her kiss blew away my strong inhibitions. When she then, ever so gently, brushed her hand sideways from my hip to my now rising member, she could sense my pleasure from its rapid response. The strength of her desire drew me closer. My resolution was weakening; my own physical desire became overwhelming. I wanted her for myself.

My hand slid down her thigh and to her knee and then stroked back up to her inner thighs which she squeezed together. 'Oh, yess! Rufus, yessss!' she pleaded. My brain registered the passion of her moans and I knew she was encouraging me. She kissed me again, ever more passionately. I could feel the rising power of her yearning for me. Lust spurred me on. Was it not part of the Olympian design to keep us in error? I was so aroused, so stirred, excited and swollen that the deed became a reality, as Lucretius had so brilliantly put it in describing this stage of sexual play. At first I think she felt a rather sharp pain. Then, as I continued to slide in and out of her as gently as I could, she began to relax and the goddess of pleasure began to work her magic. It was not long before Calliope's back started to arch. I pounded into her more forcefully. The first spasm of her orgasm shook me. I felt the jolt race through her body and she cried out the most beloved moans of a climaxing Venus. I recalled Jupiter's foam which entered between Danae's thighs like the foam which enters a cove during a storm. Her first post-coital reaction was to kiss me most tenderly, even gratefully. Then, slowly recovering from her release, she whispered lovingly: 'Oh! thank you, Rufus, and Eros too. I feel I'm in the clouds above.'

I could sense that her entire being was suffused with a sense of gratification. It was obvious that she had fulfilled a long repressed desire. Moreover, it seemed likely that she thought she had proved herself as a seductive young woman. Secretly, despite my unaccustomed sense of guilt, I was proud to have initiated her into such new horizons of human pleasure. Softly and quite calmly, Calliope fell asleep on my chest and eventually I joined her in the world of dreams.

Next morning, before we got up, she told me, her eyes blinking: 'I want us to do this very often, Rufus.'

'Hmmm,' I replied, trying to gather my senses.

'Tonight?' she asked eagerly.

'Let's see,' I replied evasively.

'I know, father, that you feel it is wrong for us to be together in this way. But I need you and I can feel that you do want me.'

My daughter, whom I so loved, was filled with desire. The fact that she yearned so openly for me was inescapably and seductively flattering. I was not trying to shift the blame on to her. I carried the vessel of responsibility. I knew I treasured her above all else. One must protect one's treasures. However, in irrational ways I regarded her and Eros to some degree co-responsible in this matter.

While considering all of this I could hear Porcius lighting the fire in the next room. A new day was starting. Reality was returning, It was time to get up, drink a glass of hot fresh milk, and then take off for the baths to perform an ablution after the evening's lovemaking. As I left the house Calliope calmly told me as usual her plans for the day: she would be playing with her friends that afternoon after her lessons in poetry, Greek, weaving and elocution. In ever so many ways, articulate as she was, Calliope was not yet mature. This made my burden heavier.

I tried to walk with a lighter step as I made my way through the narrow streets of Cumae to our own baths. The trees appeared to be stretching their branches as if waking up with the sunrise. Was I really a different man because of what had happened last night? I didn't think so. Of course my feelings for my beloved daughter were of the strongest kind. Fortunately, there was no fear of her becoming pregnant because she had not yet experienced the first of her *menses*. I did not expect, did not anticipate that initiating her into lovemaking would cause her any long-term distress. I would have liked to discuss this with Quintius, but felt it was better to work through my own rather unclear thoughts and feelings. There was no need to rush to conclusions.

Max, his Vectius (now a freeman), Peleus and Alfernus were already in the hot water when I arrived. They were all joking and in good spirits, Max in particular.

'Good-morning, Rufus. Any more risqué stories to regale us with about Clodia?' he asked, referring back to my encounter with her at the orgy. After last night, I had already forgotten all about it. I mumbled something unintelligible, even to myself.

'Say, old man, are you all there?' joked Max.

'Not even Eros minds what you do with a slave,' declared Peleus.

'Or what a slave does to you,' said Alfernus, nudging Max.

'I thought you were supposed to be blindfolded,' I retorted.

'It seems strange that now that I'm a freeman I can no longer enjoy the sexual freedom I had as a slave,' said Vectius.

Everyone laughed heartily.

'We won't tell on you if, perchance, you should revert accidentally to your submissive position,' joked Alfernus.

'It's funny. But now I somehow feel embarrassed by the very idea,' admitted Vectius.

'Isn't freedom splendid!' I exclaimed, to everyone's amusement.

And so the light banter continued until Quintius joined us. His mood was more serious than ours.

'I would be sober too if the gods did not give me sexual licence,' joked Max, who hoped for a reaction from Quintius.

'I'll ignore that for now,' Quintius replied. 'On my way here I bumped into Appius who told me that we are in arrears with our payments for his sacrificial animals.'

'How much?' immediately asked Max.

'Some thirty thousand sesterces,' replied Quintius.

'No problem,' declared Max. 'The Baiae bank will cover that easily.'

'Yes. But we also have to make some repairs to the portico of the temple. The cement of the pediment is crumbling and if we are to have an imperial visit, it must be repaired,' said Quintius.

'There's no guarantee of such a visit yet,' said Vectius.

'But when there is, will we have time to order a statue of Octavian?' asked Alfernus.

'I gather some marble ones are available in Rome at short notice,' I replied.

'Thank Jove we won't have to put up a bronze equestrian one,' said Peleus.

'That could nearly bankrupt us,' observed Alfernus.

'No way,' said Max. 'The Sibyl's coffers are full of gold and silver. She doesn't even bother with the bronze.'

'I'm not so sure, Max. Even I don't know how much she really has . . . or how much is stored by her in the bank or in her private treasury,' replied Quintius.

'Ask her to pay up for the restoration and the statue and see how she reacts,' suggested Vectius.

'I can predict her response. She will say that she is indisposed, or that she has no time for such matters, or that she will look into it later . . . or one of a hundred other such excuses,' said Quintius.

'But you are the high priest, she must listen to you,' countered Peleus.

'But I'm not her banker, her accountant or her treasurer,' Quintius replied.

'Who are?' I asked.

'She is her own accountant and treasurer, but I don't know whom she deals with at the bank,' admitted Quintius.

'I heard that she spent a fortune recently on a golden carp for her pool,' said Alfernus.

'It is indeed a strange state of affairs when a frequently intoxicated ageing recluse holds the purse strings for an entire community,' declared Max.

'We all know the two of you don't get along,' retorted Quintius. 'She may be secretive but she is extremely astute when it comes to money. Perhaps there is a somewhat retentive side to our Sibyl, but I know that if we really are in need, she will come through.'

'You hope,' said Max tersely.

'I don't know her finances, of course,' I said, 'but I sense that whenever her reputation has been at stake – money has never been a problem.'

'You are a shrewd judge of her character, Rufus,' said Quintius.

'Thank you, my friend,' I replied, but silently I asked myself if I really was a good judge of my own character.

'Since money is of the essence here, as in most Roman matters, I should like the Sibyl to approve my boat plans, because this ship truly could help our community finances,' said Max.

'There is no way she will back it until we have first approached

Agrippa and invited Octavian to a celebration of Apollo at our temple here in Cumae,' I said.

'I don't see why we can't have both,' wondered Max.

'I'm not arguing for what should come first,' said Vectius, 'but I would suggest that, with his priestly connections, Quintius should try to arrange an appointment to see Agrippa on this matter.'

We all nodded our heads in agreement on this strategy. Quintius also nodded his head above the water in silent consent. Just as I was pondering how curious it was that we reached agreement on such serious matters so readily in the warm waters of our *familia* baths, Peleus broke up our discussion saying it was time to attend to the day's descent into Hades. I reluctantly dragged myself out of the soothing waters. I was not looking forward to spending most of the afternoon underground in my dirty costume dressed up as Charon.

Peleus had filled me in on the 'training' and said that there would be three visitors: an old couple who wanted to talk to their dead son and a young Roman, Drusus, who wanted to communicate with deceased members of his family. A problem had arisen because the young man had been given far too much to drink. Not only was he feeling sick and vomiting, but it was impossible to find out exactly which relatives he wanted to contact. It seemed he also wished to speak with a lover who had died riding and who had only been in his teens. How to play him? Alfernus was for cutting it short and not letting him go down. Dardanius, an actor and a slave, suggested not to show the shade's body – only the masked head of a youth. This idea won the day as Peleus said that the young visitor was wealthy and had pledged a considerable contribution.

Later on I met up with Drusus and my suspicions grew when he asked me in an offhand kind of way whether it was true that Virgil had visited Hades?

I answered, 'Yes. It was a wonderful moment for our Oracle of the Dead.'

'Have you had many more requests to go to Hades since his visit?' he asked.

'Only a few so far, but we already had our hands full,' I replied.

'Even the Emperor should follow his example,' he volunteered.

'One step at a time,' I responded. 'One must not let success go to one's head.'

The descent of this young Roman was problem-free until we were on the banks of the 'Styx' facing the shade of his deceased darling Petronius, who was barely visible through the dense smoke of the burning torches on the other side of the 'river'. The inhabitants of Hades are without shadows – for they are shadows.

Stricken with grief, Drusus gasped: 'What happened to your beautiful long hair?' and broke down in tears.

Our Dardanius, his face covered by a mask with short dark hair attached, was silent for a few moments before replying evasively: 'Oh, I so miss you, my darling! I am terribly lonely here.'

At this, his sobbing lover asked: 'And whatever have they done to your wonderful voice?'

Obviously the intelligence we had failed to gather during his interrogation was showing. Dardanius answered cleverly: 'The smoke has irritated my throat, you fortunate angel.'

'By Jove! You have never called me that before, Petronius!' replied the astounded young Roman.

'But my feelings for you have not changed,' replied the actor.

This produced a prolonged fit of crying from the young Roman who, I decided, had been given too little to drink rather than too much. At this stage the billowing smoke cut off our vision and Petronius mercifully vanished. Drusus was bewildered by his experience, but I was sure it need not be fatal for him because no one would believe any stories he might tell.

A few minutes later one could once again make out various shadows on the walls and then the figure of the son of the old couple appeared. This time the intelligence had been much better and his aged parents were content to hear that, while he was now flitting about stoically, he spent his time hoping he would eventually enter Elysium. Such a prospect seemed to satisfy them. Apparently their son had been a truly virtuous man while alive.

My mind began to wander while this charade was going on. Soon I would be ferrying the visitors back in my coracle across the Styx and would then be able to climb up through the narrow tunnels and return to the real world. I was already preoccupied by what would happen with Calliope tonight. Instinctively I felt a sense of social concern, of moral transgression. I argued with myself that no fault could be found with this kind of intimacy on the grounds that it was unnatural. After all, goats mate with the she-goats they have sired and in Egypt the Ptolemies were commanded by their gods to marry into their immediate family. Yes, I admitted to myself, I do want her and, as a father, I adore her. It was not as if I was forcing myself on her. Calliope was definitely urging Cupid to target me with his arrows. I decided, in Roman fashion, to let what will happen, happen. Let the Fates decide. However, at some stage soon I would have to assert my authority as her father and select a suitable husband for her. That thought was simultaneously painful and a relief.

When I entered our *domus* I found Calliope preparing a chicken for supper. She was taking over from old Porcius. Our eyes met. There was nothing hidden in hers. No doubt. No questions. Just open-eyed acceptance and love for me. For the first time I saw her, through my own mounting lust, not as my daughter but as an exceptionally beautiful and utterly desirable young woman. Oh, how great are the powers of a woman's face, of a woman's body! And her glistening hair! Like most Roman men, I had always been captivated by the natural beauty of human hair; Lydia's long and golden silken tresses had delighted me, as did Calliope's inherited treasures now. I sensed a few drops of sweat forming on my forehead as I just stood there transfixed before her.

With deliberation Calliope walked over to me, took my hand and brought it to her mouth, giving it the tenderest of kisses. Then she threw both arms around my neck and, looking straight into my eyes, said: 'I love you, father, and have been dreaming all day about how you love me!' Without waiting for my reply – which was just as well because I was speechless – she kissed me passionately with both lips and tongue. Reciprocating, I simply melted. Juno had triumphed. Through her thin tunic I could feel her whole body radiating love.

That night our bodies were restless in their passion. She responded to my pleasure as I responded to hers. Breathlessly she told me, 'Your love makes me feel complete, Rufus.' And with my whole heart I replied, 'I love you, my Calliope, as I have never loved before.' I felt that every aspect of our sensual bliss was a moment of eternity; that our unbounded erotic pleasure was an absolute in itself. Later that night we were cocooned in our love. With her wicked humour, Calliope told me that mercifully I had ended her nightmare of being selected as a Vestal Virgin.

My mind wandered. I had been told when I was five or six years old that Jupiter 'likes to watch us'. A few years later he was joined by Juno and Apollo. Then Eros entered the picture: his full-time occupation was to bring men and women together. And in my more mature years, Orpheus and Bacchus became members of this curious constellation of gods involved in our sex lives. Were any of these voyeurs watching Calliope and myself? Could they even be interested parties? The whole scenario seemed highly improbable to me, but I decided to ask Quintius if the gods themselves could practise what we thought of as perversions. Could these gods really be leering? Peeping?

In bed I turned to my little wooden statues of the goddess of Fortune and Clotho, one of the Three Fates, in a recess in the wall. Which one should come first? Quintius told me it is illogical to believe in Fortune and Fate at the same time. To me, Fate does seem like a welcome escape from blind Fortune. They represent the difference between 'that was not fated to be' and 'chance would have it so'. We deem the believers in Destiny more respectable than the worshippers of Chance. And yet we are so much at the mercy of Chance that the supreme skill is to how to placate her and make her smile on us. After my second night with Calliope I was certain Fate was responsible and thus tried to diminish my own role in our illicit affair. Fate, as all Romans know, is far more powerful than the will of any man.

The next morning, on my way to the baths, I heard from the market traders that, to everyone's amazement and relief, the *pestis* which had broken out in Ostia had not spread. Instead, some of those who had manifested high fevers seemed to have recovered – which was most unusual. According to the rumours which were circulating, it was the strong west winds which had changed the atmosphere. Obviously the wind is a living force because it is blowing. It is being driven by some superhuman force we cannot see and do not comprehend. True, it whistles and sends us messages. It knocks some things down and can make others fly. I have heard it said that the end of the *pestis* must be attributed to the intercession of Volturnus, a wind god, who was acting on the orders of the commander-in-chief, Jupiter. Jove personally had ordered a prompt end to this particular scourge. Whatever the explanation, I was extremely relieved with the outcome after having grappled so unsuccessfully with the *vexata quaestio* of these terrifying epidemics.

X

I had wandered down to Baiae about a week later to buy a new tunic for Calliope in one of the many stalls where highly scented oriental women were selling colourful foreign clothes to the acutely fashion-conscious Roman matrons and their daughters. (It seemed that the shape was always the same, but the colours, the fabrics and the names of these tunics and *stolae* were as variable as the weather. One year it was the 'crocus'-shaped tunic, the next the 'loose-knot' tunic, another year the 'close-knit' tunic or the 'shift' tunic – not to be confused with the 'shiftless' tunic which came later. All these names reflected was the desire of women constantly to wear something new and different.) Passing a stall where fresh drinks were being sold, I suddenly spied Virgil ordering a lemonade. Somehow in the sunshine he looked more swarthy than I remembered him. Nobody took any particular notice of him. I thought of how satisfying it must be for one of the most renowned personalities in our land to be able to walk through the crowds without being jostled. True, the rare bust I had seen of him in the library of Atticus hardly resembled him. It tried to make him look more serene and even kindly. This was obviously flattery on the part of the sculptor. To me, seeing him there in real life, his tall figure seemed somewhat bucolic. With his irregular gait Virgil could have passed for a somewhat tipsy old farmer. His face was pale, drawn and rather melancholic. At first, I could not work up the courage to approach him. Who was I, a comparative nobody, to speak to a distinguished poet? My courage flagged. Then I reminded myself that an elder of the Orphic sect could talk to anyone, even a poet at the peak of his powers! Quite impulsively, I went up to him, not knowing exactly what I would say.

'Most illustrious poet!' I began tentatively, 'you will probably not remember me, but we met during your visit to the Oracle of the Dead. If you recall, we talked quite a bit about the Orphics at that time.'

'Oh, yes.' Virgil acknowledged, his face perceptibly brightening. 'The visit was one of the most remarkable and influential of my life.' I was pleased that he was so ready to acknowledge this.

'We also were much relieved that your descent to Hades was so successful and without damage to your health,' I said.

'I must tell you, however, that it has haunted my sleep quite often since then and I am still somewhat uncertain about the reality of it.'

'That happens to many – if not most – visitors. Very few of the Romans who have had contact with the afterlife have had occasion to write about it.'

'That is certain. It had really worried me that I might perish without having finished the sixth book of my *Aeneid*.'

'I can appreciate such anxiety,' I said humbly.

'I am pleased to meet up with you because certain questions still remain. I don't know why I feel uneasy about them. I had no such problem, for example, in detailing Aeneas's previous encounters with the unknown. Tell me: is it permitted for seekers, such as myself, to go down twice?'

'There is no rule against it, but I have to tell you, illustrious master, that it is without precedent. Frankly, I think you were lucky last time and we shortened your visit so that you would avoid the most dangerous sectors. It would be difficult to guarantee your safety should you wish to make further contact with the shades.'

'Yes. I quite understand,' replied Virgil. 'Let me ask you another question. Do you admit people who want to contact the relatives of others?'

I didn't quite know where this was leading but responded: 'Each enquirer is judged individually, both in terms of his health and suitability and on his reasons for descending.'

'I would very much have liked to contact any of the heroic figures of the Trojan War,' Virgil confided.

'That would have been extremely difficult.' I relied for my reply on past challenges of this kind posed by other visitors to the Oracle of the Dead. 'You see, most of the shades only stay in Hades about a hundred years or so before moving on. Achilles and Hector have been dead for I can't remember how many hundreds of years!'

'In truth, I had not considered this aspect,' admitted Virgil.

'But you have at your disposal the wonderful descriptions of Homer on which you could elaborate,' I volunteered, wishing to steer him away from this increasingly dangerous line of discussion.

'I am, of course, already head over heels in debt to this greatest of masters. He is very much at the centre of my epic. We are all so imbued with his poetry, that I cannot even begin to acknowledge him.'

'I feel confident that you shall be able to continue to embellish your narrative with the help of Homer's genius.'

'There are moments when I feel that the writhing snakes which were sent by Poseidon to kill Laocoön and his two sons are now wrapping themselves around me and squeezing the life out of me,' candidly confessed a rather desperate looking Virgil.

'Well Laocoön was being punished for cautioning the Trojans to reject the wooden horse that had been sent by the Greeks as a peace offering. You, on the other hand, have quite a different patriotic agenda. You are set on promoting the potential glories of a new empire leading to a more peaceful and prosperous Roman era. No god would punish you for that.'

'Thank you. You are most flattering. But my punishments are of a different kind. Writing laboriously each day is becoming increasingly challenging. I must portray how Aeneas persistently feigns hope and keeps his grief hidden deep in his heart.'

Modestly he then admitted to fading hopes of ever finishing his epic. He did not feel he had sufficient strength; he feared that the poetic powers he had once enjoyed were gradually failing him. But I liked his description of the way he worked on his verses as being 'like a bear nutures her cubs, by patiently licking them into shape'.

'As you yourself so convincingly wrote in your memorable *Georgics,* no good exists without some accompanying burden.'

'So my message came through?' he said, highly flattered. 'In my *Aeneid* I am pointing out that our most worthwhile accomplishments can come only from being ultimately tested. The emphasis must be on the journey, not the destination.'

'I remember you urging your readers to recognise the benefits of hard labour and much toil.'

'Absolutely. The bored ease of the Roman rich does not in any way advance our progress to something higher or better. This can only come from the energetic efforts of those who work with their hands. Yours, I notice, look remarkably strong for an Orphic elder.'

I was embarrassed, almost wanting to hide my hands. Rowing all these years obviously had made them rougher than the hands of the usual religious figure. It was time to distract Virgil from this line of conversation. The best way, I thought, would be to challenge him as soon as I could manage: 'I confess, I do a lot of gardening,' I said.

'There is no better salve for the soul.'

'I am pleased to hear you say that, much honoured poet.' I then boldly switched the line of the discussion: 'As you know, I belong to a religious group that adheres to the ancient Roman belief in communal property. I have been puzzled why you so openly have adopted the Augustan enthusiasm for private property? Could this truly be at the core of the much vaunted revival of Roman mores and values?'

Virgil slowly raised eyes to look at me more directly. It was obvious that he was re-evaluating me. Perhaps asking himself: who is this fellow to challenge the orthodoxy of our new empire?

'Your question surprises me, but it is a very good one. I must admit to having discussed this with some of the highest in the Empire. The prolonged strife which troubled our Roman nation in the past revolved around the conflict between patricians and plebians for control of the land. As long as any doubts remained on this subject there was room for strife. Since the civil wars, our new laws have defined the benefits and privileges which control of property bestows. In my *Georgics* I described property as the just reward for the hard labour of those who mixed their sweat with the rich Roman soil and were thus entitled to a modicum of stability. The road to legal entitlement is thus the way to peace. It is also the only way to protect the property of each individual.'

'So I have understood,' I replied. 'But where does that leave the community which is at the basis of society? The health of each bee is important to collect the honey, but it is the hive – not the individual bee – that must be protected.' I was trying to introduce an element of the symbolic into this discussion. 'Our ancient Greek and Roman ancestors had no need for private property. The forests, the streams and the fields belonged to everyone. Plato, in his *Republic*, was all for abolishing private property. He considered property to be the prime source of selfishness.'

'I can see by the determination of your expression that this issue is not going to be easily resolved,' said Virgil, 'but Plato was talking about ideals, about a commonwealth somewhat removed from reality, which had also excluded all poets!'

'True. From your class perspective as a poet,' I said laughing, 'Plato was a true opponent. Perhaps I chose my champion unwisely. Socrates, however, pointed out that the duty of the state was not to secure the disproportionate happiness of any single group, but the greatest happiness of the whole. He argued that a state which is ordered with a view to the good of the whole would be likely to establish justice; the ill-ordered state, injustice.'

'Perhaps it is impossible to have both the restitution of the sacred primitive community as well as the protection of each of its members,' conceded Virgil, looking somewhat downcast. 'I admit with regret that Romans are disposed to neglect the poor and those without property in favour of those with it.'

'And that this can only lead to the corruption of our moral attitudes,' I interjected.

'That is harshly put,' the poet declared, straightening his stooping shoulders. 'Any weakening of the principle of private property can lead to the break-up of family ties the Emperor is so anxious to prevent.'

'I recognise the importance of the Emperor's struggle to limit the seemingly rapid breakdown of the Roman family, but he fails to trace the source of this corruption to his own doorstep. You will not find such a breakdown in the farming communities of Campania. It is primarily a phenomenon of the corrupt city life of his capital: Rome. The Orphics believe that community is not a utopian vision. It is as essential to us as it is to the social insects, such as the bees and the ants. We recognise the common instinctual goals of these insects, but fail to admit to our own. We depend on community for our language, education, culture, protection and continuity. Romans accept the necessity of community action to supply clean water but not to protect our overall well-being,' I said.

'I would agree with you that all might not be well if every individual was left on his own to pursue his choices, rights and general self-interest, but that is far from the situation today. Rome is most fortunate in having a wise and concerned ruler who wants to establish justice in the land,' vouchsafed the poet.

(And, I thought silently to myself, this poet is most fortunate

139

to have such a generous patron.) 'Master, all of us agree that it is essential to establish justice. We Orphics try our best to create a community which combines certain spiritual treasures of the past with modest and natural hopes for our material future. The social cohesion engendered through belonging to such a group is much like that among actors when they stage a play. Their task is clear. Thespians work together for a common purpose: to create an illusion. As a community, of course, we must do far more than create illusions: we must advance our social dreams.'

'I am beginning to sense that we have more in common than I had previously suspected, Rufus Longius. That is heartening. I respect the forthright way you state your position. There are few these days who have the courage to confront me so directly. And I empathise with your firm stand. Indeed, I held similar views as a young man.' Then shifting his weight uncomfortably from one foot to the other, he added confidingly: 'I dearly hope we shall have further opportunities to exchange our views in the near future, but before I go on my way, I should like to ask a favour of you.' It was evident that the energy level of the ailing poet was rapidly sinking.

'Please do not hesitate to ask for our help, Publius Vergilius. Our entire *familia* is at your service. But also please forgive my lack of consideration in forcing you to stand for such an inordinately long time,' I replied apologetically and with genuine embarrassment.

'No matter. No matter,' Virgil said kindly, waving my apology aside. He drew me with him a short distance, on through the market. 'I have often found the odours flowing from foreign armpits disagreeable,' he whispered confidentially as we passed some Persian women at a stand. Then, in a more serious vein, he asked: 'What I should like to know is how I can express my special thanks to your Sibyl. She has made a deep impression on me. At times, after my dreams, I am not certain whether she is a living soul or merely a character out of my own fantasy.

I am sure you are aware that your prophetic priestess is already a person of historic significance.'

'We are all aware of her immense importance to our *familia* and appreciate her standing in the entire Roman world. As to the best way to express your admiration, great master, none would be more moving than to send her a few of your new verses in which you mention her role. Truly, nothing could flatter her more.'

'That is not something I usually do, but in this case I shall try to make an exception,' he replied.

'And I should be most honoured to have a continuation of our discussion at some future time,' I ventured with genuine enthusiasm.

'By all means. I have to stay in Baiae for a couple of days to consult with a dietician. Perhaps we could meet tomorrow around midday at the statue of Jupiter and continue our conversation? I should like to hear more about what really happens in the world of Hades.'

Virgil's last remark quite threw me off balance. How best to respond? I felt I had no option: 'Your proposal is most unexpected indeed and I shall certainly be there. It is such an enormous privilege to converse with you.'

I walked away completely overawed at the prospect. My first reaction was that perhaps I should have refused him. That would have aroused suspicions. No Roman, if thus asked by a reclusive poet of Virgil's reputation, could have turned him down. I was most concerned, however, that his true objective might be to question me at more length about life in Hades.

Staying in Baiae that night, I hardly slept. My mind was totally preoccupied with the problem of how to divert him. I decided that appealing to his intellect was the answer. I had noticed that the poet liked to hold forth at some length. He had listened to what I was saying, but was far more intent on the exposition of his own views. Best to let him talk. But then my thoughts reversed themselves again. What if he started to question me about my own experience in Hades? I felt certain he would spot at once that I was evasive. That would not do. And so my ruminations continued through the seemingly endless night.

After keeping a close eye on the sundial, I arrived promptly the next noon to find Virgil already standing in front of the Temple of Jupiter in Baiae, gazing intently at the larger-than-life bronze statue of the god. I decided to seize the initiative: 'A very good day to you, Master Publius Vergilius, but permit me to ask if you think it is artistically correct that our sculptors always portray the Olympian gods as being so perfect?'

'Good-day to you, Rufus Longius! Yours is, of course, a different perspective from mine. As a poet I know it is not easy to ascertain exactly what perfection is; how I should attempt to portray it . . . if at all? Certainly we know that all the stories about Jupiter reveal the many facets of human frailty.'

'Exactly. However, this particular Jupiter now facing us seems too calm. He appears removed from any striving. I might even conclude from this portrayal that he is not endowed with desire. Do you see what I mean?'

'Your observations are close to my concerns. I, too, have problems with which I have to contend in this sphere: How should I portray our new god, Augustus? I have not even decided if he is to be a god of the land or of the sea. I was somewhat bewildered to see him portrayed on our new silver denarius as a kind of Neptune!'

'Well, he truly occupies a preordained place in the heavens, so would it not be appropriate to show him with the radiance of a sun-god?'

'Well spoken! I shall keep that in mind, Rufus. Alas, our Roman sculptors too often favour presentation over content. Their bronzes seldom sing.'

'The Greeks, on the other hand, were absolutely in thrall to

142

the idea of the beauty as opposed to the reality of their subjects. Those who sculpt the faces of our leaders always represent them as tough, responsible, hard-working, unusually earnest men. These characteristics are conveyed by making them look 'old', with bald heads, sunken cheeks, furrowed brows, ample bags under their eyes and lots of wrinkles.'

'How true!' exclaimed Virgil, with a deeply wrinkled smile.

'It seems to me that Homer sometimes presented rather light-hearted portraits of his deities. Today some of our Roman sculptors have recast the formerly randy Priapus as a dignified Augustan father, who has young ones on his lap and is busy keeping accounts, in an effort to portray the new "morality". This is radically different from the way Plato and Aristotle tried to promote their ideals.'

'Like you, Rufus Longius, I also wonder if passion and desire are not frequently excluded from the serious likenesses produced by our Roman carvers. Apparently Plato actually saw "friezes in the sky", which he described as the "most beautiful and exact of images",' said Virgil. 'It was this power of the imagination that first enabled the Greeks to place the myths in the heavens above them.'

I took a deep breath of relief as Virgil spoke. This discussion was going in the right direction and I hoped to keep it there. 'An all too facile lustfulness would seem apparent everywhere,' I sighed. 'Priapus is to be seen jumping up and down all over the place.'

'Yes. All these phalluses seem ridiculous . . . But perhaps I am out of touch. Ovid and Catullus accuse me of trying to divorce perception from desire. I think this is not only unfair on their part, but it would also be impossible for me to achieve,' said Virgil, looking somewhat grim. 'I am fully aware that Plato insisted that beauty and desire were inseparable.'

'Men are fortunate that desire persists as long as the object is beyond reach,' I said, remembering what Quintius had recently told me. 'Does not beauty die with indifference? Is not the fulfilment of desire its very death?'

'Plato suggested that as long as we perceived anything as beautiful we acknowledged that we had not yet exhausted all it had to offer,' agreed Virgil, pacing slowly in front of the temple.

'And there is a malevolent intervention here on the part of Eros who promotes our desire to pursue both lust and pure beauty but makes it impossible ever fully to possess both in the same object.'

'Yes, Rufus. Of all the ideal forms, of course, beauty is the most arresting and capable of being grasped because we perceive it through the clearest of all our senses: our eyes.'

'When I find something "beautiful", I feel that there is something about it of which I should like to know more,' I said.

'I have always found that the beauty I am describing depends on a sensuous harmony, on equilibrium, balance and the wholeness of what I am seeing.' As he thus spoke Virgil shuffled over to a marble bench and sat down rather heavily.

I waited for him to continue, sensing it would be presumptuous and even rude of me to interject any kind of response here.

Understanding this, Virgil composed himself and then continued: 'Beauty, as both Plato and Aristotle told us, cannot be separated from understanding and desire, even when it comes to poetry and music.'

Somewhat hesitantly I asked: 'Master, in your opinion can passion gradually inspire a longing for truth and beauty?'

'It is a sensitive subject. Plato explained how the love of a particular boy or man could lead to the love of everything beautiful in the world, which for him was mostly about philosophy. Plato regarded it as an opportunity to try and understand exactly what features make a youth so beautiful as to inspire lust and desire. Plato's view, but not mine, was that all beautiful things draw us beyond themselves and ultimately into the more precious beauty of philosophy.'

'That was indeed wonderfully abstract,' I ventured, 'but as an Orphic I am far more concerned with beauty of the spirit, beauty of each individual soul.'

'There rises once again your Orphic outlook,' said Virgil with a trace of satisfaction. 'Cannot the pursuit of beauty itself be its own promise?'

'I am not a philosopher. Indeed when I try to explain why I find something beautiful, I end up incapable of uttering words that will capture my experience. I do not think Orphism suggests that beauty provides a way towards morality or is somehow aligned to an enhanced appreciation of truth or virtue. We all recognise that beauty can be deceptive. I need go no further than to point out the vacuity of feeling in the endless Roman marble copies now being made of the great Greek sculptures which were almost radiant with passion and beauty.'

'You are correct in pointing this out, Rufus. It is hard to deny that their real beauty has been debased by our copyists, who ceaselessly reproduce centaurs and hermaphrodites, Venuses and Apollos, as if new myths were beyond their power to invent.'

'Repeating them so frequently has the effect of rendering these reproductions unworthy of a second glance,' I ventured rather boldly.

'I suppose Plato would have argued that ignorance and incompetence can always debase beauty but I – ' and here Virgil was stopped before he could finish his thought by the arrival of an official, who apparently had been looking for him.

'Most honoured master,' he said breathlessly while bowing to Virgil, 'the praetor, Atreus, asked me to find you. He thought it might be possible that you had forgotten you had a meeting with him today.'

'My years are beginning to show,' said Virgil, fumbling for words of apology. 'I became engrossed in a most engaging discussion with Rufus Longius, here. And we never even broached the subject of Hades and my all too brief encounter with the shades,' he said to me, slowly rising. 'These are subjects of some importance but they shall have to wait for another occasion. Rufus Longius, it was an unexpected pleasure.' And he took my hand and shook it somewhat feebly. There was no denying this great poet was feeling his age.

As he walked slowly away I almost gasped with relief. I had been able to avoid any number of possible pitfalls. Fate had been truly kind to me in her most timely intervention. This seemed of primary importance, not the fact that I had somehow been able to hold my own with one of the most revered and intelligent figures in the Roman world. That Virgil was still obviously concerned about his underworld encounters seemed to matter less at that moment than that I had passed a challenge in a way that I would not have deemed possible just an hour earlier.

XI

At the baths the next day I reported every detail of my encounter with Virgil. Everyone was impressed but also concerned about Virgil's continuing doubts. Would he somehow recall the shadow of the falling wig? That was what we all wondered but did not voice. Worries also surfaced over Quintius's trip to Rome to meet with Agrippa's adjutant regarding our proposed celebration of Augustus at the Temple of Apollo. Quintius had true 'presence' and was a superb negotiator – but I didn't know how the reputedly crass administrators under Agrippa would respond to him. Again I asked myself, 'Do we really need this "celebration"?'

Max brushed aside these doubts. 'I'm determined to pull this off,' he told us, as he was about to set out for the thriving port of Puteoli. 'I feel the gods are with me and I'm going to persuade Annius Plocamus and the rich Nabataei (our term for Arabians) to invest in fitting out one of their cargo vessels.' We wished him well and I told him to stay away from wandering rouged lips, but privately wondered whether we, as a *familia*, could cope with a greater influx of seekers of the dead. After all, my coracle could only hold a maximum of five passengers at a time. Was this truly the way ahead?

In the meantime, I had to get back to my daily routine. There were preparations to be made for a number of upcoming trips to Hades. Peleus was convinced, after the problems we had faced in the last descent (and I believed him to be right), that we had become lax in the way we were processing our visitors. In many ways our training 'camp' was a weeding-out process. Those openly sceptical must never be permitted to 'pass'. Only the gullible, the amenable and the 'compliant' should climb into my coracle. Peleus felt that in preparing those who were about to descend, we had to listen more carefully to what they had to say: make them share their fears, find out what they wanted to hear, get into their way of thinking and be certain not to override their voices with our own. It was important to find out all we could about the person who had died. What were the feelings of our visitors about the deceased? In the three days of the 'camp' we had to pay attention to what was said and what was not said about the deceased. Peleus admitted that it was hard but necessary for us to adopt a way of hearing that was different from our own. Our way of listening so influences what we learn. The visitors always started out with endless questions but after three days they usually didn't have many. The lack of sleep, the alcohol, the doctored vapours and their increasing hunger all worked to lower any tendency towards argumentation, analysis or scepticism. In principle, our 'training' should have turned them compliant.

The latest group of prospective visitors to our underworld comprised: a rich young widow, Sabina, who wanted to contact her deceased husband who had reportedly died in a storm off the island of Rhodes; a cripple, Geras, in his thirties, who wanted to know from his departed parents if he should sire offspring; and a serious, but somewhat dubious, young Roman, Caius Antonius, who wanted to reconnect with his famous uncle, Lucius Antonius. It was rare for us to be asked by visitors to arrange contact with prominent figures from the past. Caius was all the more unusual because he promised our priests Lysius and Balbus at the Temple of Apollo a small figure of a bull in solid gold, weighing about ten libra* and worth a small fortune. This was so extraordinary that we could not help but devote special attention to him. We wondered whether he had a secret agenda?

* Editor's note: about 3.4 kilo

Peleus was at his most eloquent in welcoming these prospective enquirers to our tent camp: 'I commend your purpose in coming to Cumae. You want to communicate with those you have lost. I want to gain your trust because you may be facing anxieties about possible rejection by people to whom you may have been close and to whom you now wish to talk. Such an encounter is always chancy. I want to help you overcome your nervousness over the next three days in this camp because I know that you may have heard of the few visitors to Hades who never return. I am not about to make false promises or give you any guarantees of safe-passage. We did not offer Virgil any guarantees when the famous poet made his recent descent with us. However, your trip may prove difficult. Some of you may return from the underworld so mentally stressed and unstable that your minds will be at risk. You may even experience a general collapse a couple of weeks after your descent. That is the chance you take at your own peril.'

Here I observed Caius Antonius wincing. He was also wringing his hands involuntarily. The young widow, on the other hand, seemed as cool as ice to me. I didn't take to her. Peleus looked intently at each of the visitors in turn and then continued: 'Entering into the mysteries of the next world is full of challenges. It will take each of you considerable courage to meet these. You will have to show your mettle and your fortitude in the face of great discomforts. When you confront the shades they may at first even seem threatening. Cerberus snarling at you may give you heart tremors. It is likely that the underground visitation itself will make you feel dislocated and uncertain. What I must tell you is that you are not likely to be the same person when you emerge as you were when you embarked on this voyage. It is not too late to opt out.'

Here Peleus paused but none of the candidates made any move to leave.

'Communicating with the shades is uncertain. You must also

149

understand that the dead have a protective shield: they don't have to talk to you. They can just flit away. On the other hand, if you are trembling or crying with emotion, it is entirely possible that they may take pity on you. You must prepare the questions you have for them most carefully and we can help you frame these. Visitors often make tactical mistakes when interrogating the spirits. If you are rude or angry or shout at them, they are likely simply to vanish. In the underworld, calm must prevail. Don't attempt to touch the shades because they are always out of reach. And don't ask them, for example, if they are having a good time.'

Here Peleus smiled broadly and I noted that all of them laughed. That was a positive sign. They were relaxed enough to be able to see the funny side of their descent. Peleus then continued: 'I want to emphasise that it is important for us to know as much as we can about the person with whom you wish to communicate. What do you know about the dead person? How old were they when they died? Had they been sick? How did they die? Tell us about their voice and how they spoke. Voice is an instrument of relationship. Their way of speaking must be regarded as a reflection of their psyche. But here I caution you once again that their after-death experiences may have caused some changes in their speech. They may suddenly stutter or stumble over their words. Their answers may even seem incomprehensible. In all of this you must be tolerant and understanding.'

'But what if we can't understand them at all?' asked a highly nervous Caius Antonius. 'Can we ask them to repeat their answer?'

'Of course,' replied the unperturbed Peleus, 'but it may not be any more comprehensible the second time around. Now I know that poets and painters have for generations portrayed the inhabitants of Acheron as having human attributes. But from our experience we deem it unlikely that any bodiless, insubstantial phantom could ever possess hands, noses or ears. Shadows can't make limbs or bodies for themselves, nor can they creep into frames already formed.' Here, to relax his listeners a bit, Peleus told the familiar myth about a ghostly shade entering the wrong person's shadow. Even Caius Antonius laughed. Then Peleus continued: 'I want your agreement that you will not resist our coaching. Yes, we will look closely at your areas of vulnerability. Of course, we hope you will cooperate with us, but we shall also be judging your compliance. Those who will not touch our good wines, for example, will be viewed as resisting our coaching and perhaps will not be permitted to descend. While you are here we will provide you with much water, some wine and little food. It is a regimen we have tested for optimum receptivity. You will be pleased to hear that you will be spending much time relaxing in the baths and sleeping in our dark quarters. After three days there will be animal sacrifices and a priestly diviner shall determine whether the omens are favourable for your particular descent into the underworld.

'We recognise that you are taking a risk in undergoing this training, but you are also making an investment. We ask from you just about as much as you are willing to contribute. It is up to you to judge what is right. As you probably have heard, we accept most commodities – cows, pigs, sheep, goats, bulls, wines, oils, even salt. For example, someone brought us an amphora of that delicious *garum* [a fish sauce] from Pompeii a few weeks back. Here I must specially thank Caius Antonius for his particularly generous offer to Apollo. We also want all of you to know that our renowned Sibyl is there to answer questions, but you must realise that her Oracle merely adjoins our camp and that you must entreat her divination separately.' With these words Peleus concluded his impressive and highly professional presentation.

Sabina surprised us by the amount of wine she drank. In fact, when not sleeping she seemed constantly inebriated. Was she seeking oblivion in the afterlife? Geras was the most compliant and seemed ready to do anything we asked. His ingratiating ways turned me off. And Caius Antonius was cautious, nervous, and drank next to nothing. Lysius told me that he had a long discussion with Caius about Lethe. Caius wanted to know whether one drink from the spring of Lethe really erased all memory of the past? Lysius tried to reassure him by saying that the effects of the spring were not as powerful as the myths surrounding them. Caius then wanted to know if, after returning from the descent into Hades, it would be possible for him to drink from the Waters of Remembrance (Mnemosyne). Caius wanted to be certain to remember as much as he could of his experience. Lysius again reassured him by saying that he would be given a potion of 'the water of remembrance' after he returned, just as had been given to Virgil. Caius seemed comforted by this knowledge.

The interrogation session with Caius proved most problematic for Lysius who recounted it to Peleus, Alfernus and myself. When asked by Lysius what questions he wished to pose to Lucius Antonius, Caius said that first of all he wanted to talk to his dead uncle about Fulvia. When asked what about her, he was intentionally vague. Pressed further, he gave no reasons. Then he said he wanted to ask Lucius Antonius about Niobe. Lysius had no idea whom he was talking about, but Caius did not elaborate. And finally Caius wanted to know about his uncle's dealings with Publius Servilius Vatia, who had been his senior partner as Consul in Rome. When asked by Lysius what aspect of these dealings concerned him, Caius mumbled an incomprehensible response and seemed extremely ill at ease. Caius, when asked, said that his uncle had a rough, rasping voice and his speech was uncouth, full of swearing and anger.

The four of us discussed among ourselves at some length how best to deal with Caius. We felt that, given his promise of the gold bull, we had to let him descend. On the other hand, any reply to his questions would be problematic. The nature of his questions was in itself most unusual. What was he really after and why was he willing to spend a fortune on the answers? Was he doing this at someone else's request? Was he an investigator who had concocted a 'cover'? None of us had a clue as to what Caius really wanted. How to proceed? When Balbus was to read the entrails of the slaughtered lamb the next day, interpreting the shape and colour of the liver, what should his verdict be? None of us liked Caius and all of us were doubtful about him. Peleus suggested that Lysius should try to get Caius to bring the gold bull into the Temple of Apollo before his descent on the basis that if he never returned above ground there was no way that the temple would ever receive his gift. We all agreed on this strategy and promptly began to coach our slave actor, Dardanius, on the nature of the questions that would be posed by Caius and how best to answer them in a convincing voice.

Later that day Caius, when cautiously approached by our circumspect Lysius about his gift to Apollo, replied directly:' I thought you might be asking me about it because I fully realise I may never come back from Hades. I have prayed to Apollo and asked for his help. I heard a voice tell me a week before I came here to write a testament to the effect that this bull shall only be donated upon my safe return from Hades. In this way, I feel assured that Apollo and Orpheus shall both help me overcome whatever obstacles lie ahead.' Having said this, Caius gave Lysius a parchment testament with an official seal on it and said that a copy had been deposited in Baiae. This young man had planned his visit most carefully. Such measures further aroused the suspicions of Lysius.

The gold bull had obviously been decided upon as a way to guarantee Caius a full visit. The options facing us were to have Balbus declare the omens unfavourable, in which case we would forfeit the gold bull, or to proceed and decide, once the trip to

Hades was over, whether or not to dose him with a slow-acting poison. Peleus, Lysius, Alfernus, Balbus and I were all in agreement that something was not right about Caius, his approach and requests were so out of the ordinary. Yet we could not put our finger on it. I wanted to try and get in touch with Max's former slave, Vectius, who was now working in Baiae for Atreus. He might have some clues, but even though it was only a three-hour walk, I was unsure how to go about this without attracting attention by my absence. So I did not proceed. I considered talking to Sulpicia about it, but rejected it because I knew beforehand what she would say: 'Go for the gold.'

So we continued to observe Caius during his meals, his baths, and above all during his time in the dimly lit entrance where the haunting portrayals of grief, anxiety, disease, old age, fear, hunger, death and agony were displayed on the walls. Close to the doors there were also the skilfully executed paintings of prancing Centaurs, the Harpies, the Chimera, the Gorgons and the Hydra. They had been placed there for maximum effect. When asked about his dreams, for we Romans are fully aware of their importance, Caius drowsily told us that all he could recall was that he had become an almost invisible old man sitting under an elm tree where, to his considerable irritation, false hopes hung from each leaf. None of us could interpret this or make any sense of it. Romans, like most people, only focus on something when it captures their interest. Alas, too often what we observe is distorted through the ripples of the waters of our fluid minds. We do not see what is; we prefer to see what we want to see; to hear what we want to hear. What in the name of Pluto was Caius after? Lysius could barely conceal his worries that he might have overdosed the waters that Caius had been drinking.

When the three-day period was over, the time came for Balbus's divinations. The priest, while pouring his libations, had his head covered by his cloak. At his side were the two young *camilli* (helpers) holding the implements for the sacrifice, including a jug and a bowl. The sacrifice of the lamb had been 'pure'. After the lamb had been properly blessed by the Apollonian *flamen*, Lysius, it had been killed by a single blow to the head. If the lamb had struggled that would have been a most negative sign. Of course, nothing unclean had been permitted to defile the place of inspection. Divination through the liver is most perspicuous and this precious organ was very carefully lifted out together with the gall bladder. It is always a significant and threatening omen if the gall bladder is torn from the liver. The shape of the liver is absolutely crucial. It has a three-sided pyramidical protrusion called 'the head', but its form varies a great deal from animal to animal. No omen is more serious than the absence of such a 'head'. Caius seemed anxious and in low spirits as Balbus went carefully, step by step, through his precise ritual. Sabina was still drunk and could barely keep her head up. Geras seemed resigned as to the outcome.

As I could have predicted, because we had chosen a healthy young lamb, the surface of the liver had a fine mirror-like quality. It had no spots. This was important because the liver is regarded as mirroring life itself. This liver was not yet 'blind', that is it had not yet lost that shiny property that occurs when it is exposed to the air. Fissures in the liver are always a sign of danger. Deformity of the right or left lobes of the organ can also prove crucial. It must be understood that Romans see the liver as the most likely seat of the soul. It is therefore a divine element in all living animals which, in turn, is a reflection not only of its own life but as an indication of the will of the gods. Since the fate of all of us rests with our pantheon, it is important to try and uncover what the gods may intend. Balbus's reading of the lamb's liver might possibly enable him to divine the will of Apollo himself and make some kind of prophetic declaration.

Having finished a fortunately positive reading of the liver, Balbus next proceeded to a definitive examination of the spiralling colon of the lamb. The order, condition and colour of the seven

155

concentric coils of the lamb's colon were of import. These coils were laid out flat on the marble slab. The first coil was leaden in colour, the second more like milk, the third was a sulphurous yellow and twisting, the fourth was golden, the fifth and sixth were amber in colour and curved tightly into the others. The seventh and final coil properly reversed its course. This was an excellent omen and verified the haruspicy. The action for which divine sanction had been sought could now be pursued. Young Caius Antonius looked relieved that Apollo had given a strong 'thumbs up' for his descent. Similarly positive readings followed for the widow Sabina and the slow-moving Geras.

Caius was given the proper blessings and made ready for his descent, which meant being anointed with olive oil laced with verbena. In the meantime I had to change from Rufus into Charon: take off my toga, put on my rags, glue on my dirty white beard and cover my balding head with the scraggly wig. I then swiftly made my way down to the coracle and waited on the landing-stage for the usual descent of the procession down the smoke-filled and dim, torch-lit corridors to Lethe's bank. As was customary during this waiting time, my mind began to wander. Does the human mind, as Pindar believed, work in circular motion like the heavens? Calliope was very much at the centre of my own circular drifts. I could almost feel her taking my hand and kissing it before whispering to me: 'I love you, Rufus, and continue to want you all the time.' I replied, 'Kiss me, you fervent disciple of Venus!' and wondered whether that was really me talking or whether I had heard these lines in some theatre or perhaps even at an orgy? Reality and my longings were almost indistinguishable. I could literally feel the fuzz on her cheek and the faultlessly smooth skin of her neck. I could hardly stifle my lust. Many of those past nights Calliope had been consumed by a fire she could not quench. Such passion had me far more in its thrall than the ephemeral visit of the weird little group now slowly descending into the underworld of Hades.

We had decided beforehand that the young widow and the cripple should go ahead of Caius to commune with the shades they wanted to contact. Their sessions went without any problem. When it was Caius's turn I could immediately tell that Dardanius, who was acting as Lucius Antonius, was unusually nervous. As Caius saw the head of his uncle's 'shade' appear in the darkness, he too became tremulous: 'Uncle, I am so pleased we have somehow managed to meet again.' There was silence, so Caius continued: 'Have you been sleeping a lot?'

'E–e–e–eternally,' came the reply.

'Your voice is so different. You never stuttered. Is it hard for you down here?'

'I can–n–n–n–not speak of what I am e–e–e–xperiencing,' came the stuttering monotone of his uncle.

'I am so sorry. Uncle, I wonder, did you meet Cicero in Hades?'

'We must engage in a di–di–different kind of conversation than we used to.'

'Uncle, I came down here in part because I have to ask you a few questions about the past. Did you witness any legal agreement in Caesar's time about Virgil's father's property?'

'I have drunk too much of the waters of Lethe. I do not remember those e–e–e–e–vents.'

'Nothing at all?'

'I hardly re–re–re–cognise you. Your spirit has changed so, Caius.'

'You must surely remember Fulvia? Did you have a relationship with her?'

'I met her shade recently. But we no longer f–f–fuck down here, if that is what you mean to ask,' Dardanius said in an artificially hoarse voice.

'Thank you, that partially answers my question. But what about Niobe?'

'What a–a–bout her?'

'Did you have her killed?'

'Are you a p–p–praetor now who thinks he can subject the dead to cross-examination?' I sensed that Dardanius was really warming to his role.

'I am neither a praetor nor an officer of the law,' replied Caius. 'I am just your humble nephew trying to sort out past events.'

'Humble? Humm–mmble? You come here with a gold bull and try to bribe your way into Hades?'

The instant Dardanius said this, I knew he had blundered. Letting on too much can always be dangerous. Even though he was drugged Caius picked it up instantly.

'How did you in the underworld learn of this?' demanded an incredulous Caius.

At this question the shade disappeared in a cloud of smoke. Dardanius did this just by lying flat on the ground. Caius received no reply. But Peleus swiftly interjected: 'As we cautioned you, Caius, it is dangerous to press a shade too much or to be overly demanding.'

'Holy Jove! My head is whirling around. Where am I? Is this place real?' demanded a bewildered Caius. 'This shade, who has so little in common with my uncle and seems to know nothing of the past, is startlingly familiar with my activities on earth!'

'You are getting overwrought. The shades do learn from Hades himself what is happening above ground,' said Peleus, placing a comforting hand on Caius's shoulder. Caius fell silent but I could tell, as I ferried him back across the Styx, that even in his disturbed state he felt he was somehow being duped. He was quite unsteady when he had to climb out of my coracle and on to the landing-stage. A few minutes later he rejoined the small group headed by Lysius. Both Sabina and Geras had been deeply moved by the contact they had made with their respective shades and went through the remaining rituals in something of a daze. Only Caius seemed disturbed as they all climbed the long narrow passages upwards out of Hades and into the daylight.

About half an hour later, having given him some of Lysius's

'water of remembrance', we questioned Caius about his underground experience to make certain he would not spread unfavourable reports about the Oracle of the Dead. It was evident that he was thoroughly confused. His mind had been bruised by the experience. He told us that he felt completely 'out of time'. Part of him was aware of his body but it seemed that his soul was hovering outside his body and that death was only awaiting an opportunity to ensnare both his body and his soul. What was happening inside his head was to him unfathomable. I felt pity for this young man desperately struggling to retain his sanity against the power of the drugs.

As in all cases of this kind, Peleus, Alfernus, Lysius, Balbus and myself gathered for a decision on how to proceed. 'To Socrates or not to Socrates is, as ever, our choice,' began Lysius, who tended to use proper names as verbs. This tall string bean of a priest had all kinds of linguistic idiosyncrasies in addition to his other attributes. His nose used to bleed at full moon. From an early age, natural poisons had been a passion of his and he had become extremely knowledgeable in their use and skilled in their administration. As he proudly would tell us, the best poisons were silent, deadly and, above all, left no trace.

'From the first, I have found Caius suspect,' declared Peleus. 'If he returns to a normal life, he will tell everyone in his circles in Baiae and in Rome that the team at the Oracle of the Dead tried to deceive him. I therefore vote that he should be poisoned, for all our sakes.'

'I second Peleus,' said Alfernus, 'but I feel we must take him back alive to Baiae so that we may collect his gold bull.'

'I did finally talk to the Sibyl about this,' I said, 'and her verdict was: "Give him the honey of poisoned flowers." I agree with her, Peleus and Alfernus.'

'In that case,' responded Lysius, 'I recommend a gentle, slow-acting potion mixing Apollinaris (henbane) and extract of belladonna with a tincture of opiates and a dose of hemlock. His initial hallucinations will be light and the delirium moderate. Slowly the poisons will fill his whole bloodstream and he will die a relatively merciful death at the end of the lunar month. No autopsy can reveal anything. No antidote could possibly be found to reverse this course of events.'

'Perhaps, in your honour, priests someday may suggest that so-and-so should be "Lysiused",' joked Alfernus. Some of us laughed but Lysius responded only with the faintest whisk of a smile. There was more than a trace of the sinister in Lysius's reaction.

Soon after the poison was administered, Caius complained that he felt a growing, drowsy numbness. He also grew steadily more pale. We told him that he would be better in a few days and that we would ourselves take him back to Baiae. This proved to be a consolation, after which he calmly fell asleep. The following day he seldom woke-up, drank little and ate less. When he spoke he was mostly incoherent. Lysius observed that the poison would kill his *nous* first, his body next, and his soul would be the last to depart.

That evening, as I was trudging back home in a heavy rain to my captivating Calliope, I consoled myself with the knowledge that Caius's soul would soon enter into another realm. I wondered if Jupiter or any of the gods might have taken exception to our act. To my knowledge they had not punished my ancestors for any of their 'crimes'. After all, our *familia* had always acted in its best interests in order to preserve and protect the reputation of the gods themselves.

Calliope greeted me, as usual, with the most tender of endearments when I came home. 'All this long day, dreams of you have quickened my heart,' she admitted. Neither lust nor love grants us easy passages. True, Juno had smiled on us and so had Fortune. In bed neither Calliope nor I needed reassurance that we were truly of one flesh and blood. It was undeniable that our very bodies were being fused together. Sex is about blending, mixing, being one. There was no end to our pleasures in those days. Tasty passion was on our tongues. What I wished for was also what she wanted. I was not ashamed to love my daughter and Calliope, in turn, was not ashamed to sleep at night with a grey-haired man or to press ever so many kisses on his wrinkled hands. Desire, as I already have explained, spurred us on.

However, I did not seek the kind of communion of souls with Calliope which Plato held out as the ultimate expression of perfect love. What we enjoyed was a touch of Elysium, but I recognised this was not for eternity. I knew that I would soon have to match her with a young man – preferably one of our own *familia*. Antonius, the son of Peleus, seemed the most likely candidate. They had known each other from youth and liked each other. I would have to talk about this with Peleus. For me this would be wrenching. I could hardly bear the prospect of losing my greatest treasure. Somehow I acknowledged it would be equally hard on Calliope and I could not bring myself to talk to her about it. If love between a father and his adored daughter was an act which the gods felt must be punished, I hoped that Calliope at least would be spared.

Time is the great devourer. Over the next few days our victim's strength began to ebb. I found it painful to observe that he could not lift up his arms any more. He did not seem to be in pain, but, even if he was, we had no way of knowing. He was no longer coherent. In this condition, he was strapped on to a mule and we slowly guided him back to Baiae. On presenting his letter, Max – who had returned from his expedition to Puteoli – was able to pick up the gold bull from a grieving household. I would not have had the heart to do so. To me Caius's last offering represented a kind of a sinister Trojan gift which might release unknown poisons when opened.

XII

The anxieties of our *familia* were mounting steadily day by day. Fear was undoubtedly clouding my vision. I must admit I did not, could not see things clearly. A Roman's hostility is always aroused by an indistinct view of events but it is usually allayed by talk. If I look at the long avenue of plane trees in Cumae, close up they seem wide apart, but those at the end almost meet. We need distance and must gradually develop a sense not only of perspective but also of proportion. Those of us who hold widely divergent views in our twenties tend to come closer to each other in the course of life and animosities generally have eroded by the time we reach old age. Some of the fratricidal hatreds which raged in our blood-soaked civil wars less than a generation ago already are beginning to fade in our memories and will seem incomprehensible to Calliope's contemporaries. Intuitively, I sensed the stress we were experiencing was causing divisions within our *familia*. I could not see what I could do about this.

Our recently freed slave, Vectius, who was now working in the local administration of Baiae, reported to us soon after Caius was returned semi-conscious on a mule that this suspicious visitor to Hades was a close friend of Atreus, a praetor and adjutant of Marcus Agrippa. This news flashed through our *familia* like lightning. Agrippa was the second most powerful man in the Empire and was reputed to have always regarded the Sibyl, her Oracle and our Oracle of the Dead as somehow beyond the power of the established Roman institutions and therefore suspect. Some two decades earlier, Agrippa had come down harshly against the oriental religious cults which had been introduced by the more than thirty thousand slaves from the eastern provinces imported to build the naval base from which the Roman fleet had set out to defeat Marcus Antonius. We recognised that Agrippa's long nourished disapproval of our multifarious activities, if fuelled by convincing rumours of foul-play, could have the most dire consequences.

At the same time, Quintius returned exhausted from his mission to Rome. Through his connections at the College of Priests, Quintius had presented a formal invitation to the staff of the Emperor. He had been told that a response could be expected within the next quarter, upon the return of Augustus who was travelling in Greece. Quintius was most excited by the vast and numerous new projects which were under construction in the capital under the overall supervision of Agrippa. Quintius told us that he felt it was the beginning of a new and absolutely grand age for the Empire. 'I have seen the promise of the future – and it resides in Rome,' he declared in such a positive way as to impress and affect us all.

The new Rome, which he described as being constructed of marble with glistening baths, temples and monuments, sounded too formal to me. Would it not be lacking in spontaneity? Was the plan not overreaching in its imperial ambitions? I expressed the view that I would have preferred something more Athenian, less materialistic and more spiritual – dare I say it, more 'Orphic'? Quintius quietly agreed. Indeed, I went so far as to confide to my priestly friend, as we walked down to the beach at Cumae the next day, that I thought we too had become excessively concerned with making money. Was this truly the direction we should take? I pointed out that as 'modern' Orphics we rarely sought out 'divine madness'. By way of explanation, I told him that there are now thought to be four kinds of mania, or divine possession: that of lovers, that of poets, that of prophets and seers and that of the authors of the rites of purification. The closest our contemporary Orphics now come to divine mania is to regard 'mad' desire both as illumination

163

and as a fundamentally spiritual aspect of our earthly experience.

I was surprised that Quintius grasped at the madness of lovers: 'Whoever is in this world and does not love a woman so as to possess her does not belong to the truth and will not attain it.' Quintius considered that an active sex life within the sphere of personal commitment strengthened the integrity of those involved and was essential to being well rounded. No wonder he was appreciated by the women in our *familia*. But I was too shy to ask him if, as a priest, he had ever gone to walk at night along the infamous 'Beach of Priapus' in Baiae.

Man, as Quintius enjoyed repeating, is partly of earth and partly of heaven. Our temples are our human effort to reach towards heaven; the altars represent the earth. Our heavenly part can be increased through a pure life on earth: 'Every action in this world will be accounted for in the next.' He and I agreed that our Bacchic rituals and initiation into the mysteries set out to produce 'enthusiasms' which allow the divine to enter into us as believers, ultimately enabling us to come nearer to being at one with the Creator. As we worship we are spiritually and otherwise intoxicated by our Bacchic passions, which push both prudence and rationality aside.

As an Orphic 'elder', and that is literally little more than a recognition of my age, I have to say that our religion repudiates hierarchies, liturgical obligations and the spiritual domination of ecclesiastics. Anyone can join us in our worship: Egyptians, Syrians, Germanics, slaves and believers in other religions. The latter because we believe that all deities are but different forms of the one great power that is the source of all being: 'Everything comes out of One and is ultimately resolved into One,' said Quintius. As part of creation, men and women contain the spark of the divine within them. Although reading this you may not believe it, we are not pledged to propagate our beliefs. An Orphic can still worship the traditional Roman, Greek or Egyptian gods.

The simultaneous worship of Apollo, Dionysus, Jupiter and Isis is perfectly acceptable for individuals thus inclined. As Quintius liked to point out with his touch of wry humour: no two men's religions are identical, but those with similar inclinations or temperament often tend to group together.

Quintius seemed perfectly at ease to me when officiating in his capacity as a high priest at some of the seemingly endless festival observances or when a visiting senator or one of the pontiffs from the College of Priests in Rome passed through to consult the Sibyl, herself a priestess. The duality of practices did not seem to bother Quintius. After all, as he pointed out, Bacchus and Apollo, our leading gods, are two of the Olympian twelve. The Orphic, he had explained to me many years ago, opened up all kinds of floating possibilities that the political killjoys in the Senate were always prepared to sink. The primary objective of the politicians in Rome was to keep the ignorant masses under control and to that end celebrated religious rites which they themselves often personally regarded with considerable contempt. I write of our struggles with religion because I believe this to be of importance, not only to future generations who may be searching for meaning and direction but also because it is linked to the destiny of our own Oracle.

For three centuries the leaders in our capital have tried to subvert the orgiastic delirium of the early Orphics. The ceremonies of the joyfully inebriated devotees, trampling through the mountains singing hymns to Priapus, shouting, screaming, making music with drums and cymbals and working themselves into a total frenzy of ecstasy, were threatening to those leaders wanting control of the populace. Even before the glorious days of Athens, Dionysus had become one of the gods of civilisation itself. Later, as the god who is destroyed, who disappears, who relinquishes life and then is reborn, he became the symbol of everlasting life. Indeed our Orphic concept of him in these days of the new Empire remains that of a supreme divinity.

I knew Quintius shared my distress at the endless ritual sacrificing of animals. The sight of men prostrating themselves or holding out their hands to pray while some priest sprinkled the altar with the blood of the sheep, goat, pig or ox just slaughtered was deeply disturbing. The gods could gain nothing from such sacrifices. It was only vain believers who achieved a certain sense of communion from these rituals. Orpheus first taught that men should abstain from killing and polluting holy altars with blood. Quintius, too, felt a gnawing urge to separate the divine from its primitive and cannibalistic origins. Often, when Lysius or Balbus were taking the blood out of some animal and pouring it over the altar, Quintius would simply close his eyes or pull a fold of his toga over his head. Others thought this was a sign of prayer and of his deep belief. I knew better.

Over the past few centuries, those of us who have believed in Orphism have increasingly turned away from eating animals. This has been a struggle. The early worshippers of Dionysus concluded their often intoxicated and frenzied rituals by tearing an animal apart and eating its raw flesh. To them Dionysus appeared in the form of a bull and their ultimate aim was union with this bull-god through the sacred ingestion of the god in a blissful communion. These savage rites gradually evolved to the point of rejection by us, and today we Orphics no longer drink blood or eat meat at any of our ceremonies. Instead we symbolically sip some of Campania's celestial red wine and partake of the honeyed biscuits. We recognised that with the transmigration of souls, we could well be eating bodies into which the souls of our deceased friends or relatives may have entered.

Quintius maintained that religion had not been seen by the Greeks as a way to assuage their fears about a future after death. Their gods had not been omniscient, omnipotent or omnipresent. They were thus not unfamiliar to men and some-times mingled with them. Their all too human attributes made them accessible to the ordinary Athenian or Spartan. The important thing for men was to focus on making the most of life in this world. Although Plato maintained that the soul was the higher principle, the soul and the body could strive together in harmony.

I think that Plato, because of his eloquence, has often been misunderstood by most Romans. Of course his language is poetic, with thunderheads hovering over mountain peaks high above the rhetorical clouds. Although he was a master logician, I pointed out to Quintius that when Plato did err on rare occasions he may have done so out of a certain perversity of spirit. 'Does Plato tell men how to calm their passions? No! Does he instruct them how to dispel their fears? Never! Does he educate men to appreciate what benefits them? He can't be bothered!' I repeatedly maintained.

'Just because Plato describes the clouds does not mean he predicts the weather,' replied Quintius.

'The way he misrepresented the Jewish myth of origin in his famous *Symposium* was both mischievous and intentional. Plato suffered from his eloquence while lacking both energy and what we Orphics would call "fire in the belly".'

'Aren't you using Socrates to critique Plato?' asked Quintius, with a wry smile.

'I don't think so. Socrates didn't teach Plato that 'slaves are to be scourged' rather than admonished as if they were youths. Plato failed to face up to the reality that if our domestic slaves were freed our lives would be much changed. Nor did he ever examine our moral responsibilities to our slaves when they are sick or old.'

'I have to admit,' replied Quintius, 'that hardness of heart towards slaves is quite as unpleasant as cruelty towards dogs.'

I agreed, and went on, 'Plato, as a visionary, tried to subvert the order of things in ancient Athens and presented a model where a few white beards could flatten down society into two stale dimensions.'

'You are exceedingly harsh towards our great master,' retorted Quintius. 'You, Rufus, would like to be a Diogenes, exposing the fallacies of pretenders to virtue and philosophy.'

'What I know of Plato, and it is only a regrettably small portion of his writing, I sometimes find unconvincing,' I admitted. 'Plato said, for example, that "Souls therefore exist after death in the infernal regions", but his logic is dubious. How is one to prove or disprove any argument on the immortality of the soul?'

'There I have to agree with you, Rufus. But, if you're going to critique Plato, you must also take note of his extraordinary exclusion of poets from his Commonwealth. Here Plato was truly being the advocate of Hades. Banning poets would give them the credibility – and notoriety – they have so often and regrettably lacked.'

Here I interrupted my friend and told him how Virgil was upset by Plato's rather whimsical banishment of poets from his Republic.

Quintius empathised with Virgil but pointed out that Plato considered the gods had been degraded by Homer. 'Homer left out most of their sexual escapades which later poets embellished – but which I am sure Virgil will ignore. I suspect that here for once Plato and Marcus Agrippa are of the same mind. Agrippa also doesn't care much for poets or their works. He thinks poorly of Virgil and tells people that parts of the *Eclogues* were plagiarised from Lucius Varius.'

'Well, the way I look at it, Virgil is no Lucretius and lacks Ovid's arousing sensuality. Personally, I have found his early poetry only superficially pastoral. Despite his concern with animal husbandry, some have said this barely passes as "herdsman's verse". But Agrippa is a primitive. He's shown his prejudice against those whose beliefs don't match his own in the past. He's impulsive and headstrong. I fear that one day he'll come down on us Orphics as well.'

'Apparently Agrippa also has a fascination for dying mullets,' added Quintius. This referred to the current fashion among some decadent Romans for removing young mullets from pools and enclosing them in glass decanters. The practice enabled guests at banquets, reclining on their luxurious couches, to observe the dramatic changes in coloration as the mullets struggled for air. They found it beautiful to see the dying fish turning from red to a pale tint of grey. Between their life and death one could note a succession of the most subtle shades. Personally the thought made me sick as I recalled the gradual and painful death of my own Lydia. Moreover, I thought such a fascination on the part of Agrippa was ill-suited to the wider compassion for life any truly great leader should possess.

XIII

A week after Quintius's return from Rome, we heard that Caius Antonius had died. Quintius, Balbus and I went to Baiae to represent the *familia*. I felt I was already spending too much time pondering the afterlife while underground to celebrate it again above. It was impossible for me to believe that the closing of the eyes secured the release of the psyche from the body or that a *manes* emanated from the deceased. It is mandatory to place Charon's 'piece', namely a copper coin or *obolos*, in the deceased's mouth if Charon is to ferry his soul across the Styx. You may correctly infer that this ferryman silently rejected such superstition.

The minute we arrived in the atrium, where a fully clothed Caius had been placed on a couch surrounded by garlands of flowers and with his blanched and naked feet towards the door, we noticed that all his relatives gave us glaring looks. I felt distinctly unwelcome. This kind of funeral is a three-act drama – all about kin solidarity. I tried to keep my eyes downcast and felt slightly nauseous from the odious scent of the cheap rose oil which had been sprayed all around. Among the mourners I spotted Virgil, who was as pale as the outstretched corpse. His deeply crow-footed eyes gave me a weary look of recognition. Strictly speaking, those who have presided at the Eleusinian Mysteries are not permitted to enter a house of mourning, to visit a grave or even to attend a funeral banquet, but no one present knew I had ever conducted such ceremonies. The tedious traditional mourning and ritualised burial rites were to extend over two weeks, but Quintius had told us beforehand that although his office obliged him to stay we were free to leave at any time.

Amidst this doleful funereal atmosphere, with all the burning incense, chanting, wailing and ministrations, there was one wickedly comic moment when a cupboard which held the ageing yellow-brown wax replicas of Caius's dead ancestors toppled over and rolled on the marble floor of the atrium to the utter dismay of the grieving family. The panicked attendants crashed into each other as they scrambled in most unceremonial fashion to pick up the bruised and battered wax similitudes. The family, of course, considered the incident as bringing disgrace on them and on their poor, deceased Caius Antonius.

During a short interval in the lengthy opening rituals, Virgil slowly walked over to me and asked me in a whisper if we could talk outside. Quintius looked at me with a bewildered glance. My heart started pounding faster. I followed a few paces behind Virgil. What to expect? I felt the energy ebbing from my legs. The first thing Virgil imparted to me, after we had reached the shade of a fig tree in a somewhat secluded part of the garden, was the devastation he felt at the death of Caius Antonius.

'I hold myself partially responsible for urging him to go down on my behalf,' admitted the remorseful poet.

'I, that is we . . . did . . . did not know that,' I stumbled. 'How most . . . regrettably . . . unfortunate.'

'I felt I had only received a half-tour of Hades and missed Tartarus entirely. I wanted to have an independent account of the whole underworld experience,' confessed Virgil.

'I could have filled you in on all the details, most revered master.'

'I know. I know. I had planned to ask you the last time we met, but it was not to be. I wanted Caius to contact certain shades. It was a mistake on my part. I feel responsible for his death – he looked so unwell when he came back to Baiae.'

'That could have been from the sulphurous vapours in the underworld,' I interjected. 'At times these can make any of us ill. And the fumes can prove lethal to some sensitive visitors.'

A pregnant silence followed. Then Virgil asked in a tremulous voice: 'Can you tell me in all honesty: Was Caius poisoned?'

I had anticipated this question might be coming and answered immediately and directly: 'No. Not to the best of my knowledge.'

'But what really happened? I was told Caius collapsed upon returning to the surface and never fully regained consciousness.'

'Caius was most agitated before he went down. I heard he drank a lot of wine to bolster his courage. One can only surmise that, given his condition, the experience in Hades unsettled him. Perhaps the fumes got to him as well. I cannot tell you more.'

'Thank you, Rufus Longius. I know you are doing your best under these tragic circumstances and had nothing to do with his actual descent. What troubles me as a writer is that the reality of the underworld must be seen in the context of great uncertainty. We cannot ascertain exactly where the dividing line between what is knowable and unknowable can be drawn in Hades.' And with this profoundly metaphysical thought, Virgil walked away from me looking much distraught.

I did not return to the mourners. I felt ill at ease with the eyes of all the family members glowering at me as if I were one of those who had perhaps poisoned Caius Antonius. In our land it has traditionally been an offence against the gods to let a murderer go unpunished. Indeed the murdered are called the 'unquiet dead'. If he were now one of their company, Caius would be demanding atonement and his family were saying prayers invoking divine vengeance upon anyone who might have been responsible for his murder. A crown had been placed on the head of Caius 'for having bravely fought the contest with life'.

Quintius and I talked later. Of course he was anxious about what Virgil wanted from me. I carefully recapitulated my talk with the great poet and his concern about possible poisoning. I told Quintius frankly that Virgil seemed convinced that our Oracle was somehow responsible for Caius's demise. Considering his connections with the Emperor, I felt that the prospects for our Oracle were not looking good.

The members of our *familia* became most agitated when I reported to them that it was Virgil who had commissioned Caius to spy on our descent into Hades. Some, particularly the women, were ready to accept the inevitability of events when they thought the Fates and Fortune held sway. But human intervention seemed far more challenging to handle . . . especially when a 'god' like Augustus could become involved. All of us became aware of strange portents in the weeks that followed. Our *familia* began to discuss the significance of deep-red sunsets, frequent earth tremors and sudden showers of giant hailstones. All these phenomena were regarded as manifestations, if not prima facie evidence, of divine wrath. Were they augurs of an approaching final judgement? The ever blunt Max summed it up with the words, 'The Imperial Augustan sky is about to pour shit all over us.'

XIV

Trepidation had taken hold of all of us. What was of pressing concern was that Atreus had ordered a post-mortem be performed immediately after the public registration of Caius's death. The inconclusive results would probably be kept quiet by the praetor, so we did not expect to hear anything about it. We knew from past experience that any attempt to discover the cause of death, weeks after the slow-acting poison had been given, would fail. Our Roman law, however, contained strict provisions against all who made, bought, sold, possessed or administered poison for the purpose of causing death. The penalty, ever since the time of the dictator Sulla, was deportation and the confiscation of property. As a consequence, Lysius, who was prudent in covering his tracks, and his assistant, Balbus, carefully stashed away their most precious glass vials of poison. They placed these into three or four large amphora which had been bedded with straw and sealed with beeswax. The amphora were then buried by them in a secret place to which not even the slaves were privy. Subsequently, Lysius and Balbus set about converting their poison storeroom into a perfumery. Quickly they collected all kinds of aromatics, and in accordance with the time of the year, ordered quantities of rose oil from Neapolis not only to conceal any trace of the heavy poisonous odours which might have remained in the storeroom but also to set up their new business.

All the members of the *familia* were fully aware of the events surrounding the demise of Caius when Max called for a council meeting. I was most apprehensive about this, but from the very first moment, Max seemed to brush all concerns aside with his usual nonchalance: 'I know that some brave soldiers fight to cover themselves with glory during battle and many worthy citizens overcome great adversity by defying both the odds and the Fates during catastrophes such as fires, floods, and plagues. I have learned from their examples and so must all of you. By Jove! Damn the objections! We must forge ahead no matter what the portents. I have brought with me the estimates for converting an ample cargo vessel into a luxurious passenger ferry. That is our first priority. Second comes the proposed presentation in the Temple of Apollo celebrating both the Emperor's and the Empire's brilliant future. I know I was against this originally, but given the threats facing us I have changed my mind. Quintius has just returned from Rome and we must await what we all hope will be a positive result before preparing for a visit from the Emperor himself. Yes, Jupiter and all the gods may be laughing at our efforts, but they will admire our daring and our persistence. They have by no means abandoned us. I am determined we are going to succeed.'

I was impressed by Max's powerful delivery. Cleverly, he had switched tactics, showed he was open to change. Most important in terms of his strategy, he was trying to bring all of us into *our* rather than just *his* project.

'Max, you have proposed an endeavour calculated to attract much attention to us. I believe it may have great merits, but would it not be wiser to lie low for a while rather than to court publicity?' I asked reasonably. 'I see enormous risks in launching such dramatic and even financially costly projects when we may possibly be facing a prolonged investigation.'

'I am a soldier and as such I believe the best defence is offence,' replied Max. He had this avuncular way of brushing aside criticism and potential embarrassments, but his shaved head would betray irritation: it would turn cherry pink. The flush would just as swiftly disappear, but how the blood thus came and went only an Aesculapius could tell. On such occasions, by Jove, he would switch from artificial good humour to quite genuine hostility. This was now the case.

'You want to be awakened by a red-hot poker, Rufus?' he asked. 'Modesty and hesitancy make a man unfit for public affairs. It also makes him unfit for the brothel. Any service for a fee is now the law.'

Here all of us, except the Sibyl, laughed. Drawing herself up straight, she said in a dramatically forced voice: 'Red is the colour of Priapus, the god of the phallus, of passion and of fire. Black is the colour of Saturn, of dark nights, murders and defeats. Are not the heavens filling up with dark clouds. May not the heavens turn black? Will we not be destroyed by earthquakes? When Bacchus is sated, then blood and fire and dust shall blend together.' Having presented these portentous metaphors, she closed her eyes and sat down. I had no idea where her contribution had left us.

'It is dangerous for us to have deep divisions in our *familia*, with some taking one side and others opposing. We must be careful to avoid widening up a split,' cautioned Quintius.

'There are times when I feel that, within our *familia*, loyalties are regulated by only one constant: self-interest,' declared Mentula, who as the Sibyl's 'understudy' rarely spoke at our gatherings.

'There is some wisdom in your thoughtfully chosen words, Mentula,' retorted Max. 'But, looking at it purely from the perspective of our *familia*, can we afford not to embark on these efforts? Agrippa could shut us down. If we were bigger, more prominent, would he dare?'

'Not likely,' agreed his ally Balbus.

'It is the voice of Apollo to which we must listen, not the unspoken threats of Agrippa,' declared the Sibyl. 'His voice cautions us. We are evenly divided on our course of action. This means that our *familia* cannot take any steps forward or backwards. So be it,' she said stamping her foot with her customary finality.

'I find that difficult to accept,' rejoined Max, his face flushed red. 'You tell yourselves, "If we don't move, don't do anything, all will turn out for the best." You long for stability, for the familiarity of the past. But I can tell you one thing: that is not an option. Waiting is not the answer. It never is.'

We all looked at each other for a way out of the impasse. There was none. No action seemed plausible for our *familia*. Max was both angry and upset that consensus seemed beyond reach. He got up and walked out. Quintius remained seated, bent over in fatigue. Lysius seemed resigned. Mentula looked indifferent. And our Sibyl remained inscrutable. Her eyes were closed. Then she spoke again:

> 'Immortal Apollo, it was you who put into my heart
> The oracle divine, for I know not all the things I say.
> The divinity that is within me speaks these strings.
> And now I desire rest for my heart is weary
> Of foretelling fortunes with another's divine words.'

We all fell silent again. Weary, I walked out rather despondent about our prospects. It seemed ironic that so soon after Virgil's visit and one of the most glorious moments in our Oracle's more than five hundred years of history, criminal investigators would be coming to cross-examine us in Pluto's realm.

We did not have to wait long. Only ten days passed before a procurator from Baiae, Status Pomponius, arrived in Cumae. We had no government or judicial office in our community so, after wandering somewhat wearily for two days about the temples, the baths, our tented camp and the entrance to the Sibyl's cave and asking for guidance from various slaves and attendants, Pomponius summoned Max, Peleus, Alfernus and myself to meet him in our camp. This long-serving official had a hangdog look in his age-wrinkled eyes. It is said that Demosthenes entertained the opinion that if there were two roads, one leading to public office and the other to death, a prudent man would surely choose

177

the latter. Pomponius had chosen imprudently. He began most philosophically: 'There is a paucity of settled truths in this world and not every truth is the better for showing its face undisguised. I shall be questioning each of you individually about the tragic and problematic death of the much honoured Caius Antonius. It was Virgil himself who told his friend Atreus, our praetor, that poisoning could have been the cause. What I must uncover, in what looks like a complex case, is: Was there a plot involved?' Here he took a long, deep breath. 'If so, what were the motives? Who were the participants? What were their methods? Where is the evidence?' Here he again paused significantly. 'Reportedly, you four are the most responsible for the operation of the Oracle of the Dead. Later I shall question those laterally involved in the Sibylline Oracle itself. There would appear to be an overlap between the two, but I shall try to keep the parties distinct. First, I think it is important for me to inspect the locale – not merely approach the gates of hell, but actually explore the reputedly "joyless realm of Acheron", if my Lucretius serves me well. I am somewhat advanced in years, so I shall not be able to rush through the tour. Take me down as if I were an ordinary enquirer, eager to talk to my ancestors.'

At this point Peleus spoke up somewhat firmly: 'We should be most pleased to do as you suggest, most honoured procurator, but I must advise you that all visits require considerable preparation. Ours is a holy and much revered location. No visit can proceed without a consultation, ritual sacrifice, and favourable signs from the gods. In all of this the priests are involved. On a more practical level some three hundred candles and dozens of torches must be lit before the descent. All of this involves both time and offerings to the deities. If we are to take you on the same tour as the much regretted Caius, it would involve at least three days of preparation.'

'Yes. As I said, this investigation is going to be highly complex. Now it seems it is going to be costly as well. I must consult with our praetor, Atreus, before proceeding. That means returning to Baiae and coming back to you in a few days.'

I was about to take a breath of relief, when he immediately continued: 'But before that I should like to talk to each of you individually and privately. You, Max, as the manager of the Oracle, shall be first, then Peleus, as the trainer will be next, followed by Alfernus, and if we have time by – what is your name again?' he asked, struggling to focus his failing eyes as he peered at me.

'Rufus Longius,' I said, much relieved to be thought so unimportant.

'Yes.' And Pomponius motioned to Max to come closer and pulled up a stool next to him. The rest of us rose to leave them alone. Max's interrogation lasted more than half an hour. When he came out, I immediately asked him how it went.

'Pomponius tried to wind me up,' replied Max.

'Did you let him get to you?' I asked anxiously.

'At least credit me with being able to keep my temper,' Max replied testily.

'But what did he ask you?'

'The facts are quite clear. I can't see why he was so obsessed with details,' replied Max. Then he became more informative. 'Pomponius wanted to know what I knew about poisons. I told him "nothing": I had never handled any, nor seen any given, nor even talked about poisons – except perhaps jokingly in the baths. This procurator then surprised me by telling me he was pleased to hear this because a report had come to him from one of our slaves who had overheard me at the baths making some crack about poisoning someone.'

My pulse raced as I heard this. Slaves had been interrogated. Spies planted perhaps. How much did this laid-back procurator actually know?

'Then Pomponius asked me how many of our visitors had disappeared. I told him I did not keep track of numbers. The fate of each visitor rested with Hades and the shades in the underworld.

"Have you ever seen any of these shades," he asked inquisitively, raising his eyebrows. "Yes, many of them," I replied. He now became truly curious, but I did not tell him about our actors, or Cerberus, or the "dividing of the ways". He asked me if I knew of Homer's descent into hell and I replied that everyone knew the tales from the *Odyssey*. Questions followed about how our Oracle of the Dead differed from the version in Homer's story. I replied vaguely that ours was a Latin story and Homer's had been a Greek one; that the Greek gods differed in name from the Roman ones but their functions had been altered only slightly. Pomponius seemed to enjoy talking about religion and the historical portrayal of the underworld and became completely sidetracked. Suddenly, out of the blue, he asked me: "And how is your project to convert that cargo ship into a ferry coming along?" I replied truthfully that it was "on hold", that we simply did not have the funding. And with that his interrogation came to an unexpected close.'

'Pomponius seems to know a lot more than he is letting on,' I said uneasily.

'He is canny. He has a lot of sources. Even more suspicions. But he has no evidence, no proof, no confessions,' said Max reassuringly.

'Can they drum up some kind of a case against us?'

'If they are out to get us, they can always find ways. Cicero convincingly taught us that lesson,' said Max, brushing his hand upwards as if he were searching for hairs on top of his bald head.

When Peleus came out next from the interrogation, he looked quite pale.

'By Hades and all the shades in the underworld,' he said, 'that was an ordeal. Pomponius started off by asking me questions about the "training camp". How long was it? Did we force visitors to drink a lot of wine? How much water did they drink? What and how much did they eat? Were they permitted to sleep? On and on his questions poured. I answered straightforwardly, almost brusquely. He wanted to know: "Did your preparations for Virgil's visit differ from those for others?" I replied that they were more elaborate, but otherwise identical.

'Then he abruptly switched to ask me about drugs. "Rumours have circulated in Baiae that your associates had a storehouse full of poisons. Where is it?"

'I said that I knew of no such place.

'Pomponius gave me his characteristically incredulous glance. "Did you ever give anyone opiates?" he asked.

' "Only a few times, when there had been accidents underground and the victims were in pain," I replied.

' "Good. At least that is a plausible answer. Now where and from whom did you obtain that supply?"

' "I keep a small amount in case of emergencies," I admitted. "I bought it on a trip to Puteoli some time ago from a druggist on the quays."

' "How much did you pay him?"

' "I don't remember."

'And so it continued. Then he wanted to know which of our priests dealt with perfumes. I told him Balbus and Lysius.

' "When did they launch their perfumery?" he demanded.

'I claimed I didn't know they had one. It would have been none of my business.

' "But surely you must have heard rumours about it?" he asked.

'I pretended not to know anything; our efforts were concerned with the pantheon, I said, with Apollo and the messages he was delivering to the Sibyl. I facilitated visits to the underworld and the realm of Hades where miserable shades were imprisoned in swirling mists of sulphuric smoke for hundreds of years. That more or less concluded the interrogation, but Pomponius let me know that he might have to recall me when he had more information.'

While Peleus was briefing us, it had been the turn of Alfernus. Of course I did not have a chance to hear what he had to report because I was next.

I was nervous when I sat down facing Pomponius. I did not know what to expect and feared I would unintentionally say something which might compromise the *familia* and my friends. In truth, I did not have any experience with the law and felt a general mistrust of it and those who practised the profession. It seemed like a system which favoured the rich and powerful at the expense of the poor and less privileged. I had also heard that Augustus was trying to reform it and that, in itself, made me wonder. Perhaps even more worryingly, I had no idea how much this Pomponius actually knew about me.

Pomponius was very slow to utter his first words: 'Almost – no one knows – that you, Rufus Longius, are quite another person underground. I can hardly believe that right now I am actually addressing Charon, one of the most famous of our legendary figures. That you have two identities could complicate matters, so I shall simply deal with you as Rufus Longius, who is an actor who plays the role of Charon. This Rufus, from what I have gathered, is rumoured locally to be a leader of an Orphic group in Cumae, Baiae and Puteoli.' Here he paused and I intervened in protest.

'I am not a leader. I am an elder and mere disciple,' I corrected him.

'Who, then, is your master?' he asked quite directly.

'We have no high priests, no orders, no ranks. We are all humble seekers,' I replied modestly.

'I must take note of that. It is most unlike my own experience of religion,' he said. 'Tell me, do you believe that Jupiter is first among the gods, as most Romans do?'

This investigator was turning out to be far more knowledgeable and crafty than I had imagined. Pulling myself together, I replied: 'At one time Jupiter contained the seeds of all being within his own body and from that primal mixture emerged the whole of our complex world with all that is animate and inanimate in it.'

'Most enlightening. So how do you feel about our Roman gods? Are they to be exalted over Mithras, for example?'

'I know little about the oriental religions.'

'I do not know much about your beliefs but are there not many erotic, obscene and debauched aspects which contradict the highly moral tenets of our Roman religion?'

Challenged about my core convictions, I replied: 'We believe in cultivating and nourishing the divine element of our being. We believe that those who have lived a pure life on earth will find a better place in the hereafter. I do not think we are debauched. Our poems are filled with a sense of the mystery and the paradox of life. Most are preoccupied with the eternal question: 'How can all be One, yet remain each an individual?'

'That is a most enlightened question, but not one to which I would attempt to find an answer. Tell me, do you accept our pantheon as a whole or do you . . . pick and choose?'

'I have never heard it put that way. We certainly believe in Apollo and Dionysus, who are in the Roman pantheon.'

'Good. That is comforting. Now what is your view of Julius Caesar, whom we have just deified. Is he one of your gods?'

'He was a great Roman, of course. But I, personally, cannot see him next to Jupiter or even cohabiting in any way with Juno, despite his acknowledged history of sexual encounters.'

Here Pomponius smiled broadly. Then went on to say: 'For an actor you appear to be a most independent thinker. Tell me, what is your view of our Emperor, Augustus?'

'I admire him for trying to bring order out of chaos, for trying to give Romans pride in their nation once again.'

'Indeed. You sound to me like someone who is familiar with leadership, not merely a disciple or a follower. Now I know from my reports that you have had nothing to do with the training or reception of visitors and so forth, so I will not bother you with useless questions, but I am curious: have you heard any rumours about the use of opiates?'

'Rumours? No, I haven't,' I replied straightforwardly.

'Really?' he asked incredulously.

'On occasion I have seen them given to those who have suffered bad falls or serious injuries,' I said, remembering what I had been told by Peleus.

'Yes. Of course. Now what about this new "perfumery"? Who is running this?'

'I believe a couple of priests associated with the Temple of Apollo.'

'Indeed. And where is it located?' asked Pomponius.

'I have never been there, but I suspect it may be in a storeroom belonging to one of the Apollonian priests.'

'A good guess. We shall look into this. Now before I wind this up, I want to ask you: Are you one of the organisers of the orgies which have taken place here?'

'I am not. I have just been an occasional participant.'

'A prominent one?'

'I cannot be the judge of that.' I might have added that orgiasts do not like to be boastful. It would be unbecoming.

'Who are the organisers then? Are the priests involved?'

'I have never seen any of our priesthood there,' I replied. 'These events usually happen spontaneously. One of us, drinking wine, will say: "What we need right now is an orgy." Someone else will agree. Another will join in and say that it has been some time since the last one. And within a few minutes an orgy will have been arranged for that night or the next day. It's all as simple as that.'

'Do you realise that under Roman law orgies are illegal?'

'Yes. I do. But in the provinces and particularly around Baiae this antiquated law has rarely been enforced.'

'The Senate has offered a reward to anyone exposing such Bacchanalia,' he said gravely. 'I have been ordered to seek out the priests of these cults, whether men or women. Devotees are also to be arrested. You have been cooperative and, for the time

184

being, you shall not be put under arrest. We have bigger fish to roast here and I have been sent to uncover what we suspect to be a long-running plot. My final questions to you regard the disappearance of numerous visitors while underground. It is said that they have been taken by Hades. Have you ever seen this happen?'

'Not before my eyes. No.'

'Tell me then, how do they "disappear"?'

'As you shall see when you descend into the underworld, Hades is a murky place. Often you cannot see two paces ahead. There is a lot of smoke from the torches and there may be a mist rising from the Styx itself. Reality is blurred. In these dark surroundings, the visitor can be summoned not only by a shade or a familiar *manes* but even by a cave bat, an owl or a water snake. Who knows if these forms are not in fact spirits of the dead in disguise. The visitors, lured by the voices calling out to them, may wander off in the dark never to be seen again.' Here I paused. Then I added dramatically: 'Sometimes we find a bit of their clothing in the river.'

'It sounds frightening. I do not know if I want to visit Hades – let alone Tartarus – now that you have told me all of this,' admitted Pomponius. 'You are a brave man, Rufus, for descending so often to the Styx. My admiration for Virgil has also increased for facing all these terrors for the sake of his epic poem.' Then he paused to reflect. 'Was it not the great poet Pindar who suggested that we men are all but the dreams of shades?'

'I have heard it said,' I replied politely.

'Sometimes it is hard to divine what is the will of the gods . . . ' Pomponius said pensively. 'Why should they wish to condemn us to Acheron, those strangely alive waters of the dead?' It was a rhetorical question to which I did not reply. Then Pomponius took a deep breath and said: 'Enough for one day,' and rose ever so slowly. 'I am tired and must reflect on all that I have heard. You have been most informative and your willingness to help me will count if and when there is a judgement.'

I saw my session with the procurator was over and walked away with both head and mood downcast. Wandering over to the baths, I soon found the others. They were all discussing the procurator's visit and extremely eager, particularly Lysius who had joined them, to hear how I had answered the possibly incriminating questions about drugs, poisons and the 'perfumery'. They were rather surprised when I told them much of my examination had turned on Orphism and our orgies. I surmised that if they didn't find any definitive proof of a plot or of poisoning, they would use other means to bring charges against us. None of them had thought about the procurator's questioning in that way. Even Max agreed that all of his plans had to be put on hold. Despondency overcame us. Worn out, I did not stay long in the hot baths.

Rather than return home to the arms of my ever-light-hearted Calliope, I walked into the scented pine woods of Campania. I wanted to think clearly about my prospects. Participating in an orgy or being an Orphic were not crimes likely to result in a death sentence. Imprisonment was not currently in favour. Most likely was exile. I did not know how I would react to this – whether I would ever be able to adjust to another place or another culture. I felt I was too old to be transplanted. Briefly I tried to remember how others had fared when uprooted, but my thoughts soon returned to Calliope and how this would impact on her. Much as she would shudder at the idea of losing me and being in the arms of another, I knew she would have to accept the inevitable. Fortunately she really liked Antonius and he liked her. His predicament, with his father being in even greater danger than hers, could bring them both closer. An engagement entered into on their behalf by Peleus and myself was the best arrangement for my daughter's long term wellbeing. Oh, how I would dream for ever of the parted, expectant lips of my nocturnal lily! Walking back home, I knew I would have to tell her. I also considered her dowry. I had little to offer except the house and a small garden plot in Cumae which I had inherited from my mother. I decided that would be hers. Of course if I were exiled, she would get everything.

When I arrived home she threw her arms around me and we embraced and kissed as always. Then Calliope drew back and said: 'Father, you look like you've been to Hades! I am afraid I might be swallowed by your shadow.'

'I have voyaged far deeper than usual,' I replied. I then recounted the procurator's questions, how my answers about Orphism had been too revealing for my own good, and how it all might end with my exile. Tears choked me at the thought and Calliope burst out crying.

'I . . . I shall . . . go with you!' she vowed in between sobs.

I took her in my arms and said firmly: 'No. You will not.' Then I told a small lie, saying: 'I have approached Peleus and he has agreed that it would be good for Antonius and you to become engaged.'

'A–A–An–tonius?' she sobbed.

'Yes. He is a capable young man. Even stronger than his father. You know I cannot bear the thought of losing you, Calliope. You are everything to me. But in these darkening circumstances, I must do this for you. Antonius and you are both of age and fit for marriage. It is the best course to follow.'

Instead of replying, my young daughter, with whom I had fallen in love and who so adored me, continued to cry inconsolably. I hugged her and patted her head in a fatherly way for a long, long time. Finally she stopped sobbing. She instinctively brushed the tears from her bluebell eyes, which were now rose-tinted. Gently her small fingers touched my forehead and then brushed lightly through my thinning and rapidly greying hair. 'It is unbearable. I know that you are telling me this because you love me. And I . . . I love . . . I love you for it.'

187

XIV

The Sibyl was sitting cross-legged and mumbling incomprehensible verses when I visited her on a wet and dismal autumn afternoon. She was dressed in her bright saffron tunic and had a wild and somewhat unkempt look about her.

'Our land is brimful of sacred fury,' were the first words she said to me. 'Those who have come here wanted to find out what heaven had in store. Which god to propitiate. How to mitigate an evil curse of Pluto. But not for much longer. Pluto is angry. Neptune is irate. Apollo is furious. Why? Because there are men in Baiae and Rome who want to close the Oracle.'

I did not say a word, but sat down quietly on a wooden stool.

The Sibyl hummed for a while and then broke out in a solemn monotone:

'I can count the leaves and hear the voices
Of the drafts rushing through the atrium.
I can smell the rotting Pompeian fish
And relate these to the questions being posed.
Can beautiful kinds of mushroom bring death?
Are snails slowly ascending Vesuvius?
The late winter olives are thick and blue, but very few.'

Then quiet reigned again in her rocky chamber. The Sibyl's voice seldom dried or failed when the divine prompted her to spill forth revelations. I dared not interrupt her reveries, so I waited for her to speak. Finally she broke the silence. She merely asked for water. I motioned for an attending slave to bring her some, which she consumed greedily.

'Do you know what Sibyl means in Greek?'

'I remember that you told me once.'

'It means God's will. I have been entrusted with prophesy – which is a gift of divinity.'

'A great gift,' I nodded.

'I see the Oracles closing and the anger of the gods rising. Disaster will strike Campania. Apollo is crying out to me: "The earth will shake and tremble and untold numbers shall die." Yes. I can see it all.'

'What can we do about it? Is it already too late?'

'Let the people know. Warn them. Tell them what is planned by Agrippa. Tell them that the Sibyl has foreseen the terrible disasters that are about to happen unless they act now.'

I remained silent. I knew that spreading her message of black tidings could seal the fate of the Oracle. It could also cost us our lives.

Then she switched her tone and explained that it was Agrippa who had cut down the sacred groves on the banks of Lake Avernus fifteen years earlier and had used the timber to build his fleet. On the very shrines to Apollo, he had built dockyards.

'This sacrilege outraged Apollo,' she claimed. 'Apollo's bronze statue in his temple in Rome broke out in a sweat. And then the fiercest of storms continued for days until the Pontifex Maximus sacrificed a large number of gladiators to appease him.'

What could I add to the Sibyl's narration? I found myself incapable of speech.

'I hear silence,' said the Sibyl, dropping her voice. 'It is a void . . . It turns me cold . . . I cannot bear it. Apollo, I pray to you: bring back your music or I shall be paralysed. Please. Please. Oh, please!'

Silence ruled once more in her carpeted chamber. Then Sulpicia turned confessional.

'Contrary to the myths about me, Apollo never offered me his love,' she said haltingly, in a voice filled with regret. 'I would readily have consented to be his. My spirit, my mind were always

189

his. My body was never sought by him. He never even stroked my hair . . . ' Her words trailed off.

'Is there not an ancient story that one of your ancestors took a handful of sand and holding it forth said: "Grant me as many birthdays as there are grains of sand in this hand." And that Apollo was ready to grant this but when she refused to be his in return, and as she had forgotten to ask for eternal youth, he allowed her to grow older and older until only hair, skin and bones remained?'

'An absolutely horrid tale,' she practically spat out. 'What a lot of tripe! That old myth was a scurrilous effort to malign not only the Oracle itself but also all the Sibyls that were to follow. As for me, I do hope that some of my sayings will be immortalised – although I must sadly admit to you, Rufus, that I never had the full support I prayed for from Apollo when making my prophecies.'

'I appreciate your confidence in me, Sulpicia,' I honestly replied.

'My priests envy me my age, but they don't feel the cold. Sometimes I sense in my whole being that I can no longer appease Apollo. I wonder if maybe he too is getting tired. Why should the gods not experience fatigue? I know they feel ingratitude, just like I do. It surrounds me. Perhaps the gods are getting too ancient to inspire the Romans. They have come to believe that reality is calculable. The people are lacking in ecstasy. They have no enthusiasm. They do not even remember that enthusiasm is the god entering and dwelling within his worshippers.'

Haltingly I ventured to ask her: 'Are you . . . afraid of death?'

'Not in the slightest. I used to be. But I have waited too long, chewed too many leaves from Apollo's tree, experienced too many trips to your underworld. But the real thing could be an interesting experience, could it not, Charon? I might even talk to my dear father's shade, possibly visit Elysium and the latest kingdom of the universe.'

'That sounds like an enviable journey, Sulpicia!'

'Perhaps that is just my dream and I shall only have a companion in the sleeping butterfly . . . It has no song.'

Silence again. She closed her eyes. Then, speaking in almost a whisper, but prophetically:

> 'I am a Sibyl, born of that inspired mother, Circe,
> And father Silenus, raving drunk and brilliant.
> At that time when all things come to pass,
> You shall remember me as a prophetess of Apollo,
> And no one more shall call me a maddened she-ass
> Or an oracle singer of necessity hollow.'

Sulpicia looked drained. Silence reigned once again.

I felt my audience with her was at an end. I had wanted to talk to her about so many things that afternoon, like the consequences of Virgil's historic visit, but the Sibyl was in another realm – her own, quite special mystic realm of prophecy. As I left her chamber, I remember saying to her with great emotion: 'May the Fates be tender to you, Sulpicia!'

She merely nodded silently in response.

XV

A few weeks after the visit of Pomponius, we held a celebration of betrothal for my Calliope and Antonius at the ample house of his father, Peleus. The entire *familia* attended in the flower-bedecked atrium. A proud and happy fiancé presented Calliope with a gold ring. Looking straight at me, with tears in her eyes, Calliope immediately slipped this on to her middle finger. Everyone there thought she was crying because she was so moved. They applauded at length. I knew better. For a moment I also cried quite publicly. Calliope looked so beautiful, so tender, and so sensuous all at the same time. My Calliope was young, alive, blossoming. I felt grieving, empty, ageing. For me it was heartbreaking. I was losing my only true source of happiness, but I was losing it for the sake of the one I loved most in the world. The rites were followed by a sumptuous banquet at which, although I got rather drunk, I held my tongue. Late that night my best friend, Quintius, helped me as I staggered back unsteadily to my now lonely home. I was quite desolate and cursed Virgil for all our troubles. Quintius was distressed by my condition. He told me he had rarely seen me so drunk or so sad. I had never told the closest to me about my illicit love and could not confess it even to him. Some secrets are so deep they must remain that way, no matter what.

Peleus and I had arranged that from the moment of their betrothal, Calliope should live together with Antonius in his house. Calliope had at first objected, but I explained to her that a clean break was essential in our heart-wrenching situation. She was now mature enough to accept this but our last nights together had been among the most passionate ever. I like to think that although she had seduced me, I had initiated her into the realm of ultimate pleasures. I hoped she would treasure these as long as she lived.

It was in this disconsolate state, with only my ageing dog, Corso, as company, that two days later I had to face the visit of the praetor, Clemens Atreus, who had come to interrogate the leading members of both the Oracle of Apollo and the Oracle of the Dead. I took an instant dislike to this devious and disconcertingly suave adjutant to Agrippa. There was a perverse air of injured sanctity about him. In his highly modulated and fruity voice he told all of us, except Sulpicia, meeting in the Temple of Apollo that he had read the report of Prefect Pomponius and that while there was as yet no proof of murder, the number of those who had come to consult the Oracle and had afterwards died from unknown causes related to their visit was considerable. The figure had been further augmented by those who had perished underground. Clearly the Oracle of the Dead was regarded as a dangerous place. Although rumours had been received of a storeroom full of poison, no traces of this had been found by investigators thus far. Atreus's whitish-blue eyes were colder than ice as he declared: 'We *will* get to the bottom of this. I intend to talk to some of you privately, and I want names. I want dates. I want facts. Don't tell me long stories, myths or legends. Leave those to our great Virgil. You may have helped him along in his epic but you did yourselves no favours. Let us all remember that Odysseus was portrayed as something of a deceiver, a swindler and a charlatan by no other than Homer himself.'

Our Sibyl was to be the first to be interrogated, in her abode. We were all apprehensive about what she might say and how she would react to this detestable praetor, so different in his approach from Pomponius. The long intervening weeks had enabled us secretly to weave (no slaves were allowed within earshot) a coherent narrative to which we would all stick, no matter what. To this we solemnly swore, not only to our gods, but also on our very lives.

I was of course immensely apprehensive when it came to my turn to give evidence in private to Atreus. He started off by telling me he could make no sense at all of the Sibyl's utterances. She was in such a trance that he had had to call in Quintius to elucidate her replies.

'Is she always this way?' enquired a most sceptical Atreus. 'She seems to be suffering from a butterfly memory.'

'She can be in and out of ecstasy,' I explained, 'but she is seldom comprehensible when uttering prophecies. That is why the Oracle has to employ priests to interpret her sayings. A resort to the oblique and the ambiguous as well as the over-use of parables are common devices for Sibyls here as well as in Delphi. The interpretation of her pronouncements by the priests enables us to make sense of what she is saying. For example, the words father, mother and home frequently crop up in oracular messages. Father can mean the enquirer's actual father, or the fatherland, or Jupiter. Home could be a house, a city, a country, or even the ultimate return to the afterlife.'

'I see Pomponius was right when he said you were articulate and insightful. Frankly, when the Sibyl told me that "the little bluetit buzzes around, it is so difficult to follow", I could make no sense of it. Was she poking fun at me? Was I the bluetit? And when she pronounced that "only the garbage in Cumae sighs and stinks", I didn't know whether this was a joke, a poetic metaphor or a mystical insight on her part.'

'Perhaps all of those,' I tactfully replied.

'It makes little difference what she said,' he concluded abruptly. 'Obviously your Sibyl has become somewhat addled in her mind. Now I should like to turn my attention to the Mysteries. Pomponius suggested you could shed some light on these.'

'But how are they relevant to the death of Caius, as the Oracle is in no way connected to them?' I asked tentatively.

'I shall determine the questions,' he replied imperiously.

I was unprepared for an approach from this direction. What

to tell him and what to hold back? Atreus observed my hesitation and urged me on: 'Come now. Out with it!' he ordered.

'I don't quite know how to start. Exactly how much detail do you want me to go into?'

'As much as my interest will allow. I am personally curious, but so are both Agrippa and the Emperor himself. I am particularly interested in the initiations.'

That was the first time I had heard a reference to Augustus in this way. This was turning into far more than just a murder investigation. Knowing that a long recitation would work to my advantage, I decided to answer by beginning with historic origins.

'The Orphic Dionysian rites in ancient Greece were based on the idea of communion with god. The torn-off bits of the ritually slaughtered bull, representing the body of Dionysus, were eaten so that, according to the belief of the celebrants, they could actually become One with him, become part of the god. In Greece the bull was the chief of the sacred animals because of his incredible strength, his impetuosity, his virility and his rage. The sacrificial bull at Delphi was not merely holy but was regarded as a sanctifier who had the vital power to make men holy. To have contact with this bull was to spread his power and his holiness to the worshippers themselves. You may not know this, praetor, but Orpheus introduced the Greeks to the concept of eternal life. Orphism brought with it new concepts of man and of destiny.' Here I paused briefly to collect my thoughts. Then I continued methodically: 'The early Orphics believed that this life was a punishment for some sin committed in the past. The Orphic doctrine of personal salvation held that a life of asceticism would gradually remove the contamination of the soul and that the individual would then become as he had been before the soul sinned: pure. Later, because the Orphics would not take life, the rendering of the sacrifice became symbolic. Believers switched to a ritual of drinking wine and breaking barley cakes.' I saw the praetor's ice-blue eyes slowly begin to drift, so I was encouraged to continue. 'Initiation into the Mysteries would guarantee participants a life in the Isles of the Blessed where the sun never sets and gentle zephyrs blow in perpetuity.'

Here Atreus suddenly interrupted. 'I am not interested in the consequences of the rites. I have little more than scorn for these Mysteries, with their doctrine of exclusive salvation. How could a murderer attain bliss merely because he was initiated? No. No. No. What I want from you is to hear physical details of the Mysteries. Must participants consent to a kind of *nudatio mimaria*, for example?'

'Nothing of the kind. Theirs is not some kind of cheap, theatrical striptease performed in mime. It is the baring not only of the body but of the soul itself.'

'Why are you willing to tell me these things which the Greeks never revealed to the uninitiated? Are you not deterred by threats from the gods that spilling these secrets will render you impotent or even lead to your castration?'

'Yes, by Apollo! The gods may wreak their revenge on me, but I am old and have little appetite for life left in me.'

'But won't this affect your afterlife? The gods could take their revenge at a later stage.'

'Yes, they could. A life after death can be a punishment or reward depending on one's actions in this life . . . but then a lifetime, like yours or mine, is but one of a number of stages in the process of reincarnation which gives the soul multiple opportunities for purification.'

'Yes. Yes. I understand, but let's return to the initiation. How does it begin?'

'On the first night, at the temple, and before they proceed, the priest will ask those seeking initiation: "What do you seek?"

'They reply: "We seek the Truth."

'The priest, motioning them, says: "Enter."

'Within the temple walls a priestess in a pure white tunic with a red-wool fillet wound around her head bids them: "Fetch

the lustral water; wreathe the altar with white wool, throw
frankincense and the sacred boughs into the soaring flames."
When they have fulfilled her command, she leads them in a
ceremonial chant:

> "I am your servant,
> I am your heart.
> Womb of your flock,
> I'm eternally your part.
> Flesh of your spirit,
> Pestle of your flowers,
> I dream your dreams.
> Oh, everlasting seams,
> I celebrate your total power.
> May your boundless presence grace us – now."

'The celebrants are then escorted in silence to the bath-house
to hand in their clothes and bathe. Next they are anointed with
oils by some slaves, told to relax and given saffron-coloured robes
to put on. They subsequently spend the rest of the night and the
next day in silent fasting, meditation and prayer, drinking only
pure water. On the second night, the female celebrants often
drape animal skins across their breasts, set flowering garlands
on their heads and untie the ribbons that bind their long hair.
Then they are led out into the dark and proceed between lines of
lit torches which are held high by murmuring initiates. Their
murmurs gradually turn into chants which grow louder and
more contrapuntal as they advance towards the sanctuary. A
naked and usually ample priestess stands in front of the portico,
holding a torch in one hand. Behind her stand two priests who
hold burning incense. In a ringing voice the naked priestess asks:
"Are you prepared to enter?"

'All nod their heads and express their readiness by repeating
the salutation: "Hail, Pan! Hail, Faunus! Hail, our Fatuus!'
following the shouting of the priests.

'When all are assembled in the sanctuary itself the priestess will say something like: "We seek wisdom eternal . . . the one in all things . . . the god of unity . . . the centre and fountain of the whole." Then she will caution the celebrants in no uncertain terms: "What you will see and experience here you may tell no one. Each man must swear absolute and total secrecy on his testicles. Do you swear you will obey?" Using their right hands to hold their testicles, they all swear.'

'You seem to know this by heart,' said Atreus. 'I am all ears and most impressed. But having thus sworn, how do you dare to break your oath?'

'It pains me,' I said truthfully. 'Perhaps Apollo will not forgive me and a dire fate now awaits me in Hades. But the initiation into the Mysteries must not vanish from man's heritage. The Orphism which the Greeks launched must not only be treasured but must also be perpetuated. Romans must learn not to fear but to appreciate the solemnity of our beliefs. If the Emperor Augustus would understand this then the persecution of our sect might end.'

'Nobly spoken, Rufus Longius. Now proceed!'

'Standing in a separate row, each of the women then places both hands on her breasts and swears to the lord of all life. The naked priestess standing before them tells them: "At bond is your own life – not only here on earth but in the hereafter. You are in this sanctuary for a night beyond time, which is part of eternity – where there is no beginning and no end: no life, no death, only the absolute present and the immortality of the soul. This is as on the day of Zeus at the first hour. Let your witness be the down-flowing waters of the Styx, witness to the most dread oaths of the blessed gods, that you shall obey." The assembled women then nod their heads and say, "We do."

'Let me explain a bit here, if you will permit, Atreus.'

'Yes. Yes,' he nodded, impatient to hear more.

'According to Homer and Hesiod, time only began after the

198

sexually promiscuous Gaia and Uranus (her own son from an affair with Erebus) coupled. The result was Kronos, Father Time himself. Time is thus the consequence of an incestuous coupling. Kronos created the pattern of night and day out of chaos. He did this by polarising the universe, by separating the sky and the earth. Time was "the becoming" which causes matter and non-matter to oscillate between these two extremes of existence.'

Here Atreus interrupted. 'Enough. Let's go back to the ceremonies.'

'As you wish. So the by now slightly swaying priestess continues: "All you men, I presently offer you escape from the thralldom of your bodies and union with the White Goddess who is the source of all life. Now, in the darkness and privacy of the night, you must each proceed to pay homage and kiss my holy of holies, the place through which all of us enter this earth. Are you ready to do so and to gain access to the Orphic Mysteries?"

'All the men silently assent and one by one pass before the priestess and press their faces into her genitals as she slowly chants:

> "I come from the pure, pure Queen of those below,
> For I avow having paid the penalty for deeds unrighteous,
> Whether it be that Fate laid me low or the gods immortal.
> I have flown out of the weary and sorrowful circle,
> I have risen with winged feet to the diadem desired
> And then sunk beneath the bosom of the Queen of the
> Underworld.
> A kid, I have fallen into milk."

'I do not understand that last line,' interrupted Atreus.

'It is a Bacchic metaphor, familiar to the Orphics,' I replied, pausing in my dissertation.

'Then, in the contemporary modification of this ancient rite, there follows the drawing of blood from a young bull. It used to

199

be that all had to drink of this blood. Today we drink consecrated red wine instead.'

'I don't quite see the connection between Bacchus, the blood and the wine?' queried Atreus.

'Bacchus, as Dionysus was renamed by us Romans, has become the symbol of everlasting life, but he is also the god of wine. Put simply: we prefer drinking wine to imbibing blood. Now let me return to the Mysteries. The priestess will continue, telling the initiates to place themselves within the universe. "Is the One not the ideal identity of your inmost nature, of your soul itself? The One, the ultimate deity within you, is the essence of all mystery, of the oneness of the creator." Having thus spoken she will then shout:

"We seek to glorify you, Bacchus!
We invoke you, Bacchus, to arouse us.
We are all part of the One,
The One is all part of us.
One is the past, the present, the future and the afterlife.
Our aim must be to worship the totality: the One."

'And with this some women initiates will wail while beating tambourines with their palms. Others will begin to dance in circles, clap their hands and call out to Bacchus, or Dionysus, and to Orpheus. A few of the men will produce tunes on their provocatively curved boxwood pipes. Others will sing phallic hymns, or merely shout and scream. The celebrations will continue till early morning, but I think I have given you the essence of the Mysteries as I remember them.'

'I doubt anyone could have described the rites more clearly,' said Atreus in a most complimentary manner. 'But I am confused. If men are made in the whole's image of the One, this ultimate deity of yours, then men must be bisexual?'

'Yes. It is hard for some to accept, but we are all part man and part woman. When men and women join into one, we approach the ultimate oneness of the creator – and, let's face it, "the beast with two backs" is bisexual.' I produced the first smile of this difficult meeting.

'Did you see whether men got erections when they kissed the naked priestess down there?'

Atreus's prurience surprised me. 'It never occurred to me to look,' I replied with a certain revulsion. 'I have been describing a profoundly spiritual experience to you.' There was evidently something bent in this praetor.

Embarrassed, his reaction was to shift ground. 'How does this religion incorporate the range of deities which we Romans have come to accept and worship?' Atreus asked.

I could sense this was a double-edged probe. Everyone knows that the worship of the Emperor has become a test of loyalty to Rome.

'Each of us must somehow find the path best suited to our needs,' I replied, and then ventured into deeper waters. 'The Emperor Augustus, who is himself divine, regards Apollo as a protector of the state and so do the Orphics. In his role as the first Roman Emperor, Augustus is fulfilling the auspicious prophecies the Cumaean Sibyl gave to his ancestor, Aeneas.'

'You speak like a loyal citizen even though your views are officially heretical,' declared Atreus. 'I am amazed that someone like you, who for decades has endured the fateful currents of the Styx and sipped the waters of Lethe, could present such a compelling narrative. If I have the chance, I would like to discuss this with the great Virgil. But I shall most certainly pass on what I remember to Marcus Agrippa.'

'That is an honour indeed, praetor. I don't know if I made it clear that initiation is a concession to the notion that if one wishes enlightenment one must abandon one's focus on rationality and turn to the senses and the nourishment of one's soul. I believe initiation will help one eventually to gain a place with the Blessed in the Elysian Fields.' I stopped short at this point, not wishing to say that one might then be selected to come back as a fish, a bee or even a tree.

'None of us can guarantee what happens in the afterlife, Rufus Longius, but in this world a Roman's duty is to advance our nation, uphold our laws, worship our gods, support our divine Emperor and protect the sanctity of the family. I hope you will appreciate this when Agrippa presents his, as yet undecided, course of action.'

With these words Atreus concluded this most extraordinary session with me. I felt distress at having broken my oath never to speak to anyone about our initiation ceremony, but rationalisation soon won the day. I convinced myself that the world would gain far more in knowledge than I had lost by way of honour. Of far more immediate concern was: What would be my ultimate punishment? Would our Oracles survive? And what about our *familia*? Unable to resolve any of these imponderables, my instinctive recourse was the addictive red wine of Campania.

XVI

We waited for more than three nail-biting months after the visit of Atreus for news from Baiae. There were no further inspections by the judiciary. No further interrogations by magistrates. Quintius pointed out that Agrippa was being forced by the Emperor to divorce his wife and to marry Julia. Obviously, the co-adjutor of Rome had personal matters of greater import on his agenda. The uncertainty of it deeply affected all the members of our *familia*. We struggled to go on with our daily routines, but visitors to the Oracle had slowed down to a mere trickle. Peleus tried to attribute this to an exceptionally wet winter. Max reported that rumours of multiple poisonings had been circulating in Rome and this was obviously frightening off potential visitors. Only Lysius seemed relieved: no one had discovered his small cache of poisons and, most unexpectedly, there were now numerous orders for his perfumed oils, which Max had been promoting on his visits to Puteoli and Pompeii. Money and sales-manship seemed to hold sway much as they always had done.

Those who read this may find it odd that we, as a *familia*, were so ready to accept the inevitability of whatever was about to happen to us. But you must understand that the Parcae (or Fates), who represent the powers of Destiny, and the ever present Fortunae, whose symbol is the wheel, hold sway in our Roman consciousness. These goddesses have assigned us our roles in life; whether we shall be rich or poor, celebrated or ignored, it is our task to play out the role we have been given to the best of our ability and without complaint. Admittedly, human intervention has become ever more difficult to handle, especially when a new 'god' like the Emperor Augustus has been granted nearly divine powers. All of us accepted that our fate ultimately rested in his hands.

Quintius tried to comfort me throughout this waiting period. I had confided to him that I had broken my oath of silence during the questioning by Atreus. This troubled me immensely. It haunted me in my now lonely sleep. Quintius tried to explain that, having expected to be cross-examined on the poisonings, I had been caught off guard. I had not betrayed any member of the *familia* or implicated anyone in a crime. I had revealed no names. In any case, exposing some secrets of the Orphic Mysteries would do the cult little harm. It would only inspire curiosity. It was rumoured that Augustus himself, apparently urged on by a somewhat ailing Virgil, was considering attending a session of the cult in Greece.

It was, of course, impossible for Quintius entirely to allay my pangs of conscience. From my earliest years I had been in-culcated with the belief that, for a Roman, a solemn oath to the gods was to be broken only at one's personal peril. I could not quite understand why I had done it. It was not as if I had been tortured. And to tell it all to a state official for whom I felt such an instinctive dislike made it all the more puzzling. Was I losing my mind? Were Apollo and Orpheus now taking their revenge on me by making me doubt my sanity? My body's response also surprised me: I had begun to feel older than ever and my already greying hairs had started falling out. I attributed all this to the vengeance of the gods. When it thundered I was sure it was Jove expressing his anger towards me.

One afternoon, when wandering about in the woods, I found myself talking to a less than responsive Minerva. She represented the kind of intelligent goddess I most appreciated. I asked her directly if I should flee into the forest to escape judgement – 'You know all about that, dear Minerva.' Am I too old to use a bow and arrow to kill a deer or a bear, I wondered to myself as I brushed through the leafy wood? I still felt strong and capable. Imprisoned, I would waste away. Pondering my possible convic-tion, I even considered 'vanishing' into the Styx. This seemed highly preferable to torture or to being sold into slavery.

An increasingly concerned Quintius suggested I needed the company of a woman and urged me to seek out Clodia, who he knew liked me. In truth I greatly missed Calliope and longed for her, but could not tell Quintius.

A few nights later my best friend, not knowing what to do and sensing that his counsel was not helping me, brought me two bottles of the finest red wine from Campania. The alcohol helped more than I anticipated. That night for the first time in weeks, I slept soundly and without nightmares. I continued drinking somewhat immoderately for about a week. I became blissfully out of touch with the world about me. Then rather late one morning, just after the Ides of March, there was a loud knock on the door. Feeling still hung-over, I didn't bother to get up but I heard old Porcius greeting Mentula. She asked for me and told him it was urgent. So I roused myself, put on my sandals and straightened my tunic.

'There is tragic news,' she said, looking me over with disdain at my condition. 'It's terribly upsetting. Sulpicia is – is dead.'

I was speechless and just stood there, swaying, while tears started to well up in my eyes. 'What? . . . how?' I mumbled incoherently.

'I – I want to tell you that she died naturally – otherwise there will be a scandal and she will not be able to get a proper burial. Too many Romans believe that suicide is an evil and that it might even be contagious. Just between the two of us – and this must remain a secret – our Sibyl took a massive dose of belladonna last night. She was gone by the time Clodia came to bring her some warm milk this morning.' Here Mentula began to cry. I took a few steps forward and held her in my unsteady arms. I then patted her gently on her back for a time while she composed herself.

'Did she leave any note?'

'Yes. And a lot of dried leaves on which she had written jumbled messages.'

'How like her,' I said.

'She wrote that she could not go on. Agrippa, whom she called a vengeful and spiteful official, hated her and was going to shut down her Oracle. When she asked for guidance from Apollo, the god sent her the unequivocal message that she was going to be the last of the Cumaean Sibyls.'

'Her prophecies have most often been astonishingly right,' I nodded.

'Yes. A most remarkable and lonely figure . . . so . . . so lonely,' said Mentula, and again she began to sob.

'In one way I am glad for her that she was spared the ordeals to come,' I said by way of consolation.

'She . . . she . . . left messages. M–m–many . . . ' stumbled the tearful priestess. 'She left me all her jewellery.'

'You deserve it. You have been very good to her for many years. She saw you as her eventual successor.'

'That I shall not be. Even if the post were offered, I would now refuse it. It would go against her last wishes,' Mentula said, pulling herself together.

'Did she speak of funeral rites?'

'She wanted to be cremated, on top of a huge altar of logs on the sandy beach facing Cumae. She wanted all of us, our whole *familia*, to get drunk as the embers cooled, and then she wanted her ashes taken into the sea to meet her *manes* under the waves.'

'So it shall be. None of us will have any trouble getting drunk,' I assured her.

'You, too are mentioned on the leaves. She was very fond of you, you know. You are to receive her famous bronze tripod and two valuable urns.'

I was most surprised. I had no idea she was specially fond of me.

'In three days we shall carry her body to the sea. Our entire *familia* and all the others from Cumae, Baiae and beyond will attend.'

'Is there anything special I can do?' I offered rather feebly.

'Let me think. Yes. You could go to Baiae and round up some *vespillones*. I don't think we have any carriers of corpses here in Cumae.'

'I shall do so,' I said, determined to sober up.

Indeed, for the next three days, as all the preparations for the funeral were being made, I didn't touch any alcohol. The nights were difficult: I dreamt of our Sybil so vivdly that I believed she was alive again. When it came to the funeral itself, I was so overcome with emotion that I had no desire for drink whatsoever.

It was strange to see her small corpse dressed in her own saffron tunic and lying on a bed of garlands spread atop an altar of logs at least three times my height. There was an enormous crowd of mourners there, including many who had come to consult her, as well as Atreus and Pomponius, who had interrogated her just recently. There were a number of dignitaries, including senators who had consulted her, some of the very rich from Baiae and Puteoli, the governor of Campania, the mayors of the neighbouring cities and many more. Their attendance was a fitting tribute to the Sibyl. Virgil did not come but a slave of his brought an enormous bouquet of anemones.

It was Quintius who delivered the funeral oration. For the dead, he said, these rites are performed to release them from the evils of this world. To Plato it had been 'an ancient teaching that the souls of men that come here are from beyond, and they shall pass beyond again and come to birth from the dead'. Lucretius, Quintius proposed, argued that our fear of Acheron must be cast off because otherwise the ideas of death shake our life at its very foundations and, as that poet said, cover us with 'the blackness of death'. The correct view of death, according to Epicurus, is that death is *nothing*. He held that recognition of such an ultimate void, of this nothingness, would quench our foolish yearning for immortality. But, said Quintius, Epicurus admitted that accepting the ultimate void was a challenge not many could face.

Having concluded these philosophical introductory remarks, Quintius observed in a sombre voice how strange it was that no one really knew Sulpicia's family background. She had joined the Oracle when she was only six or seven, had risen to become a priestess, and then was selected to become the Sibyl when she was in her late thirties. She had never talked about her mother or father. It was as if she didn't have any. Nor did any relatives of hers ever appear. We, all those closely associated with the two Oracles, were her family. In her own way she treasured us because we were all she had. Of course she was immensely proud to be in the long, long succession of Sibyls. The Oracle became her entire life. And a great Sibyl she was, too. She truly communicated with Apollo and transmitted his messages to us and to the world. 'I shall greatly miss interpreting her complex, often symbolic and frequently metaphorical utterances,' said Quintius. 'They were a challenge and, if I may say so, Sulpicia was also a challenge. She was always as demanding of herself as she was of others. She was utterly convinced of the importance of her office. Anyone who ever had an audience with her was inevitably impressed, if not overwhelmed, by her presence, by her enormously powerful *persona*. Even if they didn't understand a word she said, they came away with the sense that they had encountered greatness. All of us already miss her far more than words can tell. The tears around me say it all. People far and wide will be most saddened by her sudden departure. Virgil expressed his enormous regret at not being able to attend. He is not well. Virgil was most in debt to her for her guidance and in his note has written to us that she will feature prominently in his epic. Yes, Rome too will miss her. Even our holy Emperor, Augustus, who secretly had come to consult her on a number of occasions, will miss this extraordinary figure, whose role as mouthpiece of Apollo was an ancient institution.'

Then, having finished his eulogy, Quintius picked up the burning torch which had been placed next to him, and lit the high wooden pyre. As he did so, he said: 'Fare thee well, Sulpicia, and may you long enjoy the luminous plains, the grassy fields and scented flowers of Elysium.' Then, manifesting his spiritual disposition, Quintius said, as if in prayer: 'Let us all, in our hearts, thank the eternal, whom those in heaven and on earth revere, for ever and evermore.'

As the flames leapt upwards, I felt they were consuming an entire era as well as a part of my own life. I approached Quintius, who threw his arms around me, and both of us broke into manly tears. As the pine logs began to crackle and spark, the two of us, weeping, walked away from the beach and the large assembly. We continued to walk till we reached the nearby pine forest and then sat down silently on an ancient fallen log. For a long time neither of us spoke. Quintius broke the silence: 'There was absolutely nothing we could have done to stop her.'

'True. It was the will of the gods. But that doesn't alleviate the sadness,' I said.

'It will be our time before too many Januaries.' Quintius gazed at me gloomily.

'Sometimes I think the end cannot come soon enough.'

'You should not be pushing the Fates to do our bidding,' he replied. 'There is no indication that death will be better than life. Death does not necessarily fill a void. It most likely is a void. Some part of the deceased may exist, but how, where and for how long is not in our capacity to judge. Socrates, our wisest ancestor, asked, "Who knows if to live is to be dead, and to be dead, to live?" So it is possible that really we are dead; in fact, I once heard an Orphic sage say: "We are now dead and the body is our tomb." '

I knew my friend's analysis was right and, much as I believed in the cycle of reincarnation, his quote from Plato was welcome. For a long while, in between silences, we talked about our memories of Sulpicia: of her outbursts and the commanding way she stamped her foot, of her need for approval and of her longing for physical contact, which her position had prevented her from enjoying. Much of her life had been exceptionally solitary and bleak. Nostalgically, we recalled the splendid dinner she had hosted for Virgil and marvelled how dramatically she had carried off that unforgettable ceremony.

We also discussed whether, if an afterlife existed, Sulpicia would go to Elysium or to Hades. Quintius pointed out that the Homeric dead in Hades were believed to gossip, moralise and grieve. I added that, according to the Orphic tradition, the reward for the just in Hades was 'everlasting drunkenness'. Quintius said that Hades was the more likely outcome for our Sibyl because it would just mark the continuation of her life on earth. In Elysium, on the other hand, the shades purportedly rolled dice, rode horses, engaged in gymnastics and played the lyre – none of which Sulpicia enjoyed while alive! We both laughed at our speculations.

These distracted us from our genuine sorrow.

That night I had a nightmare in which I was searching desperately for an important papyrus scroll but was not able to find it. Were the gods telling me something? The next morning as I pondered on this dream, I suddenly realised that the scroll represented Sulpicia, our vanished Sibyl.

That same morning the *familia* gathered on the beach where the fire had burned down to ashes. Carefully the three *vespillones* scooped up the still warm ashes mingled with the few remaining fragments of Sulpicia's skeleton and placed these into three urns. As all of us hummed a dirge while the urns were carried to the water's edge and emptied into the sea. Mentula, Clodia, Clymene and Cytheris wore *infula* (fillets) of unspun wool wound several times around their heads, symbolising the purity of the ritual. They all carried baskets of flowers and walked out to the edge of a large rocky outcrop. The wind being favourable, they scattered handfuls of flower petals and dried leaves to float away on the water. It was a beautiful and meaningful end to Sulpicia's short funeral which, once again, left most of us in tears. Later, when on my own, after the sea had most sensuously lapped my toes, I wrote a short verse to her:

> You, Sibyl, have left me to my sorrow.
> Prophetic one, you left me to the night.
> You, who were my candle and my torch,
> My guide to Apollo and my shining light,
> Are now departed in the everlasting dark.

The summons from Baiae came a week later. Ten members of our *familia* were to report to the glittering new villa of Marcus Vipsanius Agrippa on the following day. Extensive gardens surrounded his truly palatial residence overlooking the spectacular Bay of Puteoli. Like the rest of us, I felt quite overwhelmed by both the size and the lavishness of this establishment. The dazzling white Carrara marble made his palace seem more like a temple than a home. We were escorted into an enormous atrium in which polished wooden benches had been arranged. An attendant told us to sit and informed us that there would be a short wait. We were all understandably apprehensive. The long wait had taken a visible toll. After a while Max rose from the bench and said, 'I have to go and take a piss.'

Alfernus retorted: 'You'll be taking it soon enough.'

Despite the atmosphere of tension – or because of it – we all laughed.

Rather than talk about the unknowns facing us, Quintius, who was seated next to Mentula – there to represent the missing Sibyl – said that only now could we realise how important she had been to us. We had become dependent on our Sibyl because she had bestowed on us the authority of her divine contacts. Without such backing, we were all the weaker. Without her we were already a different kind of *familia*. 'The Sibyl's absence not only fills us with sorrow but now also deprives us of a certain freedom of action which we had previously enjoyed without even knowing it,' said Quintius darkly.

'Watch your dangling sentences,' said the hollow-faced Lysius.

'Your sentence will come down soon enough,' I retorted. Only one or two of us giggled.

After we had been waiting for more than an hour (and it seemed like an eternity to me), Agrippa finally made his entrance, followed closely by his aide, Atreus, and another official carrying a bundle of rods surmounted by an axe – the public symbol of the force of the law.

Marcus Vipsanius had the strength and the arrogance of power written all over his face and body. His strong chin, wide and powerful neck and broad forehead gave him an almost gladiatorial appearance. His thin and tightly compressed lips gave him a look of determination and signalled a strong will.

Those lips were in no way generous. I preferred the cold marble busts I had seen of this dynamic leader to the somewhat frightening reality. Agrippa carefully adjusted his spotless toga, with its blazing purple border, and sat down most deliberately on his curved seat. Atreus stood a pace behind him. It was Atreus who spoke first to express official condolence for the Sibyl's departure. 'Her fate is now in the hands of the gods and not in ours,' he concluded and sat down on his chair slightly behind Agrippa's.

Then Agrippa, his words carefully modulated, spoke up strongly and with precision: 'In the seventh year of our Roman Empire, we all thank our wise and just Emperor, Augustus Caesar, for his edict regarding your ancient and much celebrated Oracles. The regrettable death of the Sibyl makes our decision much easier. It is our belief that both your institutions must cease their operations forthwith. Not only does the Oracle of the Dead represent a serious threat to the lives and the safety of all who visit, but your managers also have been pushing for its popularisation. It is our strong sense that Rome's religious heritage should not be turned into a circus.' Here he paused significantly. I observed the top of Max's head turn purple.

'The Emperor's most urgent priority is to recover a stable and ordered citizen state. The salvation of society starts with the family. Your family, however, has tolerated orgies and debauchery in the name of Orphism. All of you have known this was illegal. The exercise of the Orphic Mysteries further threatens to debase our Roman morality. Just as adultery between freeborn citizens demeans the dignity of Roman citizenship – or, as our poet Horace most aptly describes it, 'pollutes the citizen body' – so does Orphism undermine the natural respect we owe to our illustrious pantheon. We must honour Jupiter, Apollo, Juno and all the gods on Olympus with devotion and sacrifices. We must build our divinities temples and not profane these with alien practices. Rather than resort to lengthy court procedures, this Imperial Edict intends to bring the difficult criminal investigation of the death of Caius Antonius to an end. In our judgement it would be hard to ascertain which criminal acts were committed by individuals and which by the group acting in concert. All of you have set a poor example for both the worship of the gods and the practice of citizenship. The Oracle of the Dead is hereby closed with immediate effect and its passageways are to be sealed.

'Gaius Valerius Maximus has been the general manager of the Oracle of the Dead and shoulders responsibility for all the acts which have occurred on the Oracle premises both above and below ground. Because he has a distinguished record in our army, he will be relegated for ten years to Gaul, a most pleasant province with which he is already familiar. Atenius Vatinus Peleus, who was in charge of the processing of the visitors to Hades, will be relegated for ten years to Sicily; Lysius Decimus and Caecilius Balbus, both priests of the Temple of Apollo, are to be transferred to a religious sanctuary in Rhodes;

the high priest, Marcus Quintius, who has been cleared of all wrongdoing, is to be reassigned to a new post by the Pontifex Maximus. Alfernus Italicus, an aide to Peleus, and Rufus Longius, a boatman, are each to pay a fine of two hundred silver pieces and are to be placed under observation. All slaves serving the members of the Oracle are to be freed. No new Sibyl is to be selected and her Oracle shall be converted into a centre for religious observance. So be it. By order of Gaius Julius Caesar Octavian, the Emperor Augustus, on this last day of April in the seventh year of the Empire.'

Whereupon Agrippa rose and everyone gave three shouts of 'Hail, Augustus Imperator!'

I was stunned. At the stroke of a pen I had been cut in half. Charon no longer existed. Only Rufus Longius was alive and free. Where I had expected a possible death sentence, or exile at the very minimum, suddenly to be let off with a fine came as a shock. That is the fabled Roman law for you. It did not even occur to me in those moments to wonder what I would do or how I would spend my remaining years. I was emotionally upset to hear that the underworld where I had spent so much of my life was to be sealed for ever. I had become attached to that strange alternative realm, to those labyrinthine tunnels of grief by which I had descended for more than thirty years! I was also extremely disturbed to hear that my closest friend, Quintius, was to leave Cumae. I would be bereft! There was no one else in whom I could confide. I was not concerned, however, that the Sibyl's Oracle was no more. Our poor Sulpicia would have wished it that way. To be the last Roman Sibyl, currently being immortalised by Virgil, was the best of all imaginable memorials.

As soon as the officials had left the room, Quintius came over and embraced me. He was thrilled I had been let off. I told him that for me his departure would be a painful blow. Quintius tried to reassure me by telling me that whatever his new position we would be able to exchange visits a few times a year. This was but partial consolation.

Max, on the other hand, was still beet-red. 'Money! Money! Money!' he exclaimed as soon as the dignitaries were out of the room. 'Dirty bronze, brass and silver. Those bastards wanted to do me in. They wanted my enterprise to fail. See if they don't steal my ideas, the greedy stinkers!' And he banged his fist with all his considerable energy on the wooden bench. 'I spent all my capital, and other people's as well, working to make the new ship a success. Who on earth would want to pay for a luxurious voyage from Rome to Massilia for one?' Poor, ever-ambitious Max had a point there.

Looking around at the drawn and weeping faces of some of the members of our *familia*, I felt strangely dislocated. This edict had destroyed our entire community. Most of us had grown up together, much as our parents and grandparents had done. The Oracle had an oral history stretching back more than nineteen generations! We had been one of our peninsula's most prestigious and long-lasting institutions. Ours had truly been a community because, although we suffered all the arguments and differences families always experience, we also had a noble common purpose. We may have been out to survive and to make money, but more importantly we truly believed in the value of the Graeco-Roman mythology we had been furthering. It had been essential to appease the gods in order to protect their reputations. The occasional and painful deaths of some men had been seen by us as necessary sacrifices to Pluto and Hades. By our acts and by our acting we had re-enforced the ancient beliefs held by most Roman citizens – beliefs which Augustus and Agrippa were also struggling to maintain. Alas, our efforts were now at an end. I was convinced theirs were just beginning. As I walked disconsolately out of Agrippa's palace, the first bats were fluttering into the rapidly darkening but still shimmering indigo sunset.

XVII

The daffodils are furious this year. There were late frosts in Campania.

The present, like a flower, does not long endure. It is now three years since the Imperial Edict was delivered. I was given an unexpected lease on life – but not, I suspect, a long one. No summary execution. No exile. Even now I am not sure why. I felt guilt at not being exiled like Max and Peleus. This haunted me for many months. Yes, the edict had been right on a number of counts. Crimes had been committed and I had been more than an ordinary boatman. I had been party to many of the decisions to drown or poison those who might have ratted on us. Did I escape serious punishment because I had been more open in answering questions posed by Pomponius and Atreus? Did others, like Quintius, testify to my innocence? Had the Fates intervened? Or was it just the luck of the Roman law? Are we Romans perhaps not pushing excessively at the limits of human understanding?

Three years after Agrippa's stern pronouncement some phenomena now seem more comprehensible to me. I feel time is vanishing. The hours of the flowering honeysuckle and the centuries of the cedar must be nearly of equal duration in the circling of the heavens. I sense that time itself may be as illusory as creation. There are only moments of eternity. If time were eternally present would this not point to an instant where both past and future were one? Now that is such a complex thought I shall not try to elaborate on it for this could whirl me into a state of mental paralysis. Is it not more likely that my own incarnation will be one where past, present and future are united? Being without the daily contact of my former extended *familia* does give me much time for metaphysical reflection. Perhaps I have become the carrier of Lethe's forgetfulness? A haunting thought. Yes. When trying to recollect past events there are fleeting moments when I yearn for some of the more powerful waters of remembrance.

Virgil has not been so fortunate. He did not live to see his fifty-first birthday. He had been ailing for some time. He died in Brundisium on his way back from Athens where he and Augustus had been privileged to witness the ancient Mysteries. His ashes were taken to his estate in Puteoli where they were ceremoniously buried. Unfortunately, Virgil had not completed his *Aneid* and his dying wish was that the manuscript be destroyed. The Emperor apparently reneged on his own pledge to Virgil to execute this wish and the epic work is reportedly being edited and will be copied hundreds of times by the end of next year. I must admit that Octavian (I still refer to him by his old name) has encouraged the literary talents of our age and was exceptionally solicitous of his favourite poet. Naturally I am looking forward to reading the *Aneid* to see how our Oracles are portrayed.

Because Virgil had been able to draw on his own experiences in our underworld, I hope he developed Homer's shadowy conception of Hades into a far more impressive vision. Did Virgil accurately describe the parts of Hades that we showed him? Quintius sensed that Virgil may have devoted too much of his energy to style to command the divine ease and fluid genius of a Homer. He believes Virgil may have destined Augustus, after his human reign over the Roman Empire, to be the divine ruler of the earth, the sky and the sea. Quintius openly wondered whether this worship of the Emperor was worthy of the poet.

Virgil's visit was our historical high point, but ironically it was also our undoing. It brought such unfavourable attention to the Oracles that Octavian himself approved of their closing. Fame, as I always suspected, can also portend disaster. People are so drawn to it, they are like moths attracted by fire.

I am proud to have been the last Charon. My small coracle shall remain floating at its docking place until it rots. When I think back upon it, I regard my coracle as a wondrous boat; in my heart I feel it is still afloat. I did not have the opportunity to say goodbye to it.

Agrippa commandeered hundreds of prisoners to carry backload after backload of gravel down the narrow corridors. This marked the end of an era, but it is going to take a number of years to finish blocking all the passages. I do not miss the penetrating stench of the underground waters. Perhaps moths will continue to swirl about at the entrance for some years to come. From now on Hades and the fabled underworld shall exist only in the imaginations of our descendents and in any future literature about our past.

The dreams of this old coracle captain are no longer filled with the shadows of Hades. I do not miss the play of bogus wraiths in our make-believe underworld. I no longer regret my constant character shifts from being feared underground and beloved above. In my dreams I know not if I am still on earth or living below it in the tomb of death. At odd times I dream of joining the phantoms floating in our underworld. There are nights I still converse with Sulpicia. When I wake up, it sometimes seems very much as if she were alive. I usually see her with a heavy touch of mascara around her dark eyes. We talk about all kinds of matters in a perfectly normal way. She asks me how I am getting along with Antonius, my young son-in-law. I ask her, in turn, if she still feels lonely in her cavernous lair, as if she still lived there. She confides that she feels a bit like the last autumn leaf on her quince tree. Sometimes, early in the misty mornings, I walk to the water's edge in Cumae and reminisce about the Sibyl's dramatic immolation on the beach and the scattering of her ashes on the sea. Then a trembling tear may form in one or both eyes.

I recently was able to read a copy of Ovid's portrayal of Hades, which I suspect will be judged as being much more fanciful than Virgil's. I have always preferred him to Virgil, whose poetry is rhythmic but rocks me to sleep. Ovid's muse is wanton. His Hades, his underworld, is a rambling city and newly arriving shades have trouble finding their way around its dark alleyways. Hades doesn't quite welcome the newly arriving 'fresh' shades, he merely acknowledges their entry into his dim and gloomy urban limbo. Ovid openly marvels that although Hades has a steady stream of newcomers, it is never overcrowded. (Unlike our Roman cemeteries!)

In Ovid's underworld, the three heads of Cerberus bark in consonance! What a musical pandemonium that must be! His Furies blithely spend their time combing the snakes out of their hair, turning Hades into something of a circus ring. I suppose our past myths are popular because they are flexible and without any hard and fast rules for the teller. Each narrator can revel in his own version and listeners are happy as long as they remain spellbound at the new spin of the storyline. There are no bars on the imagination, no inevitable endings in our myths. No wonder Cicero was able maliciously to describe Hades as an old wives' tale!

The heroes of the past are kept alive only through myth, literature and story-telling. I wonder how Charon will be portrayed a few millennia from now? I am not overly concerned about it. Since the time of Homer there has been an ever increasing longing for celebrity that will permit a man to live beyond death, as Hector suggested in the *Iliad*. Odysseus discovered that the echo of one's name in this world is not always gratifying: it can easily backfire. Hercules was the prime example of a mortal who, by his efforts, as evidenced by his twelve labours, became an immortal like the gods. Achilles, Agamemnon and Odysseus all portrayed the glorious heroism of personal combat for which there is no match in our day. Alexander the Great was un-remitting in his pursuit of immortality, but I wonder how long the memory of his conquests will last? Our own Augustus is no Alexander and hardly rates as the man-god he has declared himself to be. There is much pretentiousness in those mortals who aspire to divinity.

In real life I do have an excellent relationship with my son-in-law, Antonius. He feels bereft by the relegation of his father, but has found more than solace in my wonderful daughter. He adores Calliope. I don't know if he knows anything of our past relationship and I don't ask. They are happy and that is all that matters to me. She has told me how good Antonius is to her and how appreciative she is now for all that she learned from me.

Antonius has apprenticed himself to an architect in Baiae and earns something in copying the plans. He enjoys doing this and is learning a trade. One can only imagine where this will lead him. I expect to be a grandfather before the end of the year and it is my pride to see how Calliope is thriving. I think about what Plato said: 'Now is the beginning of another cycle of mortal generation where birth is the beacon of death.' The new replaces the old. Calliope and I love each other most tenderly but what is past is absolutely past. Gone are the days when my reason faltered at the sound of Calliope's name or when I was aroused by the gentle touch of her small, lithe fingers on my temples. Indeed, I now feel that I had been a ready victim of Eros in my love of Calliope.

Eros still flutters about, but does Eros still want me? At the urging of both Quintius and my faithful dog Corso, who took a liking to her, Clodia has come to live with me. She is unlike Calliope and no Lydia. But her face expresses such happiness at being with me that it lifts my wrinkled spirits. Clodia became a freed-woman through Agrippa's edict and this has transformed her life. She expresses herself much more clearly and is no longer as cloying as when she was a slave. I am most fortunate to have someone to look after me. That Clodia does this of her own free-will is a boost to my failing self-image.

Alas, Augustus is making it extremely difficult for slaves to be freed. He has ruled that no slave who has ever been in chains or subjected to torture can become a citizen. This is a spiteful law. The private lives of slaves have traditionally been looked down upon as being of no consequence. Babies born to a slave mother still belong to her master, regardless of who the father was. Any master can drown them, just like unwanted kittens, if he so desires. This makes me realise that the Roman institution of slavery must be abolished, but I doubt our writers or even philosophers can achieve this. There is no public desire to change this iniquitous state of affairs. I fully recognise that the end of slavery might not mean the end of servitude. Our attitude towards women is also strangely anomalous: they are overtly respected by men at the very same time that they are looked down upon. At different levels of Roman society they are simultaneously weak and incredibly powerful; the incongruous laws protect them and subject them at the same time. At least we Orphics are more all-embracing. However, I somehow doubt our religious beliefs will ever appeal to our slaves in any great number. They seem to need a faith that exhorts them out of their misery.

But I remain sanguine: I still envision Orphism as the great hope for Rome if we are to rise to those heights that are in us to attain. The Orphic religion promises immortality and perfect purity to the initiated in the groves of Persephone. For Orpheus, rebirth and reincarnation were the norm. Life could only come from life . . . new souls are old souls reborn in an endless cycle. This leads Orphics to believe that what we create should aspire to eternity in accord with the harmony of the spheres. How high should we aim? Higher than the flight of the lark, whose song was created out of sight in the blue beyond.

Indeed, what can the future hold for the new imperial Rome? Could we really invent more wonderful gods than those still resident on Greece's Mount Olympus? Can any architecture improve on that of the Parthenon? Could any more noble sculpture ever be created than that of Praxiteles? Or more powerful tales be told than those of Homer? No Roman is likely to surpass the great Greek dramatists. And as to the constellation of immortal Greek thinkers, stretching over centuries from Pythagoras to Aristotle, I doubt we Romans could ever match them. The question poses itself: Why? What do we lack? Are we less noble or talented as a people? So it would seem. We are becoming too preoccupied with the material things of life, with money. Frankly, I am doubtful much good lies ahead of us, irrespective of all our engineering feats and military prowess. I think that the degeneracy, so accurately portrayed by Catullus and Petronius in my own time, will come to haunt a Rome obsessed by gladiatorial combat and inane circuses. The decline that we are experiencing banishes both morality and soaring spirits to far distant lands. It seems to me that we are in for bad times from the barbarian within us unless some unlikely supra-divinity truly takes pity on us.

Everything about us is changing: our world is no more capable of freezing its form than could a cloud in the sky. Our Roman cities churn in an unending process of decay and renewal. Our old elite, 'the nobility', has gone – destroyed by the civil wars. It is hard these days to find men who have the self-confidence of our ancestors. But change can never be halted. I have come to recognise that with the closing of our Oracles.

What will remain of Agrippa's Pantheon or our triumphal baths in a thousand years? And in three thousand? Egypt's pyramids may still be there, but I suspect the names of commanders like Agrippa will long have been forgotten. Ultimately Lethe triumphs, as Quintius reminds me on the infrequent occasions we are able to meet. There are now deep corrugations on the forehead of Quintius. He is busy as the supervisor of the Collegium Pontificum, our most important religious college. I like to view the new Rome from the ancient terraced gardens of his residence. The glistening marble temple of Minerva shimmers on the horizon while the exhilarating, tart-sweet scent of lemons drifts upwards from his orchards. This soothes my dismay that a new Rome is rising as my own life ebbs away. On my last visit, Quintius took me to see Rome's ever-larger mausoleums, which are but pretentious guarantees of posthumous grandeur. I am not personally thrilled by all the Corinthian columns in the new Rome. I am more impressed by the deep ruts engraved by the passage of thousands of carriages into the stone slabs of Rome's paved streets. Words give more meaning to life than stones and life itself animates our expressions. For me, the clarity of Quintius's words, as well as his strong voice and calm demeanour through all our tribulations, gave true meaning to spirituality. One of his last pronouncements to me was: 'Make the eternal purpose your own by joyously willing that which the One wills.'

Just as the River Tiber flows out to sea, so my thoughts are ebbing out of me. Despite the urgings of Socrates, I find myself less questioning these days. My curiosity is diminishing. Perhaps I imbibed too much from Lethe those many years ago. I have spent a full year writing on *pergamena* whenever I can get it and on rolls of cheaper papyrus when I cannot. What quantities of black powder I have had to mix! How many goose quills have gone into the writing! I shall have two copies made: one for Quintius, who will place it in the collection of his Collegium (from where I expect it will promptly vanish), the other to be placed in a sealed amphora which I myself will bury in one of the dry caves near to where the Sibyl lived. So much for immortality.

I firmly believe that in my earthly end may be a new beginning, It is true that death, a stranger, is most often regarded as an unwelcome guest. What we Orphics call a beginning would often seem to others to be the end. For us, to make an end of this world is to make a beginning in the next. Is history not a pattern of rebirth and timeless moments? Each end is where we start anew. And, even for the Romans, heaven is both the ultimate fulfilment and the end of all possibilities. To paraphrase our departed Virgil:

> *Nunc animis opus, Rufus, nunc pectore firmo.*
> Now for the opus of the spirit, Rufus, now for the firm chest.

The air is filled with spread wings. The vultures are slowly, slowly circling.

∅

> *'Bury me with all speed that I may pass the gates of Hades; the ghosts, vain shadows of men that can labour no more, drive me away from them; they will not yet suffer me to join those that are beyond the river, and I wander all desolate by the wide gates of the house of Hades.'*
>
> HOMER , *Iliad*, Book XXXIII . Patroclus speaking.
> Translated by Samuel Butler